MERMAIDS IN
Paradise

Center Point
Large Print

Also by Lydia Millet and available from
Center Point Large Print:

Magnificence

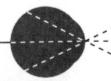

**This Large Print Book carries the
Seal of Approval of N.A.V.H.**

MERMAIDS IN *Paradise*

LYDIA MILLET

CENTER POINT LARGE PRINT
THORNDIKE, MAINE

This Center Point Large Print edition
is published in the year 2015 by arrangement with
W. W. Norton & Company, Inc.

The text of this Large Print edition is unabridged.
In other aspects, this book may vary
from the original edition.
Printed in the United States of America
on permanent paper.
Set in 16-point Times New Roman type.

ISBN: 978-1-62899-424-7

Library of Congress Cataloging-in-Publication Data

Millet, Lydia, 1968–
Mermaids in paradise / Lydia Millet. — Center Point Large Print
edition.
  pages ; cm
Summary: "Mermaids, kidnappers, and mercenaries hijack a tropical
vacation in this genre-bending satire of the American honeymoon"—
Provided by publisher.
  ISBN 978-1-62899-424-7 (library binding : alk. paper)
  1. Newlyweds—Fiction. 2. Caribbean Area—Fiction.
    3. Large type books. I. Title.
  PS3563.I42175M47 2015b
  813'.54—dc23
                                                        2014037680

CONTENTS

MERMAIDS IN
Paradise

I.
NEWLYWEDS

*C*hip picked out the destination for our honeymoon. He'd always wanted to take a cruise, just like Middle Americans. Middle Americans love cruises, Chip said ardently. Chip's a romantic when it comes to the people of the Midwest, and also those dwelling along the Rocky Mountain front, the landlocked parts of the South, things like the Dakota area or what have you. Those places are somewhat mythic to Chip. He has what I suspect is a fanciful idea: people that live away from New York or L.A., D.C. or San Francisco, maybe in a pinch Boston or even Seattle—those people are modern-day pioneers.

The Middle Americans are resolute, Chip thinks, living by choice in that vast featureless space, that oddly irrelevant no-man's land. They have their reasons, Chip believes, reasons we couldn't understand, or moral fiber, possibly. To hear Chip talk you'd think every Nebraskan male knows how to put a horseshoe on a mule. They know how to bring forth grain from dirt, or what a combine harvester is. They get what happens to that brought-forth grain, the steps before the Cheerios. The women knit long under-wear and are adept at fruit canning.

The best Middle Americans are like this, any-way, pretty much old-fashioned, according to Chip; their kids make charming toys from wooden boards, often with poking-out nails in them. Not only that, those children are delighted with the products of their ingenuity; they go ahead and play with them. Those children wave a splintered board and think of marvelous fairyland.

But Chip doesn't want to travel there, in person, to Middle America—that wasn't one of the honey-moon options. Chip's a romantic, not a moron. You don't have a Brentwood zip code and choose to spend your wedding vacation in Dayton. Literally no one does. From what I've seen, few people travel toward the middle of the country for personal reasons, unless a parent is dying. (The two of us won't have to do that, since my parents, may they rest in peace, are interred in the Bay Area, Chip's father was a deadbeat dad who left when he was ten, and Chip's mother, more's the pity, has a condo near here.) Chip just wanted to meet some of the hardy pioneers; he didn't want to physically *go* to the puzzlingly dull places where they live. He feared the religious hysterics, in addition, who inhabit the boring wastes and can be alarming. They frighten a person, when gathered in groups or hordes. Or individually.

Chip talks about that quite a bit, when not

gaming: the fact that honest Middle America, once plodding along reliably with combines for the menfolk, homemade preserves for the women and for the children some highly entertaining planks of wood, is now threatened by a growing subculture—a subculture so large it's bigger than the rest of us, actually, which maybe means it's not a subculture at all, says Chip with a worried aspect. That's where the fear comes in.

The non-subculture is made of people who believe that fossils are a trick. These people are suspicious of biology and mortally offended by an ape. Also they're angry about it.

On the one hand moral fiber, possibly, but on the other hand madness.

In any case I said no to the cruise idea. I couldn't think of a worse prospect, a floating plastic city full of food-eating vacationers, with potential for massive water shutdown, decks to be littered with plump orange bags of human waste. Closed spaces, planned activities, nausea, the smell of greasy carbs; families wearing bright primary colors or even vibrant fluorescents, heaving themselves into a pool.

Among those families wearing flashy Day-Glo clothes, those clothes that actually assaulted your eyeballs with their hideous fluorescence, there'd have to be some victims of the morbid obesity pandemic; and with the possibilities of food poisoning, sewage overflow and tragic obesity, a cruise was something I couldn't face. And so I went to Chip, I sat down beside him and took his hands and said: "Chip, I'm glad to be marrying you. But no cruise ships. Not a single one."

So Chip moved on to other honeymoon concepts.

He found a French driving tour involving Maseratis and Formula 1 racecars, where pros would drive a newlywed couple many times around a racetrack, superfast. So fast their heads would have to be spinning, their innards turbulent. Not so auspicious, Chip, I said, for honeymooners, in my humble opinion. He ferreted out a "Peaks of the Himalayas" voyage next, with visits to monasteries, meditations and nosebleeds from the lack of oxygen up there.

I always think I would have been a monk, a nun or some other holy person, in another life. It turned out I was modern, well-dressed and fairly talkative, but that's a quirk of timing. If I'd been born in the medieval part of history, I hope I would have been a monk or nun, quiet and wearing a certain mantle of wisdom.

I hope I would have used the time to think, possibly more than I do now, as a medieval-type person. I see myself singing in chapels, light streaming down on me. The singing of hymns, the kneeling down to pray, the walking with a proud, erect posture. I wouldn't have been a peasant, I hope, busily sweeping mud off pigs, possibly dying while grunting as a baby's head stuck out of me.

However currently I'm not a nun/monk, and neither is Chip, and chances are we'll never be. I thought maybe the monks would turn out depressing, with their enlightened, humble existence. What came up for me, considering those Himalayan monks and the gonging sound of temple gongs, the gong, gong, gong, what *I* thought of was the suspicion a person might start to have, in the monkish setting, that marriage overall might be a bad idea. The inner peace a monk projects, combined with never having sex, I don't know if that attitude is really honeymoon material.

You do hear about people—sure—who visit someplace Asian and scenic at a certain altitude, Asian or Indian, and then decide to go native. In one fell swoop they copy the whole Buddhist or yoga idea, they give away their worldly goods, move to a mountain hut where baths are taken in the snow and then pretend they never heard of home equity lines of credit or eyelash extensions. Next comes the cross-legged chanting, the wearing of loose and flowing robes, the eating of plain brown rice; some of them eat the rice just one grain at a time, holding that single grain in long, delicate chopsticks.

You hear about it and, despite your incredulity that a person would ever give up the bounty of our modern life, a minuscule part of you can almost see the seduction. Just minuscule, but still. I didn't want to run the risk. I'll take a pass on that serenity, I said to Chip, I'm just not in the mood for it.

I think, to be honest, Chip really wasn't in the mood either, once he did more research and got an inkling that the monks wouldn't be like monks in videogames. I think he'd been half hoping for monks with supernatural powers—at least flying kung fu. He first expected temples you could run through, surmounting obstacles and solving puzzles as you went. Then it began to seem as though extremely wise monks might be the best he could hope for, and I think at that point his interest waned.

Next he got pretty enthusiastic on the topic of a shark-feeding situation, a shark- and stingray-feeding package, with round-trip fare included, optimistically. You put on rubber fins and swim around with hostile marine life. Next came a thrill-seekers' week-long Air Safari, where you jumped from high places such as airplanes and treetops, wearing harnesses clipped to parachutes or bungee cords. Plummeting, plunging, then bouncing; screaming, then laughing in relief at not yet being dead. No, Chip, honey, I said. Some other time though, we'll do that.

My point was, I don't need to be reminded I'm alive, I'm well aware of it. Catch me later, when I'm fifty, by then I may be on the fence.

Volcano bicycle camping, snowshoeing on glaciers, ruined Cambodian temples. All had their downsides, believe me. The volcano bicycle camping was too sweaty, I thought, we'd be so grimy in our tent at night, not showered, not fragrant, no clean linens; that also was not a goal of honeymoons, was it? And the glaciers—don't get me started there. The glaciers had crevasses that could crop up suddenly, icy-blue traps of freezing death. And lonely! After I fell down the crevasse, crumpling a leg, splinters of bone confronting me, I'd sit there all alone in the darkness of the deep, cold earth. I'd sit there wracked with pain while frigid glacial meltwater washed over me, until, blessed release, I died of hypothermia.

I could picture Chip attempting a rescue, but finally it wouldn't work. Chip's not a mountaineer.

The picturesque ruins in Cambodia were a better alternative, but I happened to read a blog by a Canadian who visited Angkor Wat, got dengue fever and bravely survived it. But then she slipped on a rotting mango and snapped her neck like a winter twig. It might have been a hoax, I wasn't sure, you never know with blogs: in this case the blog started quite normally, one of those travel blogs you see so many of, and she talked about the dengue fever, she took pictures, even, of both the ancient impressive buildings and her dengue fever rash (labeling the contrast "Macro/Micro"), and put up blog posts every day. Then for a couple of days there wasn't any new entry, and then someone purporting to be her sister typed in a sentence saying she was deceased.

Anyway, hoax or no hoax, it's all the same to me, isn't it, in one sense, since I was never going to meet the blogger in real life anyway. Still it soured me on the ancient temples of Cambodia, or Khmer, as they apparently call it, I knew I'd be there eyeing mangoes suspiciously. The memory of the travel blog woman, first stoical, then dead, would make me wonder about other maverick fruit, sudden misadventure generally.

Chip yearned for daring exploits; I didn't so much yearn as just not want to have any. My vision of a honeymoon involved some relaxation, possibly spa treatments. I suggested he could do his adventure on a separate trip, a trip for bachelors—or men, at least, supporting his final bachelor days, wanting to flex their muscles, commit some acts of bravado. They didn't have to be unmarried themselves, although, let's face it, the trip would be more exciting if they were.

Chip's very friendly, most everyone agrees on that, but still he doesn't have what you might call a group of close friends—not exactly. He has pals he plays racquetball with, he has his coworkers, and he does some multiplayer online games with guys from college who live in other cities.

One of the racquetball players is an anger-management student, that is, he goes to seminars on anger management, to learn to manage his anger. Chip says the racquetball can get a little edgy because of this, when the managing isn't going smoothly. I ask Chip why he even plays with him, he shrugs and grins. His name was in the racquetball pool at Chip's gym, Chip picked him at random and got into the habit so now he doesn't want to disappoint the man. You have to wear goggles in racquetball anyway, Chip said, or you could lose an eye. I said, But Chip, aren't there some other places an angry racquetball could hit? Do you wear goggles on those too?

Just your typical Nutty Buddy, says Chip.

This guy, Reznik, he really likes to win whereas Chip's mostly playing to get a good workout in, so Chip hits energetically till near the end and then he misses on purpose. Still though, he didn't want Reznik managing anger at his bachelor party.

Chip's coworker buddies, well, in terms of other men there's Sandy, which sounds like an easy-going blond woman but is actually a man and not a blond at all, and there's Tariq. Sandy is delicate, a germaphobe who buys his antibacterial hand gel in bulk—probably not the type for derring-do. Tariq is married to a woman his family sent to him. He'd never met her before the day of their wedding but the two of them are stuck like glue. He doesn't go on trips, or even out to restaurants. He's more of a homebody. You'll see him at office functions, but only because they're mandatory. He'll be the one over beside the water cooler, holding a nonalcoholic beverage and smiling nervously. The unasked question in his mind is, *Can I go?* You see it when you look at him.

Chip likes Tariq a lot, he admires him; he always mentions Tariq when the talk turns to Arabs and terrorists. Then it's "Tariq tells me," and "according to my man Tariq." If anyone has a negative word for an Arab, a Muslim or that situation there, Chip rises to their defense. He trots out Tariq to show that not all Arabs are religious hysterics. We have them too, is what he likes to say, each country has its own hysterics, doesn't it, its own growing majority of straight-up insane people? Let's throw them all together on an island, a big one like Australia or they wouldn't fit, and then take bets.

Chip's usually hamming it up at that point, admittedly. He likes to play the fool, sometimes, likes to act less intelligent than he is. It makes other people feel *more* intelligent than they are, and then they find themselves liking him. Liking him quite a bit.

Look at the fundamentalists *we* have, says Chip, they may not put incendiary devices in their body cavities but they get up to their own shenanigans. They try to gaslight the whole culture, claiming the dinosaurs were here last week, going around to the museums—when they come into the cities—and scoffing at a T. rex skeleton.

Chip says he talked to a guy once who insisted T. rexes hung around in pilgrim times, hiding behind the trees so Founding Fathers didn't see them, probably—slapping their tails at Pocahontas, stepping on teepees and roaring.

Not all Muslims even believe women should live in sacks, says Chip: sure, we all know that in some sandy, oily countries women walk around wearing baglike garments over their whole bodies, including their faces, with just a slit over the eye region, because without that slit you'd have these women bumping into things and breaking their noses. In those countries the women look like boulders, walking around like that. Long boulders, Stonehenge style. Crowds of these women in their dark sacks are like a field of oblong rocks.

Of course, it's not a bad look, those dark robes, says Chip. Although the face covering, he could do without that. Chip's confused about why the women agree to the face-covering part. Seems punitive, says Chip, pretty hard to rub your nose, if you needed to for an itch, though on the upside, it wouldn't matter at all to have a piece of food stuck in your teeth. Those women don't need to worry about that *ever*.

He's an open guy, but he's been reluctant to bring up the face-covering issue with Tariq, rightly fearing it might offend. He'll ask Tariq about the politics, but not so much the face-covering.

Tariq's a paragon of virtue, he does the prayers, he kneels on a small rug, and his wife doesn't dress in sacks or look out of an eye slit; she wears regular U.S. clothing—though, since I'm being honest here, she could use some fashion tips. I know because I met her one time at an office party; it was St. Paddy's Day, and people were lurching and weaving around vats of green punch and beer, floating shamrocks and leering cardboard leprechauns. There's no one Irish who works at Chip's company, the closest they ever got to Ireland was making fun of Riverdance, but Chip's boss says it's a U.S. holiday now and the point of it is License to Drink. But Tariq doesn't drink and neither does his wife, so at the St. Paddy's Day party she stood beside him at the watercooler, wearing that same trembling smile. It begged us all to release her. *Just let us go now, please,* that smile said. *Please and thank you. I do not wish to be at this "party."*

It was a bittersweet situation, I guess, because I looked at her and even as I knew exactly what she was thinking, I also knew she wouldn't be released—no, she would hover painfully for at least another ninety minutes before she was set free. Everyone has to stick around, at these office parties, until Chip's boss, drunk as a lord, blearily notices their presence and marks it on his list of reasons not to arbitrarily fire them. She would hover there politely, her eyes as dark and wide as a deer's, trying to fathom the vulgar customs of her adopted country.

If Chip could, I've thought sometimes, he'd carry Tariq around with him for showing off when the talk turns to terrorists, since Tariq's a guy who's attractive and very warm. He smiles a lot; with Tariq you almost wish he'd hang out more, he seems like such a sweetheart. But Tariq has other fish to fry and by the time Chip's bragging about him, he's off being his usual homebody.

Then for Chip's college friends, you've mainly got Rocket, Eight-ball and BB3 (short for Beer Bong Three, as I recall). In their day those guys liked to tie one on and get into a hazing mentality, which could work well in a bachelor party setting. But Rocket tweaked his back on a mechanical bronco in a bar and doesn't do much physical these days, Eight-ball is in recovery and avoiding old patterns, and BB3's afraid of velocity. He doesn't travel much. That's a phobia of its own, I guess, the fear of velocity; BB3 doesn't get into anything that goes faster than walking. If he gets into a car and it speeds up past about 5 mph, he starts to squeal like a four-year-old on helium. Chip says he pictures an impact, can't help it. Even a bike ride is too much for him, if BB3 gets on a bicycle he immediately pictures his face pulpy. No skin on it at all.

Nothing specific happened to BB3 to cause this,

Chip tells me, he just woke up one morning frightened of velocity.

So in the end Chip couldn't get a group organized. Instead he signed up for an extreme half-marathon in the mud with obstacles—barbed-wire fences, tunnels you slither through on your belly, flaming bales of hay and 10,000-volt electric shocks.

But for the honeymoon, we decided, we'd go in a simpler, more tropical direction.

I'M GETTING AHEAD of myself, though, skipping ahead to honeymoons when Chip and I weren't even married yet. Chip's training for his race took up a few hours every day, at first just mornings and then evenings too; at times he'd come home bleeding from the earholes, with dirt leaking from his nose. He had one elbow in a sling, then fractured toes; his kneecaps were scab pancakes. He called it "necessary toughness" and told me men who finished the race often got the name of it tattooed on their biceps.

We had the bachelor party issue decided, so the next thing was my side of the schedule. I'd never been a fan of bridal showers, or baby showers either, really. A shower of any kind seems like a place for brain deficiency—women squeal during those showers, squeal at the sight of trivial objects. A bridal shower features frilly underwear to make the new wife look more like a prostitute; a baby shower peddles frilly bonnets you drape around a newborn's face to make it look less like a garden gnome. I skipped right over the shower option to its faux-raunchier counterpart the bachelorette party, whose most revolting facet is the name *bachelorette.* I'm as fun as the next California gal, or try to be at least, but what I don't appreciate is the infantile aesthetic. Lacy frills, voluntary brain deficiency and words like *bachelorette,* what they add up to, let's face it, is basically an infantile or possibly pedophile aspect.

I've got no problem with the male-stripper custom. It's a conundrum though, or maybe a complicated joke—sometimes I've thought the whole thing is 100 percent gay, style-wise, with all those middle-aged women smiling and clapping as though the gay male spectacle was just exactly what they came out for. Because let's face it, in most cases the stripper dance moves are cruel and unusual punishment, for your typical straight woman. Other times I've thought maybe the moves aren't gay at all, maybe they're designed to be embarrassing. Maybe *no one* likes them. Maybe the point of them is male abasement, female pity/superiority. Could that be it?

Thankfully, none of my friends insisted on the stripper theme. They were OK without strippers, also without a gigolo.

Once I knew I was safely clear of the acrylic talons of the sex industry I handed the planning over to my maid of honor, Gina D. She wasn't a maid of honor in the traditional sense, after all she's a grown woman, as many of us are, nowadays, who choose to get married. There isn't a maid around. The only one who *called* her a maid of honor was Chip's mother, who I could write a book about. Chip's mother also called me "the bride," just every chance she got. As in "Well here's the blushing *bride!*" when I walked in the front door in gym sweats with dark armpit stains, lugging five heavy bags of groceries and a case of beer. Or "Is the *bride* a little bit under the *weather?*" when she heard me in our bathroom during a bout of Thai-restaurant food poisoning. She said that through the bathroom door, where she hovered while I was in there making noises like a chimpanzee screaming.

But she was my second in command, Gina D.— my best friend from way back and my wedding lieutenant. I call her Gina D. because when we met, in seventh grade, there was another kid named Gina, Gina B., and so we used their last initials. But they were oh so different, those two Ginas. Gina B. later became a successful quilter. Her quilts are everywhere, at least, if you're the type that visits community centers, women's art cooperatives and crafts conventions. If you're a person who notices quilts, you'd certainly notice hers. Hard to miss them. The quilts have quotes, such as, for instance, *I dream of giving birth to a child who will say to me: "Mommy, what was war?"*

Gina D., though, is starkly opposed to quilts—really to most things that are handmade. She openly despises pottery. I saw her laugh in a potter's face. I was relieved she didn't spit; to Gina D. the stink of earnestness is worse than rancid milk. Gina D. wants household items to be mass-produced, ideally of a polymer, and if they're not she tries to throw them out. One time she walked through my kitchen and trashed three items in five minutes flat: a potholder decorated by another friend of mine's kid, a floral apron sewn by a long-gone great-aunt and a glazed ceramic planter I really kind of liked.

She's funny, Gina D., with a carrying personality that makes you half forget she's harshly obliterating your possessions. Everything's performance art with her, she lives in a world of irony. If a gesture's not ironic, why make it at all, is her philosophy. Gina's a failed academic—at least, that's what she calls it. Last time I checked she made a decent salary and had tenure in American Studies.

Gina claims the term *failed academic* is redundant. That's why she uses it.

She promised me no male strippers, ironic or otherwise. Gina's the type who, left to her own devices, would have to raise the stakes on male stripping—regular male strippers would never be enough for her, she'd shake her head in boredom at that idea, instantly dismissing it. Gina would have to get some paraplegic ones or maybe amputees. And she'd probably end up making out with at least one of them in a broom closet. Gina's got game.

She and I brainstormed awhile, with her arguing at first for a pilgrimage to the theme park Dolly Parton owns. She said the infantile or pedophile aspect of weddings made Dollywood the perfect place to go—a whole family amusement park, with millions of visitors a year, based on the image of a woman known for abnormally huge breasts. The whole thing doesn't fit together unless you factor in its standard deviation, what Gina calls SD. SD is the perversity of everyone, Gina says, which everyone totally ignores. "We'll fly on the wings of an eagle," she quoted (Gina loves to quote). "Dollywood, sweet promised land of giant breasts," she rhapsodized, "the land of friendly, singing breasts. Land where the large breasts sing."

Gina is fond of perversion, although, since her fondness is ironic, you can't pin her down for being an actual pervert. Quite probably, you'll never know. That's the hard part with irony. But I said no to Dollywood; we're keeping it local, Gina, I said. Chip would be heartbroken if I went without him to not only an amusement park but also Middle America. Tennessee has to count as that; the name of the town is Pigeon Forge. Meanwhile Chip would be clambering over

26

spirals of razor wire. He'd feel left out, and I couldn't do that to him.

"I'll take a rain check," said Gina D. briskly. "Oh, I know—we'll go when Chip's busy doing his midlife thing. There'll be a free week in there, maybe a few, while you're deciding if you should go the couples therapy or divorce route." She flicked on her phone, opened the calendar. "Hmm, seven years. I'm putting a reminder in. Back to the party, then. You sure about the travel ban? Because Precious Moments™ has its own chapel in Missouri."

WHILE GINA WAS planning my party, my almost-mother-in-law was also making plans: Chip had asked me to let her help. Chip's an only child, and his mother had retired the previous year from what was, as far as I could tell, a Nurse Ratched–type position. She worked at an old folks' home where, before she left her job, we used to drop in on her sometimes; I saw some elderlies who quaked at the sound of her footfall. Around the time of our engagement and wedding her main hobby was going to hear motivational speakers, and after each one of them she'd bear some pearls of self-help wisdom home to share with Chip and me. Chip's mother brings motivation to the table, that's for sure. She buckled down to setting up our reception, and if she wasn't bringing me a swatch of this it'd be a forkful of something else.

I told her that I didn't want certain so-called traditional aspects of wedding receptions, that is, the aspects that are repulsive. No feeding each other wedding cake, for instance, then mashing it around the oral region like giant babies. Strict pedophile/infantile thematic. Also no disturbing miniature bride and groom dolls perched upon the cake with glassy smiles, a serial killer's dream of love.

Chip's mother wasn't happy about this, of course, she feared the opinions of the other relatives, some of whom would be hailing from Middle America or Orange County. I shouldn't say she *feared,* on second thought, since Chip's mother has never been one to frighten easily; more like she shared their views and stoutly wished us to conform to them. People don't even perceive the standard deviant quality of wedding receptions— to them it's cute, the cake-on-face smearing, the frozen serial killer dolls with tiny startled eyes and pink slashes where the mouths should be. Not for one second is your wedding-going public bothered by things' actual meanings—and by *public* I mean those women who pass amongst each other all the information about what weddings and receptions should be, spattered across the generations like so much female deodorizing spray across the shelf at a Walgreens. These women are the clear standard-bearers of the nuptial industry a.k.a. basic wedding perversion.

To them a wedding theme is "starry night," "angel" or "antique vanilla." Yes, they firmly believe vanilla is a theme, along with warm yellow, mauve and tangerine. To them the sight of a full-grown man and woman mashing white-frosted cake into each other's nostrils and chin pores is traditional plus heartwarming. If it were tradition to eat human intestines at wedding receptions they'd garnish the plates with curls of spleen. When these ladies happen to glance at the food-ravaged faceholes during the cake-on-face smearing and feel a shiver of revulsion, they simply disregard that shiver and smile as though, somewhere within the floral centerpieces, iddle fairies are giggling.

Gina maintains the standard deviance is Freudian. To her, breastfeeding is non-ironic, earnest and the child-raising equivalent of making macramé wall hangings; also to her, all children wish to nurse at their mothers' breasts until the age of at least six, and not being able to do so makes standard deviants out of them. Gina's not bothered by her own conflicts of opinion, though: another benefit of the irony position. You can be a walking pastiche of opinions, if you're deeply committed to irony. If Gina is drunk she'll get even more into it, telling all those who care to listen—and many who would prefer not to—how our free nation is a carnival of stunted mental growth. "Arrested *adolescence?* We *wish,*" she'll slur loudly, Gina, my wedding helpmeet, when she's in her cups. "We never made it out of elementary school, buddy."

It's not always clear what Gina's referring to.

Chip's mother kept trying to shoehorn items into the reception, slip in repulsive elements without me noticing. For instance, party favors such as star-shaped fairy wands with a label on them inviting guests to WISH UPON A STAR. When I said no to that one she left me five messages, each one more indignant. Then she wanted bottles of bubble bath with swans on top, their necks disturbingly entwined; then a white-silk flower with CONSIDER THE LILIES stamped on the stem in gold.

I told her no favors, since Chip and I had passed beyond that phase. We were adults, I told her calmly but firmly: when we attended a party we didn't expect to go home with sparkle-filled bouncy balls or a handful of Tootsie Pops. We were no longer impressed, like so many gentle natives on the wrong end of a cargo-cult trade, by the magical wonder of the monogram. Black and silver matchbooks, floaty pens, even high-priced cake knives or serving spoons engraved with *Jon & Minky* or *Dick & Billy* left us completely unmoved. My personal impulse, upon receiving such items as a guest, was to hurl them into the nearest trash can as soon as I exited the function.

No, we were perfectly pleased to leave a party empty-handed, our blood alcohol content somewhere above .08.

BY THE TIME the various events fell into place, my party was slated for the day after Chip's race. He'd need some time to recover before the ceremony, with morphine derivatives for pain. Then the rehearsal dinner and then, on a Saturday in late July, our small ceremony and reception.

It wasn't going to be easy to spectate, at the mud marathon, but I drove with him anyway; the course had been set up at a ski resort in the San Bernardinos. Once we were up there in the pines, checked into our hotel room, I took a shower while Chip listened to rabble-rousing music with his earbuds in. Then we went outside and I watched as runners milled around at the starting line for what seemed like an eternity, stretching, high-fiving, chugging sports drinks and eating astronaut food.

The weather wasn't sunny, in fact a thunderstorm was threatening, which seemed to please those extreme sportsmen and sportswomen: they sought every encumbrance possible. Many would happily have run the distance on hot coals. A number sported rubber bands around the thick parts of their arms or rings from multiple piercings—rings that, I imagined, could easily get snagged on the barbed- or razor-wire entrapments and rip off a lobe or a nipple. Several participants bore large ink designs from previous years' events, one on the top of his shaven head; I saw two others comparing mud-race burns and scars, one on the neck, the other across the ribs.

"Chip," I said—as Chip, standing on one leg like a stork, pointed and flexed the airborne foot repeatedly, writing the alphabet upon thin air with his toes to loosen his ankle—"are you completely sure? I've got a great idea. How 'bout you just *don't* do this race, and we can tell everyone you did?"

"I'm not going to wuss out," protested Chip. "Babe. Babe! Are you kidding?"

"It wouldn't be *wussing*," I said. I hated the thought of Chip with a tattoo on his head. Till death do us part, and all, but with the head tattoo I wasn't sure. It didn't appeal to me. "Not in the least. This would be more like, you doing me a solid."

"Now honey," said Chip, de-storking his muscular legs and coming over to put his arms around my waist, "I know you support me taking this on. It's going to rock. It'll totally rock, OK? You'll see."

When I first met Chip, on a speed-dating lark that Gina dragged me to as an ironic gesture after I'd gone through a bad breakup, I had the impression he was a handsome guy but seemingly indifferent. It turned out he wasn't indifferent at all; when Chip gets a far-off look in his eyes it's not coldness, it's more like an echoing. He forgets what's in front of him sometimes, does Chip—goes to a dreaming place, a dreaming environment. In that land flags are flying over tall-grass meadows; men are Vikings, women like ornaments on the prows of ancient ships, their hair long and wavy. Chip's a dreamer and if he could, he'd make the world a place where questing videogames became reality, where he could wear breastplates and a deep battle horn would sound over the white-peaked mountains and lush green valleys. Stags leaping in the woods; fording of streams by warriors and their warhorses, decked out in glorious regalia; possibly mythological creatures.

But if you can't make the world into a videogame, and if you're not a full-on geek but fifty-percent jock too, I guess the next best thing is a mud marathon.

"I do support you, Chip," I sighed. "Just— would you do something for me? Don't get a head tattoo. Look at that guy. With the name of the race beneath that stubble on his scalp? He looks like he's here to kill minorities. Chip, I don't favor a man with head tattoos."

"You've got my word on it, sweetcheeks," said Chip. He disentangled himself from my embrace and returned to his warmup/stretching routine.

"Chip," I went on, as he storked on his second

leg and peeled back the wrapper on an energy bar that looked like something dark nestled in cat litter, "you know, while we're on the advisability subject, I sometimes have a thought. My thought is that, with the planet at seven billion people and counting, hundreds of millions in abject poverty, my concern is that extreme sports are maybe a red herring. If people want to put so much effort into testing their toughness, if they want to prove they're not afraid of hardship, why not travel as Good Samaritans to famine-ridden or war-torn countries? Or for the rebel, punkrock types, maybe bomb missile factories? You know—do something productive?"

"Huh," said Chip, looking surprised and a little worried as he chewed the protein bar with his mouth open. "Man, Deb. Should I not have booked the honeymoon package for Virgin Gorda?"

"Honey, my point is—"

But the pre-starter sounded then, a five-minute warning. Chip gulped down his soy protein, kissed me, took off his ultra-featherweight jacket, adjusted the tube on his backpack hydration kit (giving it a practice suck or two) and the angle on his headlamp, and made for the starting line. I raised my phone and called out to him as he went, snapping a picture when he turned to smile at me. He looked like a combination football player/ spelunker/Green Beret, his broad grin a Cheerful Chip special.

Chip's a positive guy, one of the things I value about him. Events don't tend to get him down for long. He cries a lone man-tear now and then, when he sees a commercial with starving babies or remembers watching the planes hit the buildings—Chip doesn't have a problem showing emotion—but he snaps out of it before he reaches a level that's maudlin. Chip snaps right out of it and switches into basketball, World of Warcraft or having-sex mode. He's quite accomplished at all three.

The hotel had screens set up where spectators could watch the feed from various cameras positioned along the route; I wasn't sure, though, how to pick Chip out of the rest of the crowd. He'd tied a bright bandanna loosely around his neck, colored a putrid yellow-green, but it would soon be brown as Chip got mud-covered and then it would cease to distinguish him. I bought myself a drink at the ski resort bar and sat down to watch the proceedings.

The first obstacle was ropes over a pond; the runners had to walk along thin ropes strung slightly above the surface of the water, one rope per runner, like a tightrope, plus a second rope to hold on to above their heads. Several of them splashed down in rapid succession. They were falling readily from those ropes, dropping like flies. Meanwhile I slowly drank my margarita, there in the ski resort bar. There was abundant salt on the rim of the glass, and I liked that; I liked the margarita quite a bit, I realized pleasantly, as the extreme athletes balanced, then wavered wildly, as they splashed into the pond and struggled to climb out again, covered in scum.

Yes, I nodded to myself, the margarita was tasty.

Between leisurely sips I tried to make out Chip on the large screen, Chip balancing on a narrow rope or toppling into the chilly, brackish water, but I really couldn't see him, and in the end it wasn't worth the effort. There were so many men on those ropes, so many strong, tough men out there exemplifying toughness—surely these men were heavy as iron, with that muscle mass on them, and yet to me it almost seemed as though their bodies were puffy, as though they might suddenly rise into the air, borne heavenward like so many man-shaped muscle balloons . . . a few woman balloons, here and there, but mostly it would be men.

I ordered a second margarita, then, thinking of a future time when muscular man-balloons might rise into the air, eventually popping. By the time I focused again, the ropes-over-a-brackish-pond obstacle was history and they were just running in a pack, a crowd of heads moving up and down, bobbing, some with wide grins—a pack of humanity. Some wore glued-on handlebar mustaches or Scottish kilts, others were painted all over their bodies in various colors, resembling zebras, tigers or indigenous tribesmen. One joker wore a Louis Quatorze wig.

The running part was, to me, tedious. I recalled someone saying people had perished, during other mud marathons—and more than one, even. Some people perished, in the course of proving their toughness: well, so it went.

It was a rumor, anyway; Chip said the paper they'd made him sign was purely a gimmick, a legal form known as a death waiver.

Someone remarked that it would be another ten minutes until the second obstacle, so I decided to take a walk outside to look at the party prep. The organizers were throwing a big bash after the race, with live bands and plenty of alcohol, where tattoo artists would put a tattoo on a runner's head for less than fifty bucks. I walked across the grounds—I'd poured my second margarita into a plastic cup and carried it with me—and glanced into some of the body art tents, thinking fearfully of Chip's scalp. A guy like Chip, if he's in a triumphal mood, can be tempted. He's not a rock, Chip, in the heat of the moment, when it comes to aesthetic decisions; he's fallible. Chip's only human. He never claimed not to be.

I saw photos displayed of armpit work, photos of naked-chested people raising their arms above their heads, and in those armpits were tattoos. In one pair of armpits there were grinning skulls, while in another two large eyes popped out to look at the viewer, one in each pit. They seemed to be the eyes of snakes, perched balefully on scaly lids. One man had women's legs tattooed in his fishbelly-white armpits—a pair of disembodied legs in garter stockings and red high heels, one leg-pair per armpit. The legs were spread wide, one pointing up the inner arm, the other down the ribs, to reveal betwixt them both a nest of springy armpit hair.

I turned away from the tattoo tent, feeling one's idealism might be sullied there. Before I left the area, though, a tattoo artist called out and propositioned me, jauntily offering his body-scarifying services free of charge if I would be a little more outgoing. Although I felt gratified and waved amiably, I wondered if my jewelry had been a factor in the attraction. I've heard that, on a male finger at least, a wedding band can be an enticement, alluring as a loaner puppy. Was it the same with engagement rings? I thought of asking the tattoo artist this question, since surely there could be no harm in it, but when I turned around, my plastic cup newly drained, he'd already gone to ground.

I got back to the screening room in time for obstacle number two, called "Radioactive Jacuzzi" (although, as far as I know, there were no actual particles of thermonuclear fallout). It was a wriggle on the stomach across a long vat of ice cubes, with barbed-wire netting close above them.

This time I really would have liked to catch a glimpse of Chip; he's always been sensitive to cold. He doesn't eat ice cream, even, claiming it freezes his brain near the forehead. But once again I failed to spot my soon-to-be husband: there was too much humanity, it all looked the same to me and I lacked the necessary patience. Instead of squinting and studying those figures of athletes, I bellied up to the bar.

And so it went: obstacle, drink, obstacle, drink. The men and several women ran through lines of flame; they carried logs up hills on their shoulders, abraded their knees and elbows climbing through massive corrugated pipes, and scaled treacherous vertical surfaces. As they became exhausted, injured and covered in mud I threw back margaritas, added some nachos to the mix. I flirted with several other spectators, even got my palm read by someone taking methamphetamines; it was oddly relaxing, even luxurious. A girl with blue fingernails did numerology, while off in the corner a group of wholesome, rich-looking men wearing Harvard letter sweaters chanted ominous runes in some foreign and possibly ancient tongue . . . the point was, it was a party scene, and we the audience even forgot what we were there to watch, after a while. Few of us even glanced over at the screens; it was like being at a party on election night, supposedly "watching" the "returns." We paid no attention to the faint sounds from the speaker system—squeals, screams, and bells ringing repeatedly.

I drunk-dialed Gina on my cell; she'd been passingly interested in seeing the mud marathon and Chip had invited her, but as it turned out she had a scheduling conflict—free tickets to a special showing of an old Karen Carpenter movie. Now, tipsy and at loose ends, wanting Chip to be finished so he could join me at the after-party, I hit the speed dial. It was the intermission in the Carpenters movie so I gave her the room run-down. That's what Gina calls it when you're surrounded by people you don't know in a social situation and feel compelled, whether under the influence or straight lonely, to dial a friend and callously describe the other people at the scene. I meandered out to the finish line eventually, with Gina still on the phone; in the lobby of the theater she was talking to me rapidly, even as a random hipster guy tried to persuade her to go with him to a glow-in-the-dark tap dance show.

"It's a critique of Bush v. Gore," she said.

And then I saw Chip, though at first I barely recognized him. I'd promised him to snap a cell phone pic, a photo of him completing the mud marathon, and so that's what I did. I raised my phone. He was beaming with joy through the mud plastered over his eyebrows, cheeks and chin, a Stevie Wonder look. But as he ran toward the finish line, right through the final obstacle, his arms raised to greet me, just beaming like a child, he got an electric shock. I think the wires hit him across the lip; maybe the tongue. His mouth was open for the smile. I saw him jerk back like a spastic.

Then he crossed the line and was with me: he shrugged off the shock, hugged me and lifted me off the ground, making me filthy. Soon he collapsed in a heap, and when he recovered it was time to celebrate.

In the end I was able to prevent him from getting a tattoo, but only by the skin of my teeth. As I'd predicted, he ultimately declared he wanted one—not a head tattoo, he knew he couldn't shave his head before the wedding, but maybe a back-of-the-neck adornment. He saw the other extreme athletes taking swigs of whiskey and going under the needle; with a few beers to his credit Chip turns into a joiner, that's his way, and soon he longed to top off his own effort with a marking ritual too. He joined the tattoo line and requested that I catch his branding on my phone's video.

Instead of debating the merits, I had to distract him. I lured him out of the line, then led him into a dark stand of trees and had my way with him. That's how it works with Chip: you have to skip the preliminaries and bring out the big guns. You don't waste your time, and his, with words and sentences.

Argument's a dull blade, when it comes down to it, and I like to be efficient. We both left the party satisfied, me because I'd pulled out a last-minute win on the inking crisis, Chip because he was drunk, certified tough and newly laid. There's not much more a man like Chip asks for.

Or any man, possibly.

THE NEXT DAY he was pretty achy; he had a long bath, popped some muscle relaxants and did the couch potato thing, gaming. By the time I left for my Ball-and-Chain Party, as Gina was calling it, he had a bowl of popcorn at his elbow, a console on his lap and was gazing wide-eyed at the large screen, where one of his many avatars flew into a fanciful moonrise/sunset on a steampunk zeppelin, pulled by a team of elegant purple dragons.

Gina had found the perfect venue for the festivities—perfect for her, at any rate. The rest of us were just along for the ride. She had us meet her at a generic wine bar, probably so that no one would instantly bail; then we trooped over to the nightspot, Gina in the lead. It was instantly obvious I hadn't gotten clear of the sex industry after all: this was some kind of Goth, medieval-bloody S&M fetish club with the tag line "The Decadent Seduction of a Horrific World." I was glad I hadn't invited members of the older generation, though it did give me a bit of pleasure to ideate Chip's mother entering the place.

There was a band playing dirge-like atonal music whose singer had multiple studs sticking out of his cheeks Chia Pet–style; in cages hanging from the ceiling, ghoulishly clad people danced in zombie-style slow motion. Holes were strategically cut in the dark, shining costumes they wore, which made them resemble enormous spiders, albeit with hanging or popping characteristics. On the walls played grainy, obscure movies of what seemed to be morgue attendants plying their trade; and then, of course, there were your basic whip scenarios, masks and black latex.

"At seven we have the Ravage Room booked," said Gina. "A private show. *Just for us*." The prospect filled me with creeping dread—at that point I would have welcomed a few basic, beefcake male strippers—but I ordered a drink and played it casual, as Gina demanded. One woman in our party, the only person I'd invited from my office, was openly terrified, eyes darting around like those of a hunted herbivore. She said she was feeling sick, slunk off to the bathroom, and did not return. I felt bad and made a mental note to reach out to her when I went back to work; she had photos of poor kids tacked up on the walls of her carrel whom (she believed, at least) she was sponsoring with monthly payments to a multinational charity. Seated atop her computer were several "cute" bobbleheads.

"Gina," I said with some audible irritation, because Gina only intimidates me sometimes, "congrats. One down, thirteen to go. You really outdid yourself this time."

"That woman's got an actual PBR can stuck through her giant ear-pierce hole," mused Gina. "You think it's got any beer in it?"

"Seriously, Gina," I said, shaking my head. "I swear."

"Absinthe for everyone!" she cried.

Nearby stood our waitress, waiting for orders with tears of blood flowing from her eyes. She was wearing a skin corset, that is, a corset whose dozens of opposing hooks, between which dark-red-and-black silk fabric was stretched, went into her actual skin in two rows up and down her back. I stared at the hooks, goggle-eyed.

"First round's on me!" crowed Gina. "Let's raise a glass of the favorite drink of Aleister Crowley, the Great Beast! To Debbie and Chip! Absinthe for everyone!"

44

"Could I please have a wine cooler?" asked someone timidly.

"I'd like a Budweiser Chelada," said someone else to the torture waitress. "Do you have Budweiser Cheladas? Those ones that come in cans?"

"Pimm's Cup," said my college friend Ellis, a good-looking dentist.

Ellis pretends to be a Brit, doing an accent he learned from *Masterpiece Theatre*, but his deal is he won't admit he's not English no matter what you say—despite the fact that his parents were born and bred in Teaneck, N.J. The mother chews enormous wads of bubblegum-flavored bubblegum. Though technically a prosthodontics specialist, Ellis is really more of a method actor. He never drops his English persona, going so far as to eat cottage pie, Marmite and large jars of pickled onions; he even leaves his bottom teeth slightly crooked. He makes annual trips to London, ostensibly to "see some West End theater" but really for language immersion, honing the accent. I think he tries to pass there, and where he fails he makes adjustments. The upshot is it works perfectly for him, here in the Golden State, where based on his Englishman status he sleeps with dozens of women.

No one was jumping onto Gina's pretentious absinthe bandwagon. Everyone was annoyed they even had to be there in the first place, all they'd signed on for was a harmless bachelorette party and instead here they were at the Plague Death Tavern, where rooms off the main area had blood-dripping signs in visceral designs that read RAVAGE, BLACK TUMOR, and PUSTULE.

Also, the cover charge wasn't nothing.

I sympathized with my guests, hell, I agreed with them, so that when it was Gina's turn to make a bathroom run I smiled at their plan to get back at her. And when we did—before too long—file into the private space referred to as the Ravage Room, several of us were feeling better than we'd felt before, newly brimful of liquid courage.

A minute later the red lights in the Rav. Room changed to a purplish-blue and an amateur theatrical began, involving a peroxide-wigged woman in a white dress, behaving fakely innocent, and a muscular man, possibly garbed as some kind of primitive metalsmith, who wielded a battleax-like tool and seemed to have small nubs of horns implanted between his skull and his scalp. I couldn't figure out what they were enacting, but I got the message that it was both purportedly twisted and achingly stupid.

"You're kidding," I groaned to Gina. "The pedophile theme? Really?"

"It's tradition," said Gina, smugly.

She wasn't so smug a minute later, when the guy with horn implants turned his attention away from the pretend virgin and focused it on her.

One thing about Gina is, she talks a great game and she'll even walk the talk if she can do so in private, but she doesn't like to be in the spotlight. It's a secret weakness that can, if necessary, be turned against her.

The horned man in his satanic leather stylings had a piggy, solid kind of face on him, a face that signaled openly that he was a minimum version of a *Homo sapiens*—not unlike the gay male strippers we *would* have been watching if Gina were more of a Republican. And when he turned that dumb face on Gina, then knelt down and began lavishing attention on one of her feet, she turned red as a beet. Not only was he lavishing slavish, adoring attention on the foot, he actually slid one of her boots off and buried his face in her toes.

"Oh! No!" protested Gina, trying to shrink away. "I've been wearing leather all day with no socks on. Jesus, it's gotta be—I mean—"

The horned man took a deep sniff, like it was manna from heaven. I watched her face closely as she struggled to regain her composure, reject her own unguarded, sincere alarm and reconstruct the ironic distance.

". . . totally rank," she said faintly, as the panic faded and the irony returned.

It wasn't much but it was enough to cheer most of us up just a smidge, so that we coasted through the remainder of the show with lighter attitudes.

47

All part of life's rich pageantry, I reflected, life's rich pageantry.

For the next hour my mind wandered as I plotted how to mend fences with my coworker who had fled, the one with big-eyed bobbleheads. Technically I was her superior in the corporate hierarchy, earning several times what she did since she was a secretarial type. The contrast was stark at times, me with my spacious corner office and panoramic views of cityscape and sky while she worked in a shared cubicle out in the open. Her only view was of an old Accounting lech we called Tricky Dick for his habit of sliding his hands into his pants pockets while he was talking to you and then moving them around, furtive.

I don't want to come off arrogant, but I'm not apologizing for it either: the kind of business I do comes pretty naturally to me. The Stanford MBA was pretty much a sleepwalk through the borough of Lazy Ass. We all have our skill sets, right? At least, some of us do. Some of us don't, I guess.

Chip has plenty of skills, just different ones; he has me outclassed in at least six categories but he couldn't perform a basic cost-benefit analysis on a supercomputer named Deep Blue. He's great at other computer stuff, but nothing too financial. So I've got the corner office and I've got the decent salary, where Chip at his workplace, and my young coworker at ours, have their desks out there in the open like any Tom, Dick or Harry.

48

My point is, I had to stop by my office first thing in the morning—I had two days off before the wedding weekend, but I'd promised a colleague to look at some numbers for him on the way to my mani-pedi. And there she'd be, this sweet young woman fresh from her southern sorority, looking up plaintively from her cubicle populated by orphans with missing appendages to whom she, full of naïve hope, sent her hard-earned cash. She was trying to make for them a better world—even if eighty percent of her gifts *did* go to pay the admin overhead of a fundraising department in Chicago. And there I would be, too, the callous exec with no pictures of orphans tacked up at all, not one single orphan on my wall—just a defiantly ugly print of Hulk Elvis by Jeff Koons.

Me, the callous exec that had taken her to an S&M den, which she'd run away from, probably weeping. If that wasn't a litigation scenario I'd never heard of one.

Plus which, I liked her quite a bit, though admittedly I only knew her because, before we both went on the patch—I was a light, social smoker but had promised Chip to give it up entirely—we used to slink out to the pre-cancer ghetto every day or two, with the comfortable solidarity of the self-condemned.

"Damn it, Gina," I said in the cab home. "You screwed me this time. I *work* with that girl Suzette."

"If you don't have regrets after a bachelorette

party," said Gina, "you're doing something tragically wrong."

"I didn't say anything *about* regrets," I said. "I said you screwed me, G."

"Same thing," said Gina, shrugging and scrolling on her phone.

I growled and lowered down my window, sticking my face into the wind doglike. Gina doesn't accept responsibility; that's not the way she rolls. She also doesn't apologize. She says it's a sign of weakness, like an animal peeing on itself.

They tried to teach us that in B-school too, but what can I say: at the end of the day, I choose to leave my power-mongering at the office, where it belongs.

"If she even *comes* to the reception after this," I said, to the passing street, "you better make nice. And you better hope she doesn't sue the company for sexual harassment. Or emotional distress."

"Where's my thank-you for the kickass party?" objected Gina, pretending to be hurt.

Gina hears only what she wants to hear. So that night, already a little tipsy from the Plague Death experience, I drowned my sorrows over a bottle of good wine with Chip. Unlike so many other heterosexual men, Chip enjoys hearing a woman bitch at length about her acquaintances and friends—he's fascinated by the daily machinations of the fairer sex. It's not the details he's interested in but the passion women bring to their interpersonal dissections. What amazes him the most, he often says to me, is how much we seem to actually *care*.

"Don't you get tired of it?" he asks. "How can you keep it all in your head?"

I WENT INTO my office the next day with a sense of foreboding about Suzette, afraid she'd be presenting with PTSD. But as it turned out I didn't have time to think about it: the numbers consult was a ruse so they could throw a surprise party for my nuptial occasion. Suzette was nowhere to be seen; I heard later she'd had a dentist appointment. (Was it my imagination, though, or were the orphans sadder and thinner than usual as I walked past her carrel, the bobbleheads bobbling with new mournfulness?)

They'd made a waterfall of mimosas, a catered spread of baked goods and resplendent fruit platters evoking ancient Greece.

After that the two days until the rehearsal dinner were a whirlwind of activity—the kind you remember too blearily to describe. There were the female-objectifying beauty rituals; the cathartic taboo-lifting of friends taking depressants and/or stimulants in my immediate vicinity and then expressing boundless affection for me; the token out-of-town family (mainly Chip's) alighting at local hotels, some of them choosing budget establishments, others opening the ostentatious rooms of their luxury accommodations to large groups of guests.

There was also the lingering presence of Chip's mother, who benefits, in life as well as on special occasions, from the fact that Chip believes she's sweet and funny and should be humored smilingly. Most other humans tend to see her as more of a wrinkled mythological harpy, old, partially digested worms smeared over her clack-clacking beak. Once she openly bragged to me that when Chip was a baby she made it a rule to embrace him once a week, rain or shine.

Chip gazed at her beatifically when she said it, like hers was the gold standard of attachment parenting.

It's a wonder he emerged from that sharp-twigged, bespattered nest with both his balls intact. It's a wonder he only flies off to dorky utopian dreamlands during the odysseys of his gaming, instead of 24/7 at a mental health facility.

And yet, and yet—it's oddly comforting that a Nurse Ratched harpy could raise a man like Chip. If a man like Chip can emerge sane and whole from eighteen formative years with a Nurse Ratched harpy, there's hope of redemption for each and every one of us. There's hope the sun may not burn out after all, some billions of years hence, transforming into a giant fireball that obliterates the planet.

So I try to see his mother less as a malevolent, live person and more as a short, gnarled, wooden figure hulking in a shady corner of the room, a kind of totemic minor demon whose presence inoculates innocent folks against the purer forms of evil.

Well, there was Chip's mother—call her, say, Tanya, since that *is* her given name—following us both around and imbuing the atmosphere with a perfumed unpleasantness, but other than that it was pretty much how I'd hoped it would be. There was champagne, there were margaritas, there were blurry rites of passage. By the time the rehearsal dinner rolled around I'd literally forgotten Tanya was there, even though, technically, she was located four inches from my elbow. All the faces were good faces; there was no ugliness anymore. Ugliness had vanished with the acuter of my senses, ugliness had made an exit from the stage of my perception, and all I could see were smiles. Love was around me—of that much I was certain.

Ellis made a long toast in his flowery, posh accent, quoting what must have been a famous British individual—Churchill or Kipling, someone like that, or maybe one of the war poets who wrote from the trenches about sad homosexuals dying. Even as he said it I had no idea what he meant; I was too busy relaxing. Gina, partly rebuffing him, said something about mad dogs and Englishmen that may have offended a great-aunt of mine, who bustled out loudly in the middle of her speech. My thought, watching the great-aunt go, was, *Wow, I had no idea she was invited. My second thought was, Is she supposed to be alive? Hmm, hmm. Is that the one who lives somewhere?*

By that point Chip was nudging me to smile or possibly respond to his mother's verbiage, which had the scent of Hallmark to it, so I waved at the assembled company much like an empress on a boat tour of the colonies. Beneath the tablecloth, one of my shoes was off and I wondered if a cat was licking my toes. A cat? Or was it a pervert? There'd been one like that at the Plague Death Tavern . . . you had to hand it to Gina, I thought, she knew what memories were made of. I hadn't enjoyed it much at the time, no, enjoyment hadn't occurred, at the Plague Death Tavern, but then again here I was, only a few days later and already reminiscing.

I should be sober, I thought, for the ceremony

itself; for the ceremony, sobriety was the right choice. Later, at the reception, a person could drink to excess again. Although, now that I thought about it—Tanya was standing, raising her own glass, I hazily noted—was the wedding-ceremony sobriety not just another robotic nod to senseless tradition? A drunken bride would look bad for the patriarchy! Yes. If the sacrificial virgin is a staggering souse, not so good for the fleshly property exchange, awkward to think of babies: uncomfortable to picture child rearing, conducted by a staggering floozy.

But was I actually *worried* about that? Was Chip, even?

Chip didn't have a subjugation agenda; Chip wasn't a patriarch. In fact Chip liked the matriarchal animals, smart elephants and randy bonobos. He even liked the pregnant male seahorses we'd seen at the big aquarium in Long Beach. Chip was benevolent on gender issues, one of his sterling qualities. Sitting beside him at the table, I gave his hand a squeeze, thinking fondly of how, despite his muscular physique, he wasn't the subjugation type. His mother's beak was clack-clacking again: if I squinted I could imagine the crushed worms, half-eaten beetles peeking from her teeth . . . she was clacking the beak in my direction now, so I raised my glass toward her in a salute.

Maybe I didn't have to be *exactly* sober for the ceremony, I said to myself—a few glasses—well,

I'd check in with Chip on it. Not to get his *approval* to drink beforehand, don't get me wrong—that's patriarchal, completely—but we could put our heads together on the subject, see if we had a consensus.

Chip's mother was seating herself again amongst her flock of Orange County dowagers, most of whose husbands had preemptively perished. Here you go, said those old, sweet geezers, I'll go ahead and die, so you don't have to do it first. Like opening the door for the ladies, I thought: gentlemanly. Chip had more relatives than I did, or, that is, his mother actively talked to them and knew their children's names and sexes. My own parents, may they rest in peace, never really showed an interest in the whole fraternizing-with-relations thing—the second cousins, step-uncles by marriage. As far as I could tell while I was growing up, a relative, to my parents, was like Middle America to coastal dwellers: only existent in the abstract. That was why I was surprised to see the great-aunt from St. Louis had snuck in. The last time I'd seen her had been in a Christmas card photo.

I imagined Tanya had showed me some kind of potential guest list, and to get away from her I'd probably nodded.

"Remind me," I whispered to Chip, amongst some clapping, "talk to great-aunt. Thought she was dead."

I was telegraphing a bit—slurring, I admit.

"Your Aunt Gloria? From St. Louis?"

"Yes!" I cried, deeply impressed at his knowledge of the furthest, smallest, most insignificant branches of my family tree.

He patted me on the wrist.

"You already talked to her, babe," he said. "On a couch. For like three quarters of an hour. You were telling her all about Gina. And the Ravage Room."

I sat back, pensive, and held my water glass firmly.

I'D GONE WITH a dress that was more of a cream than a white, even toward the beige family— it didn't have a white feel at all, really. Tanya almost vomited when she first saw the garment, apparently thinking her age group would view a non-white wedding gown much as they would a large sign reading I ALREADY PUT OUT. But by the time the big day rolled around she'd assimilated, trying to hide the outfit's non-white identity by making sure none of the décor was white either. Creamy beige was everywhere, down to the tablecloths at the reception. Tanya was trying to trick the eye.

She even asked the photographer to go mostly for black-and-white pics: sepia tones, she said. She didn't personally like that look, she was more of a primary-colors type, but she'd read in a wedding planner book that sepia was classy.

Like the trooper that she is, Gina took all the heat off anyway: when I refused to wear black, as she was goading me to, she bought as her own reception garb the kind of evening gown a hooker would wear in the Addams household. There were feathers involved, spraying over one shoulder like the black-and-red plumes of some fiendish hell-fowl, and her spike heels were daggers pointing toward the floor. Gina enjoys high fashion, steeped as it is in irony. The excellence of a friend like Gina is that she'll take the hit for bad behavior every time.

She didn't wear the vampire dress to the ceremony, fortunately, where, as the so-called maid of honor, she agreed to wear something less funereal/whorish. But the ceremony itself was on the informal side of conventional—held in the gazebo of a well-landscaped garden overlooking the Palos Verdes bluffs, the ocean crashing below. Chip had initially wanted one of those Renaissance faire weddings, until I told him I'd rather get a Renaissance faire divorce. I could live with the gaming, I told him—though it was going to be a stretch, sustaining sexual desire for a mate with multiple cudgel-bearing avatars. Over time, the gaming would be a liability where my libido was concerned: I was already making a major exception for Chip by agreeing to share the remainder of my time on Earth with an active fantasy enthusiast.

Chip didn't understand the psychology involved,

didn't see how his alternate life in the land of heroic centaurs could possibly be a turnoff, but he took my word for it. He accepted the fact that I was making an aesthetic sacrifice. So there was literally *zero* potential, I told him, for me to go even further and cultivate an attraction to a Renaissance faire husband. Not in the cards. You have to draw the line somewhere, and I personally draw that line well before wizards and bawdy wenches. I draw the line between medieval reenactments and me, and I draw it firmly.

So we looked pretty normal, I'd guess, standing there with the ocean behind us, our gazebo festooned, garlands in various places. Chip wore a charcoal suit and silver tie, and he looked very, very good. Chip's the kind of man who might have been a male model, if he weren't so innocently unaware of his own looks. He's one of those rare people who actually go to the gym for pure enjoyment, not vanity. I felt fortunate, standing there, holding his hands, gazing at him. I thought, Well, I'll be blowed. (If a ship's captain can use that fine expression, I thought, then so can I.) I further thought: Few women have the kind of luck I do. And I wasn't being sentimental. It was more of a statistical analysis.

Other than that, I can't say a lot happened. A breeze blew the dry grasses along the bluffs, making them dip and sway. Music played. There was the sense, all around us, of the kind of momentousness that is also completely trite. We were at our wedding.

I was glad I'd limited myself to two flutes of champagne in the dressing room, and that Gina, a few feet behind me, had amused herself by getting her eyebrows dyed that morning instead of snorting the mound of fairly pure cocaine left at her house by a trust-fund grad student she'd recently stopped sleeping with. There was a pleasant quality to being balanced and calm, to not wobbling at all on my heels, to hearing with dull precision the droning voice of the officiant.

Standing on the bluffs, I thought of where we were, Chip and I, and how beneath our feet was a tectonic fault block of seafloor sediments atop a submerged mound of metamorphic rock that had risen out of the Pacific beginning one to two million years before. I didn't have an opinion about it, really, though it recalled me to an early class in geology, how the only part of that class I'd really enjoyed or retained had been the cross-sectional drawings of the layers of the Earth. I hoped there wasn't anything symbolic in the fact that the ground beneath our feet was eroding. I thought of how it was impossible to form any particular impression at times like this; how, at a time like this, you had a tendency to think of yourself in the third person, if only fleetingly. I thought of not thinking.

Shortly after that, the ceremony ended and we kissed.

• • •

LATER, AT THE reception, Ellis and Gina hooked up. I hadn't seen that one coming, since Gina ridicules Ellis openly for his faux-English identity and he calls her a stupid cow. Still, when you're carried away on the romance of an evening, I guess, a cow can get less stupid. A fake Englishman can start to look like the real McCoy.

Actually, as I said to Chip when we passed them dry humping behind a port-a-john, something about the hookup made a certain sense; Gina loved the inauthentic and the absurd, and Ellis was both of those. In turn, though you couldn't call Ellis ironic—his Englishness was the most heartfelt thing about him—his life was definitely a gesture, and Gina may have briefly mistaken it for an ironic one.

All in all it was a good party. The band was fun, the food was tasty, the weather held and the drinks didn't run out (Chip had wisely bought ten extra cases of wine in case his mother's estimate turned out to be too meager—check. His mother's cheap to the point of felony. To her it's more moral to steal something than pay too much for it).

Suzette from the office showed up with no obvious psychic scars and seemed to enjoy herself, talking for long periods, Chip told me, with an ex-military cousin of his from Duluth. Although Chip and I got away with no cake-on-face smearing, not everyone was so lucky: a cohort of Chip's coworkers used the dregs of the cake in a food fight of their own. The fight was instigated by Chip's drunken boss, who as far as I knew had invited himself to the reception.

Thankfully that was in the wee hours, after most of the more fossilized guests had already left. Gina took footage of the hijinks "for the capsule," as she always says. (For as long as I've known her—I'm talking, since seventh grade—Gina's been amassing the contents of a time capsule for future inhabitants of Earth to see, she says, why our civilization tottered and fell. She's always threatening to put some artifact of me in there; when I get on her bad side she prints out one of my emails.)

Chip and I were exactly where we wanted to be. We drank, we laughed, we danced—and I was reminded how I'd first fallen for Chip, out on the town after our five-minute encounter at the speed-dating session: he's a great dancer who's never embarrassing. It's shocking in a heterosexual white man, and far more so if you add *gamer* to that list of adjectives. I thought of his elegant moves—as I gazed at him making them—as his mother's one gift to me, because when he was a child she'd forced him to take ballroom dancing lessons, out of some antiquated notion that one day he'd have to escort the great-granddaughters of slaveholders to debutante functions. As a social climber, she wanted to be prepared for that eventuality.

Well, the debutantes never materialized, and the lessons tortured him while he was a baseball- and soccer-playing boy, but they proved useful in the end, imbuing him with an easy grace he was later helpless to suppress—though he might have preferred to be seen doing a grudging, apathetic shuffle.

I had myself a small moment of clarity under the stars, walking out from beneath our soaring beige tent after midnight, Chip with his arm slung around my shoulders. He's a tall man, Chip, about six foot three. *Is this what happiness is?* I asked myself, and the answer seemed to be: basically, yes.

It came to me that we might be asking too much, often, with this pursuit of happiness deal. We acted like happiness was a consumable good, stashed on a shelf too high to reach. But at midnight on my wedding day, coming out from under that beige tent with its various garlands dangling, I saw that happiness was a feeling, not a deliverable. We pursued it all our lives as though it were a prey animal we needed to pin down, shoot and eat. But all it was was a feeling—a feeling! It rose from us, from nowhere else; the thing did not arrive all wrapped up like a gift. No use waiting for home delivery. Not coming. No tracking number to look up. You had to open the door and step out into the street.

It made me feel free, to realize that. The Big Happy was not an achievement. It wasn't a goal.

It was just an emotion.

Chip didn't see my point. I guess he'd already known it. That's the thing with these moments of clarity, you have one, you get psyched, and then it turns out the person standing next to you already knows the thing. Your newfound clarity's old news to them. They act like every six-year-old had that knowledge in hand long before you, that's how minor your clarity is. Other people are a letdown, when it comes to clarity. And sure, technically I had to admit, *happiness is an emotion* isn't a groundbreaking discovery. And yet: knowing this and *knowing* this are not the same.

I wasn't willing to let go of the moment right away; I was determined to show Chip that the clarity meant something. At times, when it comes to telling my thoughts to Chip, I'm like a dog with a bone. Chip's more than a sounding board to me; Chip is the *universal ear*. That's the job of a spouse, isn't it? You find someone to be your universal ear. So I'm a dog with a bone when I have an idea, a dog that keeps on gnawing/talking until Chip accepts the bone/thought as the big gift that it clearly is.

"See, Chip," I said, "this matters, because, Chip, people are out there thinking they have to *pursue* the happiness, like it says in the Declaration of Independence or whatever, they think it's not only their right but like their *job,* Chip. See? They think it's their *job*. Those poor fools think they have to be constantly pursuing it! Of course they *fail* constantly, too, because the problem is it can't be caught, you have to make it yourself! You have to just fabricate that feeling out of *thin air!* You get it, Chip? You have to conjure it like a white rabbit!"

"Uh-huh," said Chip. "Definitely."

"So the pursuit thing is a fool's errand! A fool's errand, Chip! The rat race! The push for richness! The pressure for success!"

"No, yeah," said Chip, but he was fumbling with the strap on the back of my camisole, mistaking it no doubt for something else.

"You make it, Chip! You make it!"

"Come on, let's get you up against that tree," said Chip. "The bark's not too rough, is it, honey?"

"You *decide* to feel happy. Sure it's fleeting, but you can do it whenever you want to! *Joy,* Chip! You make it up out of thin air!"

"I'll make something up," muttered Chip.

And so forth.

Well, the particular, perfect angle of my clarity slipped away, as clarity tends to. You know the rest. But it was enough that I'd had it. I would remember, I promised myself. *Out of thin air,* I whispered, in my mind. *Out of thin air.*

PARTY AFTERMATHS HAVE never sat well with me. At least in this case we didn't have to do the cleanup ourselves, plus we were leaving two days later on our honeymoon, so we had that to look forward to. Still, waking up the morning after the wedding, hungover, with the task of saying goodbye to out-of-town guests hanging above our heads—I didn't love it. I fortified myself with aspirin and water chased by a nice, fresh bagel and coffee; Chip elevated his mood with a brief voyage to some pseudo-Celtic kingdom populated by slutty forest nymphs strumming on dulcimers.

They lived in treehouses, with wooden foot-bridges swaying between them. Impractical, you may say, but nymphs don't give a shit about practicality. Chip defended the slut-nymphs, if I'm not mistaken, with his bow and arrow as they came under attack from swarthy brigands.

After that, we hauled ourselves reluctantly into day. Soon we were driving, making the round of the hotels.

This was how it would be, I figured, from now on—the two of us side by side, discharging obligations. I considered asking Chip if he was disappointed, this next morning, if he'd thought being married would be more like the half-naked wood nymph community, more like the piercing of brigands' hearts, less like just being in the car, sitting there, seeing the other cars, passing buildings.

Next I thought: Well, sure, but no need to force the issue.

It struck me that we'd probably never see some

of these out-of-towners again, since families meet for weddings and then the next time, after the wedding get-together, memorial services. I wondered which of our friends would fall by the wayside, about which of them we would find ourselves saying, ten years down the road, When did we last see Kevin/Dave/Krishnamurti? Wait—no way—was it at our *wedding?*

Hard to tell who would fade out of sight. But odds were that someone would. Perhaps many.

We left my great-aunt for last on the list of stops, since I didn't want to go. I was ashamed of whatever I might have said to her in my drunken confession. I didn't know her, and I was ashamed of that too, though I couldn't say why—it wasn't like she'd ever reached out to me either, except for the surprising move of coming to my wedding. Her name was Gloria; she lived in a city. Or town or state. Lewiston, possibly. She'd been married to my mother's uncle. He'd been in commodities—seeds. Maybe feeds. Something with sacks of grain, but where you never see or touch them. She had a skin tag on her neck the size and hue of a purple grape.

I preferred to call in an excuse and let her slip quietly away to LAX, but Chip is annoyingly decent about appointments: he has an "honor code." To Chip, blowing off a great-aunt from Louisville was a failure of ethics; to me, not blowing her off was a failure of intelligence.

Sober, it was going to be hard to think of conversation topics.

"It's really too bad," I said to Chip, "that you can't just be honest about this stuff. Like, why can't I say to her: Aunt Gloria, we don't know each other from Adam, and chances are you'll die soon, right? What are you, ninety-one? Eighty-three?"

I'm not that good with ages, once there's a critical mass of wrinkles on a face it's all the same to me.

"And even if you don't die shortly, we're not going to see each other again because I'm not flying to Louisiana unless someone hijacks my plane. So let's cut to the chase. What does it mean, really? This extended family thing? I mean why did you come? Why are you even here talking to me?"

"Maybe if you don't say that about her death coming," suggested Chip mildly. "That might come off a little cold, I think. But you could maybe do the other part."

"Some people talk like that, don't they? Some people have the guts to talk like that, I bet," I said.

"I don't know if it's *guts*," said Chip.

In my mind Aunt Gloria had turned into a bit of a battleax since the rehearsal dinner, judging me harshly for my indiscreet tales of black-plague-celebrating pseudo-bondage dens, but as it turned out she was a gentle bumbler. She said almost nothing of interest the whole time we sat awkwardly in her hotel room—once she looked for her bifocals for a painfully protracted five minutes, another time she offered us a dog-eared tourist brochure from a table. It was about an amusement park with giant bunny statues that celebrated Easter all year round, but Chip turned it over in his hands as though it were made of delicate filigree, nodding respectfully.

After what seemed like an eon we walked her down to the lobby, where an airport shuttle van waited. She clutched her vinyl purse; Chip carried her luggage and tossed it up to the driver. Before she stepped in after it, she put out her hands and touched my shoulders, then cupped my cheeks. The hands were softly trembling, and when she smiled it was the saddest smile, and her eyes were watery.

"You were the *sweetest* child," she said.

Then the doors folded closed and the van pulled away.

GETTING ON THE airplane to the Caribbean I was nostalgic for the days of Eastern Airlines, how when I was a young girl, flying for the first time, the pretty stewardesses in frosted lipstick had smiled so much and been so kind to me. One of them had given me a plastic pin with wings on it, a cellophane-wrapped pack of cards for me to keep; she'd led me into the cockpit to meet the pilot, like a VIP. Those days were gone for sure—it was a wonder the surly flight attendants didn't kick us in the shins as we boarded. One of them, a weak-chinned man with thinning hair, shot me a baleful look.

I'd much rather have the frosted, buxom women, I thought. Did that make me a sexist? Was I some kind of gender traitor?

"We'd get better service on a Greyhound, Chip," I said.

I'd been thinking how *good* Chip was, just *good,* ever since he'd made the right call on feeble Aunt Gloria. Chip was often correct, I was thinking, he often made the right call, whether by means of the cheerful optimism he always had, sound instincts or plain dumb luck. I felt a wash of terrible fondness for my tiny great-aunt, now—how often Chip showed me the good path, how often he took the edge off me.

I'd started feeling downright grateful about the marriage arrangement, once my hangover was gone—almost as though I'd taken Chip for granted earlier, but now I wasn't anymore. I say "oddly" because you'd think it would be the other way around: before the wedding, appreciation; after the wedding, complacency. But so far, the reverse seemed true. Chip held my hand as we sat there. I searched his face for signs of his own budding complacency, but didn't find any.

And as we waited for takeoff, the mid-sized

aircraft stuffed to the gills, tepid, fluorescent, with a kind of cattle-car vibe presiding, I almost understood—thinking back to air travel in the 1970s, when I was but a babe in the woods—my husband's nostalgia for a fake-medieval wonderland of magical beings. It wasn't the same deal, of course, my own stewardess memories being grounded more strictly in what many would call reality, but still, all at once the idea of a charming, lost past was resonating with me. Whether it was half-invented or cut from whole cloth, the point was: that other life, that other world of wonder and possibility, what a warm, golden glow it had.

What a glow.

II.
HONEYMOON

I'd never been to the Caribbean before. The closest I'd gotten to a tropical island was the Florida beaches, swarming with the retired and half-naked. But the British Virgin Islands were different. For one thing, seminude humans weren't littering the sand; the turquoise bays were frequently deserted, the white sands smooth.

I noticed right away that I liked it.

As we motored in on a ferryboat from the airport, which was on a nearby island named Tortola, I pictured pirate ships anchored in the bay. In my mind's eye I saw the pirates drinking rum in a carefree fashion on the shore, their Jolly Rogers rippling in the breeze, the great sails on their ships billowing. The sleeves of the pirates' white shirts also billowed, fallen open over muscular chests. This was the kind of thing, I knew, Chip also liked to imagine—how dashing our fellow humans might once have been, in bygone days, even the criminals.

Chip said there was good rum nearby—not far away grew the sugarcane, of whose byproducts that famous rum was made—and we would partake of it. From our resort, a former yacht club with cabins built onto a hillside overlooking the sea, we would visit the Baths, a boulder-strewn shallow-water grotto. We would swim and snorkel. We would receive pampering services. We would be drink swillers and food eaters.

"This is what I was talking about," I told Chip approvingly, as a servile-acting individual drove us over the resort grounds in a rickety golf-cart rig. Side by side in the back, we jiggled inertly like the human cargo that we were. "*This* is a honeymoon scenario!"

"Whatever makes you happy," said Chip, and smiled at me.

It was a shame the whole world didn't resemble this resort, I thought fleetingly as, still jiggling inertly, we passed the immaculate landscaping and fragrant flowers brimming from Japanese-influenced rock gardens—that would be nice. Was it so much to ask? How hard could it be? Yes, yes, there *were* some obstacles, but still—thinking of how the whole world *didn't* look like this resort, I felt faintly aggrieved.

The golf cart ascended a steep paved path and then halted in front of a scenic dwelling with wraparound covered porches and resplendent greenery.

"Your cabin, sir," said the servile individual to Chip.

The manservant addressed his master, not me; he respected the hierarchy, the very reason for his job. Was there a difference between truly being servile and just pretending to be? I asked myself. Servility was the pretense of being a servant, wasn't it, I answered me, but at the same time, you actually were a servant. The damn thing was the pretense *of itself.*

I'd make a note of that conundrum, I'd bring it up to Chip when he was bored. There was the problem of service and servility, and then the problem of human cargo. Some people were paid to act servile, others paid out to be human cargo, the burden borne by the payee. Chip and I had paid for the privilege of others' service; therefore, on the back of a golf cart, we sat and jiggled inertly.

I thought of where the fat was, in this world, and particularly in our home country. In fact the fat was mostly settled on the poor people, the poor and the working class. The poor and the working class jiggle inertly, I thought, more than the middle-class people like Chip and me. We jiggle inertly on vacation, though neither Chip nor I is per se fat—still, what fat we *do* have jiggles, much as inanimate cargo shifts. In short we have some pretty inanimate qualities. In the past, the fat of the human world settled on kings, queens and a few wealthy merchants. But they didn't have fast food back then. Fast food turned the fat balance upside down, at least in our country. In our country the rich and middle class are thin now and the working poor jiggle inertly—or no. The poor jiggle, but not inertly like the rich. The poor jiggle *overtly*.

Plus also there's the fact that, among the tragically, morbidly obese in our nation, especially the white people, many are also religious hysterics. There seems to be a link, statistically, between the obesity epidemic and the religious hysterics, morbid obesity and extreme right-wing politics, and then again between those politics and stupidity, or at least "low educational achievement." What's more, many of these aspects are also linked to what Chip liked to call Middle America. What can the meaning of this dark pattern be?

I didn't pretend to understand it—whether the hysteria was caused by the fatness or vice versa was a mystery to me.

This is your honeymoon, I told myself. Try not to think of the fat tragedy. Try not to think of the thin tragedy either, don't think of the starving millions or the young middle-class girls with self-loathing. Try not to think of tragedy at all, the vile bookends of the fat/thin tragedy. Don't let it nestle in your mind there, as it tends to, curled cozy like a squirrel. When you go home, then you can think of tragedy. Plenty of time for that.

No sooner had we settled ourselves in the beautiful rooms—where breezes wafted from huge French doors and there were enormous ceiling fans, on top of the natural seaside air currents, fashioned handily of picturesque woody fronds—than another servile professional entered. This one was female, bearing a tray upon which stood frozen drinks and a spray of gargantuan flowers. She walked sinuously in from the terrace, where the reeds of our palapa rustled in the wind, and Chip and I gazed at her like she was Eve in the Garden of Eden. Not in the sense of being tempted by the snake and bringing about the fall of man—no. More in the sense of embodying a primordial womanly grace, with her darkish, gleaming complexion and earthen-toned sarong. With her high cheekbones, bright eyes and regal bearing, she wore the servility lightly, as though it weighed nothing.

I wouldn't blame Chip, I thought, I wouldn't blame him at all.

But Chip had eyes mostly for me, as soon as he hefted his long-stemmed, fruit-adorned cocktail glass, trying not to flinch at its excessive femininity, and thanked the Ur-woman.

It wasn't that I felt like less of a woman, next to her; more, less of a human. She was the one who bore the burden, I was the one who jiggled inertly, and the burden looked better on her than the jiggle did on me.

"Were we supposed to tip?" Chip asked after she left.

"Yes," I said, though it hadn't occurred to me before. "Yes! We have to tip! And the other guy, too. We just *insulted* them, Chip, by not tipping. It's like we slapped that beautiful woman right across the face."

We resolved to tip twice as hard next time we saw her—unless she was replaced by another majestic female being paid to act servile, which we hoped she wouldn't be. We prided ourselves on loyalty.

I wanted to ask Chip if he thought the fact that the whole world doesn't look like a beautiful resort was just a question of money—grinding poverty vs. repugnantly excessive wealth. Was it just money, or was money not really the main problem? For instance, I often hear it said that people don't starve because there's not enough food in the world, they starve because the food's not always in the right places. Is it the same way with beauty? Is there, in fact, plenty to go around?

But we got involved in other actions, it was our honeymoon, after all, not some kind of policy debate forum, it was high time for fornication, so we got that out of the way.

Or no, it wasn't fornication anymore, I realized— we were married. Disappointing.

I HADN'T THOUGHT of people, when I thought of our tropical-resort honeymoon, and the initial pure, scenic expanse of beach sands had encouraged me to continue not thinking of them. But as it turned out there *were* some other people at the resort. And wherever there are people, Chip will talk to them.

We're not the same, in that regard. Chip possesses a wealth of interest in his fellow man, harbors a fascination with his own species, whereas I tend to see the prospect of small talk and tedium. It's not that I don't like people overall; I just like to personally *select* the ones I spend time with. I favor screening techniques that don't involve random proximity.

Chip's more of an equal opportunity converser.

Even before the first night rolled around—roaming the grounds as I napped and showered—he'd made friends with no fewer than five people including two couples: a same-sex and a homely. He sketched them out for me: they were two well-dressed men from S.F., broadcasting an artsy quality, one in home furnishings and the other in the *independent film industry;* a spinster biologist specializing in reef fish; and a quiet, nerdly heterosexual duo celebrating some anniversary, whom Chip took under his wing no doubt because they were, as he put it, "from the Heartland."

"What's the Heartland, Chip?" I asked him right off, because the moniker has always puzzled me.

"The place in the truck and beer commercials," said Chip promptly. "Where they like New Country, isn't it? Those guys that sing about *proud to be an American, where at least we know we're free?*"

"It's the *at least* part that's genius," I said.

"It's kinda defensive," agreed Chip.

"But anyway, I don't think that's the definition," I demurred. "I mean some people in New Hampshire like New Country too. They like it a lot, I bet."

"Yeah, huh," said Chip. "I bet they do."

"But New Hampshire's not the Heartland, is it?"

"That's true," said Chip. "Or—I don't know. Can you have a Heartland that's kind of spread out, maybe?"

"Maybe the Heartland is spread out," I mused dreamily.

"Sweetie, you'll *like* talking to them. You'll have fun. They're really interesting."

"I doubt that, Chip," I said. "Look, I know how much you've dreamed of making friends with the natives of the Heartland—discovering what makes them tick. I know that about you. But are you sure you'd get an accurate *sense* of them in this setting? Wouldn't it be better on their home turf, in a way? Like, their natural habitat?"

"But we never go there," he objected, beating me on a technicality.

"It's such an artificial situation," I persisted. "I mean, think of this resort as kind of a zoo. Consider the animals in zoos that stalk and pace, wishing to sink their teeth into a passing five-year-old's carotid artery—or the others who, more the truth-in-advertising types, throw their own feces against the glass. I mean can we really *know* those animals, when we see them in prison like that? No, right? And isn't all this"—I raised my hands to indicate the splendid hotel—"kind of the same, without the electrocuting fences and the misery? I just wonder if, meeting these people as tourists so far, far away from where they *evolved,* you're coming anywhere *close* to getting the real Heartland experience."

When Heartland people vacation in the coastal cities, we're certainly zoo animals to them, I was thinking. Despite the fact that it's our native habitat, they ogle us as though we're exhibits. Those Heartland tourists strap on their fanny packs like ammo belts. I've seen them trundling along the Walk of Fame, admiring the movie stars' names on those pink terrazzo stars with their faces wreathed in smiles, then looking up and, on beholding average citizens, shutting those faces like barn doors.

"It's second-best, I totally see your point. But it's only dinner, babe," said Chip, and put a strong, smooth arm around me, nestling me in. He smelled his best smell. I don't know how he does it—must be a mixture of soap and pheromones.

I have my way of ending arguments, and Chip has his.

So there we were, our first evening in the newlywed utopia, fresh from a dip in the warm, aquamarine ocean, sitting around a table with five strangers. I have to admit, the setting had that odd combination of the picturesque and the asinine you sometimes see in vacationland: the restaurant was built over the water, not *jutting* over it but actually on top. It had platforms like little islands, allowing groups of diners to float in the bay as they ate. Chip and the Bay Arean designer talked about the engineering that must have been required to build this marvel of tourist novelty.

Meanwhile the "dining islands," as the restaurant called them, made me feel seasick, bobbing around like that. I tried to believe in the romance of it all, and maybe I would have been able to if I'd been alone with Chip, candlelight shimmering over the gently lapping water of the cove as we drifted beneath the lavender sunset. But with all seven of us sitting there raising our forks to our faces (the Middle Americans, the film industry/decorators and the parrotfish expert) we seemed more like a flotilla of pigs. I noticed plenty of the other islands *were* tables for two. And here we were with our table for many, long enough for the Last Supper, practically. We were the biggest floater in the pond.

The dining islands were mysterious, seeming to move around freely, yet whenever a waiter wished to serve us, bringing us near the home port to receive heaping platters of seafood, the ocean's marvelous bounty deep-fried into oblivion. Then away we floated again, to gaze down, whenever we might wish, at a sea slug glistening on the sandy bottom.

It struck me I should take a trip to the restroom, which thankfully had been built on solid ground, to rid myself of queasiness for a bit. So I made my excuses and stepped off the island onto one of the cunning raised pathways of white, broken shells, smoothed into softness by the tide, which ran like tendrils into the small bay where we floated. I struck out for the ladies' room like I was fleeing a beheading, concentrating on not turning an ankle as I picked my way over the shells on my platform mules.

I'd already drunk some wine and felt the pleasant, half-drunk turmoil of time passing, that rush of buzzed debasement/elevation that's so perfect and delicate a balance. As I wound my way through the restaurant's more landlocked tables I felt that swift bittersweet isolation, weightless and delighted—here I am, I thought, like all the others before and after me, my brother and sister drunkards, I salute you up and down the generations, from ancient Rome unto the palace of the future—those decayed palaces, those cities overgrown with the weeds and monuments sunk beneath the waves. I floated through my fellow humans in their multitudes—how sweetly, how thinly the blood ran in my veins!

Inside was where the families with children or elderly members dined—the ones who feared some of their number might topple off the islands if they ventured out there, topple and quickly drown. I envied them their nausea-free location, as my buzz faded slightly. Along the corridor to the restrooms I passed an over-the-hill-looking man wearing bulky suede sandals on his hairy white feet, and my heart went out to him—some people have no sense of anything. That was the thought that came to me.

He stood rocking back onto his heels, his hands linked idly behind his back, gazing at a map on the wall; I saw it was one of those cutesy 3D maps they print for tourists, showing poorly drawn pictures of buildings with banners like SUSIE'S SANDWICH SHOP written on them. Sweat stains were visible beneath his arms on the unfortunate T-shirt he sported, which bore on its wrinkled back the legend *Freudian Slip: When You Mean One Thing and Say Your Mother*.

It was only a matter of time till Chip made friends with him.

In the bathroom a similar-aged woman stood in front of the mirror, doing something to her eyeballs. Something with contact lenses, judging from the plastic paraphernalia on the sink counter. I could see at once she was a matched set with the Freud T-shirt, her hair a mixture of gray and brown, wearing a frumpy dress from some place Guatemalan or similar, Nicaragua, I don't know, a place where underpaid women bend over wooden looms, honest and kindly, with their whole bearing giving the impression that they welcome a life of fruitless toil.

A muumuu deal, it had embroidered flowers and a pear-shaped quality. I tried to like the outfit, though, as I beheld it—mainly to counteract Gina. Gina's opinions rent out a space in my brain, and try as I might I can't ever completely evict them.

"Isn't it *gorgeous* here?" the muumuu wearer half yelled at me, as I tried to sidle past into a toilet stall.

"Mmm, hmm, wmm," I said, or words to that effect. I don't want to talk on my way in or out of the stalls. Not to a stranger, possibly not to anyone. It's a moment for keeping your own counsel.

As I peed I thought of how probably, when Chip made friends with the sweaty Freud T-shirt guy, I'd have to act pally with this woman, his bookend, who now wished to prattle on to me as urine streamed between my legs into the toilet bowl. Well, sure she did. Why not? I was a person; to go with my urethra, I had ears. Urethras were for peeing, ears were for receiving the random chatter of orbiting life forms. Her own life-form equipment included a mouth for talking from—a generous mouth above a muumuu of embroidered flowers, as it happened. Red, green, yellow, purple, and blue. Yes, she was a life form displaying other life forms and reaching out to even more life forms, willy-nilly. Out there, beyond the metal door, she was saying something about Pacifica or maybe spina bifida—I couldn't hear past the rushing sound of pee. I wished she would stop, though.

I'd known Chip long enough to predict when he would make friends with the strangers I'd spotted; what it came down to was simply whether the person in question would consent to talk to *him*. Because Chip *was* going to talk to them, it went without saying, so if the other party was *also* a scattershot, arbitrary extrovert like Chip, nine out of ten times they'd connect. And here was my answer, right in front of me: the woman, who had never met me before, was talking about spina bifida, or possibly the beer Pacifico, as I peed.

And it was all for naught, I thought, as I loudly, deliberately flushed—on the subject of spina bifida I was a blank slate. No help to give. No expertise at all.

There was a pregnant pause as I came out, as though she'd asked me a question.

"Sorry?" I said.

"Have you been to the Baths yet?" she asked eagerly. "A*maz*ing!"

"I saw them in the ads," I conceded, turning on a tap and beginning to wash my hands. I was still trying to evict Gina, or rather the goblin Gina, perched cozily on my shoulder and glaring down at the perfectly friendly woman's shoes. Like her dress, they seemed to partake of a peasant motif, homespun or at least cheaply manufactured. They were fashioned of myriad strings of knotted leather or possibly vegan leather alternative, none too clean, flowers sprouting, tassels hanging, hither, thither and yon, tendrils of shoe twining around her ankles and up her calves like so many creeping vines in a movie where plants come alive. Or wait, plants are alive. But you know what I mean. The shoes were unflattering, with soles flat as pancakes that showcased the woman's large, pale toes, the female equivalent of her partner's; they were nosing out of the Jesus-style footwear like rows of eager hippos. Albinos.

The Gina goblin wanted to torch the sandals. Failing that, the goblin wanted to take the sandals, along with the chunky ones worn by the Freud T-shirt man, and nail them up on an offensive sign. HIPPIES GO HOME, something like that. Mean-minded and impeccably dressed, the goblin chittered on my shoulder—chittered unpleasantly.

How many times, I wondered, as the woman said words like *mindfulness* and *fully present,* had that Gina homunculus hitched a ride on me? I didn't always like it, but I couldn't shake it off, either. Chip and Gina were angel and devil on my shoulders, basically, and there were things I loved about them both. I went Chip's way when I could—maybe prolonged exposure would encourage me. Gina insisted on judgment, an us-and-them mentality, while Chip, with his earnest friendliness, tried to lead me down the path of brotherly love.

But brotherly love was sometimes wrong.

Take the toe situation, I thought to myself.

When we were kids, Gina and I, and even through college, which we attended together, I'd had some creative ambitions. Young people often do. I wanted to write songs and also sing them for a living, had singer/songwriter fantasies. I took lessons, I wrote songs and forthwith I sang them; excitedly I made demo tapes, performed for myself in mirrors and in showers, concocted videos. Later I put on shows for others, at college bars and grungy yet pretentious cafes.

But finally Gina showed me the error of my ways, pointing out quite rightly that the world was full of singers already—showcasing the foregone conclusion of my artistic and professional failure. Don't be a wannabe, said Gina impatiently. It was Gina who persuaded me to go the MBA route, whereby at least, she said, I could grow up to be a loser with money instead of a loser without it. And we'd be at the same school then, she said, because she planned to go to Stanford too and get her PhD. She wasn't born to make money, she said, because to make money, one way or another, directly or indirectly, you had to build people up. She was born to cut people down, she said, and that's what she was going to do. Criticize.

Therefore: a PhD. But about the singing, we can always do karaoke, she said, we'll go to karaoke bars whenever you want!

We'll get wall-eyed. We'll belt us out some Bee Gees *shit*.

Since then there's always been a shadow Gina following me, even when the real Gina, in her physical body, is absent, such as during my honeymoon. (Gina, I happened to know from texts received on my cell phone, was enjoying her own honeymoon of sorts with Ellis, whom she'd decided to like for several weeks at least, she texted me, before *bringing the hammer down.* She also texted me that he was surprisingly good in the sack, *you know, for a faggot.* She said his *Eurofag fashion sense* meant he'd given her good advice on buying a new bag. Also, the décor of his apartment was actually half-OK, she reported, if you ignored the *fake-punk boy-teen completely faggy Union Jacks.* Other than me, all Gina's closest friends are gay guys; she's less a homophobe than a victim of Stockholm.)

I acquitted myself with a compliment on my way out of the restroom—you can distract a woman lickety-split with an unexpected piece of flattery about her appearance; it's the interfemale equivalent of a sucker punch—and booked it past the Freud T-shirt in the hall, who was still rocking back on his callused heels in front of the 3D map like he was contemplating the Mona Lisa.

I headed for the restaurant's shining bar, figuring I could while away another five minutes waiting for a new drink before I had to step onto the nauseating island once again.

"Do you sell Dramamine?" I said, after asking for wine.

Startling me, the bartender whipped out a pill in a paper slip and ripped open the package. He dumped the contents neatly into a glass of seltzer and pushed the glass across.

"We get that all the time," he said, and leaned over the counter, voice lowered. "I'm going to tell you this because I think you're a fox. Don't like to see a beautiful woman puke."

"Uh—"

"And I don't like to watch it being cleaned up, either. So here goes: there's a switch you can flip under the table, on the central post that holds the table up. You find it with your foot. It's supposed to be for emergencies, but if you want to stop that thing moving, just flip it. You saw how shallow it is out there—there's a little anchor-type deal on the bottom of the island that drops and locks into the track. The hostess can override, and she *will* override eventually so you can get served and like that, but meanwhile you guys'll stop moving."

"Knight in shining armor," I said sincerely. "Serious, here. Really."

So I felt pleased on my return to the table, possessing the secret weapon as I did.

• • •

THE MARINE BIOLOGIST sitting next to me was a woman who loved fish. Fish in general, parrotfish in specific. They're thick-lipped reef fish in bright colors; I saw some later, but at the time I didn't know a parrotfish from a hump-head wrasse. She was a parrotfish promoter, the biologist.

"You see that beautiful, fine white sand all around us?" she asked me, over dessert.

I nodded, though in the dark, to be precise, the beach sand had faded from our sight. Along the dark shore a row of tiki torches flickered orange.

"You've got the parrotfish to thank for that," she said, and nodded emphatically. "Bioerosion. *Major* contributors."

"Ah!" I said. "Bioerosion!"

"They eat the reefs! They make the sand! They chew it up and excrete it. A single parrotfish can make two hundred pounds of fine white sand per year."

"I *see!*" I said.

"You like the beach? Then thank a parrotfish. That's what I always say," she went on.

She was eating a flan with gusto.

Still, I was happy to be talking to her, because the husband from the Heartland seemed to be at loggerheads with one of the Bay Areans, Chip standing by neutrally. The Heartland wife looked embarrassed, but the Heartland husband was sticking to his guns—something about global warming. He said it seemed to be nature—that various Ice Ages, also, had taken place now and then, and the warming was a non-Ice Age.

His logic went: It has been colder before, and now it will be warm. The film-industry Bay Arean, enraged by this, was raining thunder upon him.

Meanwhile the Heartland wife and the other Bay Arean were making small talk off to one side, trying to take the edge off any free-floating climate-change aggression with harmless domesticity. The Bay Arean designer recommended air plants for the Heartland living room, which could be placed in clear-plastic globes that dangled from shelves or light fixtures. They required no soil. You watered them with a spray bottle, he told her; couldn't be easier. The Heartland wife received this wisdom with earnest nods.

Presently Chip latched onto a couple of words in the Bay Arean filmmaker's angry tirade—the words *carbon dioxide,* I picked up—and used them to launch a friendly digression. Chip plays the fool to make peace, often, as well as to make people like him, and in this case he asked if carbon dioxide was the gas from car tailpipes that killed depressed people. If so we *should* reduce it, Chip suggested with modest buffoonery, absolutely—no one should die in a garage. Least of all a person who's goddamn depressed. In my garage, went Chip's transitional patter, there's a garbage can that smells, some old strips of moldy carpet and an aging Nissan Sentra. Is that a fitting sunset to a life?

This led to a lighthearted discussion of which cars would be the worst to die in, with "minivan" leading, and the conversation was thus steered into the social safe house of irony.

All of this I heard in the background, in pieces, as the parrotfish expert enthused about how coral went in the fishes' mouths and white, tropical sands came out their ass-ends. We wouldn't have the tropics as we knew them—with highly visible reef creatures swimming over a pale background in water that looked turquoise—if not for parrot-fish and other "bio-eroders," she chin-wagged to me. The tropics would look very different with no white sand, wouldn't they, and without the reefs and their nibbling fish that sand would dis-appear, said the biologist. In fact, she elaborated, gesturing at the Bay Arean off to her left, what he was talking about, the warming, the rising acid of seawater, all that would kill the parrotfish, she said, in the event that it continued.

". . . generate models with fairly narrow margins of error," she was saying through her final mouthful of crème caramel—because by then I'd realized it wasn't a flan, strictly speaking. "Of course those models have been completely disregarded. Because, as I'm sure you know, an effective political response to the science, on the time frame needed, was always an impossibility."

I was thinking of flipping the table switch, because the truth was that most of the wine glasses and beer pitchers were still full at our table and we wouldn't be leaving that table and hitting dry land anytime soon. Yet once again nausea was rising in me, as we floated past a two-top where a poorly dressed couple seemed to be dipping fried squid rings into a pot of onion-scented sauce. I felt around with my foot for the center post of the table, but all I got was air; I was near the end of the table. So I had to scoot my chair over a few inches, then a few more, to come within range of the central post.

I didn't want to call attention to my activities, though; I didn't want to seem like a schemer, so I went on nodding and talking to the biologist while this was going on. Above the table's edge I was normal, albeit feeling increasingly queasy; below it I was little more than a stuck-out limb with a sneaking, feely foot, making forays.

When my toes finally touched the table's main post I cast off my shoe and inched the toes up and down the post, looking for the telltale bump of a switch. Listening to the biologist I got distracted, though, so it took several moments for me to notice the post wasn't as smooth as it should be, the post was in fact furry, and furthermore it was a leg.

The leg extended from the Heartland man. He

whipped his head around like it was being spun on its neck-stalk by a Linda Blair Satan.

I was startled by the abruptness of the head spin and snatched my foot back with a speed that rivaled his.

But it was too late. He was smiling at me. The Heartland husband thought I was making a pass at him.

And here's where I made my second mistake, because instead of coming clean and admitting I'd been looking for the anti-vomit button, I lost my way in confusion. There was a guilty look on my face, I know, as I averted my eyes in embarrassment from his strangely avid gaze. I had to reach out my bare foot a bit in his direction yet again, in order to snag the abandoned mule and tumble said mule back toward me with my toe tips. Then I wriggled the foot back into it.

Making matters worse, I shifted my body neatly away even as I did this, recommitting my attention to the dismal future of parrotfish. For all the world as though I was either ashamed of my footsy overture or, worse, coy.

My eye-contact avoidance convinced the husband, I believe. He knew me for the strumpet that I wasn't.

AS WE WERE leaving the restaurant, the Heartland guy got next to me while Chip strode ahead listening to the Bay Arean designer orate on the subject of high-end prefab sheds. The Heartland wife had gone to the restroom with the parrotfish expert, so her husband and I were, unfortunately, alone and bringing up the rear.

"So, hey," he said. "You don't say much, do you?"

"I say a lot," I said. "Sometimes too much. Believe me. When so moved."

"But back at the table there, you let your twinkle toes do the talking."

For a second I thought the barkeep would get to clean my sick up after all.

"Twinkle . . . ?"

"I like them," he said, in a fruity voice.

I glanced down at the offending digits as we walked, needing somewhere to rest my eyes. They still sported their wedding pedicure; the nails were salmon-pink. Seen from a Heartland viewpoint, I guessed, they could be deemed trashy.

"I'm a toe man," he said, dropping the volume. "And yours are top-notch. Grade A. *So* hot."

"You're kidding me," I said. "Is this something—is there a hidden camera?"

"A lot of people feel it's not cheating if it's the toes," he went on, fruitier and juicier by the second.

"So did Chip mention we just got married?" I rushed. "This is a great place for a honeymoon, I think. Don't you? Really perfect."

"Many people say if it's just the toes, anything

goes. There's an increasingly—call it *liberal*
approach, since you're from California, ha ha—
to when it's just the toes."

"Just the toes that *what?*" I said, and then
regretted it.

"That *share intimacy,*" he said. *"Toe-genital
intimacy."*

"Oh my God," I burst out, and practically stam-
peded over the Bay Areans in my haste to get next
to Chip.

As soon as he and I split off from the others to
make our way along the lighted footpaths to our
cabin, I gave him the lowdown. He seemed not to
completely believe me, before I reprimanded him.
Chip tries pretty hard to see the best in folks. But
he came around when I supplied a few details,
and he promised me we'd try to eat alone—at least
in the evenings, when darkness was all around.

"I'm not hanging out with that guy again," I
said. "I'm not sharing another meal with him. No
meals of any kind. And no day trips either, Chip,
because I know how you like to invite strangers
along. Not him. He made me feel like my toes
were prostitutes. Like my *toes,* Chip, were dolled
up in Frederick's of Hollywood. That's not right."

"Your lips say no, but your toes say yes," said
Chip.

I hit him for deadpanning, but it was weak.
Still, the words of the toe man haunted me as I
tried to fall asleep. I thought to myself: *Are* my

toes sluts? *Were* my toes asking for it? It kept me up after Chip had fallen asleep, even, because I worry about these questions. In the broadest sense, of course, no woman should have to worry about whether her toes are asking for it—in the most lofty, the most righteous sense. But on the other hand, in the more narrow, specific context of personal choice, was I responsible for debasing my own toes? Were the toes, in essence, fashion victims, like those newborns with lacy headbands strapped around their craniums, fluffy rosettes affixed, to broadcast femaleness? To function as blaring signs that read: *I am a female baby, what so many call a "girl"; moreover, it is absolutely vital to my parents that even perfectly indifferent passersby should know this instantly. For that reason, and that reason alone, I have been tagged with this most hideous adornment.*

Had I visited that kind of sad, pimpish outrage on ten innocent dactyls?

It wasn't till the next morning, when I woke up to the sound of steadily plashing waves, and then the sight of Chip bringing me my morning coffee with his shirt off, that I felt completely nausea-free again. I sat propped up on the pillow, drinking my coffee, watching the fan whir overhead, and I reassured myself. The toenails were pink. That was the whole story.

We set off for the Baths not long after, where we spent the morning walking between gray, wet boulders, on top of boulders, and beneath boulders. There were narrow crevices to walk through, sand beneath our feet; there were ropes to hang onto as we climbed; there were wooden ladders. It was a group of boulders, with the ocean washing in and washing out again. That was the situation there.

We sat on top of a boulder, just the two of us, and looked out to sea one time; after that Chip kissed me on the sand, an inch or two of tide lapping at our legs. I had sand on my calves, sand on my knees, and I thought how much I enjoyed the sight and texture of sand on skin, how satisfying it could be to roll the grains beneath my fingertips, two sleek expanses of my skin with sand between them. One day, I ruminated, that skin would be wrinkly. That skin would be baggy as a pachyderm's, and possibly gray, too. The sand wouldn't be as satisfying then.

"You think we'll still like sex when we're old, Chip?" I asked romantically, while one more time we boulder-sat.

"I'll take me some Viagra," said Chip. "I don't care. I'll pop it like vitamins, if need be."

"I'll be all wrinkled, like an elephant."

"Me too."

"Wrinkles get a bad rap. Don't they," I said.

"If you think about it, what's a wrinkle or two," agreed Chip.

"I think it's probably an evolution, reproductionof-the-fittest type thing. I mean we probably want to mate with wrinkle-free people so they're still fertile, for one thing."

"Good point," said Chip, nodding.

I was contented, sitting there with him. And yet I had a sense that nothing was happening—that nothing, possibly, would ever happen to me again.

Curiously it was then, sitting on our boulder, looking out to sea and thinking of being elderlies together, that we caught sight of a small power-boat churning into the harbor from the direction of the reefs. In that boat was a newly familiar figure: the parrotfish expert. She wore a black wetsuit and stood looking off the bow, a kind of rigid tension in her posture; when the boat passed close enough that we could see each other better she jumped up and down, waving wildly. She was yelling, but I wasn't able to hear the words. Then the boat veered toward the docks.

"That's weird," said Chip. "She didn't seem the excitable type, so much, when we first met her. Did she, Deb?"

We got down off the rock and strolled along the intertidal zone toward the marina. We weren't in a hurry—we held hands, we held our shoes in our other hands, we looked for crabs and shells, scooping up water and wet sand onto the top flats of our feet, then letting it trail off. It wasn't long at all, though, before we saw the parrotfish expert again, and this time she was running toward us.

She still had her wetsuit on, which made her run in a held-back, goofy-robotic way that looked like a form of slow torture. But she was doing it anyway. That expert was determined. And it was a sight worth seeing.

By the time she got up to us, though, she was huffing and puffing so hard I thought she might be having an attack. The biologist could hardly breathe, much less speak. But she waved us away and bent over, hands braced on her thighs, catching her breath. She shook her head when we asked if there was anything she needed, just shook her head, struggling to breathe. Finally she wrestled the breathing under control and straightened up, her face beet-red. Her cheeks and forehead still bore the deep, bruising marks of a snorkel mask, which made her look deformed.

"In the reef!" she said breathlessly. "You've got to come with me! I have to show you! I saw them!"

"Those colorful fish you like so much?" asked Chip, genuinely interested.

She shook her head rapidly, emphatically.

"Mermaids! There are mermaids! Mermaids are swimming in the reef!"

SHE WAS DISTURBED, of course—we hardly knew the woman. Maybe it was a schizoid deal, we figured, or maybe a drug problem, we didn't have all the info yet, but the situation had to be handled humanely. If there's one thing Chip is, it's game. He's game for almost anything, and so much the better if, later, it might make good material for an anecdote to tell at a party.

So he humored the delusional scientist, and I went along with it cheerfully—because, of all the people we'd had dinner with, she was the only one I kind of liked. That meant that, after Chip, she was my favorite person for a thousand-mile radius.

She said she'd booked a 7 a.m. seat on a snorkel boat, and it turned out she was the only one booked for that slot, so the boat's captain took her out to the reef by herself, muttering something about swimming in pairs. But he didn't want to give her money back; it was just snorkeling after all—child's play. So he took her by herself, without a second paying customer. And that was how she came to see the mermaids. The boat captain hadn't seen squat.

We were sitting in the boat ourselves by that time, being ferried back out to the reef. She'd offered the captain more money for the second trip; she talked a blue streak while we were motoring. Also she ran around collecting parts of wetsuits for us to wear, a top and bottom for Chip and a one-piece suit in my size. I obliged her by changing in the boat's tiny bathroom, enjoying the privacy; I figured we might as well get a free snorkel out of her sad mental incapacity.

The night before, when I'd been assuming she was sane—an absentminded type, but with all the usual marbles—I'd viewed her as a normal, if geeky, woman. Now she took on a kind of homeless aspect to me. I studied her face trying to pick out signs of that unhinged quality. She didn't tweeze her brows: well, that one was inconclusive. A crazed person might tweeze or might not tweeze—might pick the brows off hair by hair, even get rid of them in one fell swoop like those women you see who shave off their brows on purpose, then pencil them on again, making you wonder: grotesquely ironic? Or ironically grotesque?

If I looked at her brows for too long, they started to seem like centipedes. I was afraid they might start moving their legs. And they had so many!

Nancy, the biologist, wore no traces of makeup, which I'd first thought signaled a feminist: laudable. I like a touch of lipstick and a subtle brown eye shadow myself—I rationalize it as less an attempt to attract males than as a kind of ritualistic tribal decoration/shamanistic warding— but I also enjoy the rare sight of a naked face. Still, now, with the insanity rearing its head, I wondered if the no-makeup thing was less a stance than a sign of neglect. Maybe Nancy was the type who wore her underwear for weeks on end, or stored her cut-off fingernails in jelly jars.

Apparently there was a sunken airplane on the reef, a small plane from long ago, and Nancy said she'd been slowly following a princess parrotfish as it weaved among the corals and then, out of the corner of her eye/mask, had seen something far larger flash through one of the holes where the airplane's door used to be. Excited to think she might have her first local encounter with a shark or large ray, she abandoned the fish and swam cautiously over to the rusting plane. It was there that she saw it: the tail. Only the tail was visible inside the plane, from her vantage point, she said, until she swam up close and stuck her head around the brown and corroded metal door edge.

And that was when she realized that the tail, covered in silvery scales, was surmounted by a humanoid torso. Atop that sat a neck, and finally a head, out of which long hair grew—modestly, and a little too conveniently, covering the impossible creature's breasts.

"What color was her hair?" asked Chip, like it mattered.

"Yellow!" said Nancy. I couldn't tell if she was indignant or just enthusiastic.

"Of course it was yellow, Chip," I said.

"I don't know about *of course,*" retorted Chip. "There are multiplayer games I do where mermaids have blue hair. Green. Even purple."

"This wasn't an MOG," said Nancy, a little prudishly.

"So what did she do?" pressed Chip.

"Put out that cigarette!" said Nancy sharply, turning to the boat captain. "Please! I suffer from asthma!"

"Nancy?" I chimed in as the captain, looking resentful, flicked his cigarette over the side of the boat, thus littering. "So what did the mermaid do?"

"She swam away! She was quick. Really quick," said Nancy. "I followed, but I was a lot slower. But I saw there were others like her. I saw their shapes in the water before they got away from me. A pod, if you can call it that. It was a pod of mer-people."

"Well, if they swam away," said Chip gently, "they may not be there when we get there. I want you to be prepared for that. We won't judge you, Deb and I, if we can't find them this time. You know—no judgment."

"None at all," I said. "I'm sure they don't stay

for long. Once they've been spotted. I mean, they must be secretive types, right? Or people would have known about them long ago."

"We do know about them," said Nancy.

"But I mean, know they were *real*," I said.

"Colossal squid," said Nancy.

"Pardon?"

"Well, they were 'mythic' too, till recently. Then their bodies were found, dead and floating. Finally one was caught live. Forty feet long. Weighed one thousand pounds. The oceans are very deep, you know. The last frontier. Still largely unexplored. New discoveries happen daily, new species are identified all the time. Maybe this is a similar situation."

There was no reasoning with a deranged marine biologist. I nodded agreeably.

Before long the captain was throttling down and Nancy was eagerly pulling on her fins, positioning her mask.

"Come on, come on!" she urged, as Chip and I struggled with our own masks and fins. And then we followed her off the side of the boat, which had a slide built into it. Swoop and splash.

I have to say it was gorgeous down there, a place where beauty clichés came true. Light filtering, colorful blobby formations, glamorously decorated fish flitting about—all in all it was exactly what you'd hope it would be. Chip and I followed Nancy, waving our flippers steadily. She turned out to be much better at the free-dive thing than either of us; Chip had to be impressed.

Again and again she dove, fishlike. Or seabird-like, possibly.

Chip tried to copy her after her first few dives, when she turned her goggly, tube-sucking face toward us and made a gesture of impatience. Seemed like she didn't know what we were up to, snorkeling around on the surface, wimpy. I could tell Chip felt he had to rise, or rather dip, to the challenge. Chip's fit but he's no scuba diver; I hoped he wouldn't get the bends. I didn't even try to dive deep, myself—I had a mild case of swimmer's ear. So I floated, waggling my flippers as Chip did his best, coming up to breathe through his tube, then dipping down again and again in the parrotfish expert's wake.

The airplane was maybe twenty feet under. You couldn't even see into its decrepit cockpit from up at the surface, where I was. But no yellow-haired mer-people must have been languishing there, because Chip shook his head when he got back up to me. He stuck his head out for air, then came back under and gave me a slow-motion headshake.

But Nancy didn't give up easily. She kept on going, round and round the reef, to each new nook and cranny, then out past the reef to a cluster of underwater rocks. The variety of fishes thinned out and there were fewer of the bright, darting ones and more of the flattish, dull-colored numbers camouflaged by sand. I was waiting to signal to Chip that I was heading back to the boat—I thought I'd get a drink of water, take off the borrowed wetsuit and put my feet up for a while—when down beneath me, where he and Nancy had most recently dived, came a silvery explosion of bubbles, a confusion of flippers. Streams of froth surged up and made it impossible to see anything but white.

I hoped they hadn't met with a jellyfish or been barracuda-bit. As I peered down and saw nothing, I ideated blood and teeth, severed digits bobbing and leaking crimson in the surf, like in so many shark movies. I started to feel panicky as the cloud of bubbles in the water beneath me refused to clear, and finally decided to free-dive down—my swimmer's ear be damned. What if Chip was caught on something and running out of air? What if the crazed biologist had suddenly attacked him? There could be anything happening, below that blinding screen of turbulence.

I gulped air from my tube, held it, and gave what I hoped was a powerful flip of my fins. Down I bucked, feeling pressure inside my head and not liking it a bit. I swished myself around the bubble cloud, instead of through the midst of it, so that I wouldn't crash into anyone coming up; I tried to force myself down, though my body resisted. Still I could see nothing except a rock with brown and yellow barnacle-type things on it that looked like rotting teeth. I bobbed up again, gasping.

Luckily, a few seconds later Chip surfaced too, and then Nancy, all of us popping our tubes out and sucking in air.

"Jesus!" cried Chip, spluttering.

"You saw them! Didn't you?" asked Nancy, spluttering too.

"I gotta go down again," said Chip, and without waiting for me to answer, down he dove.

I followed him, of course, because at this point curiosity was killing me. It was frustrating, though, because I was in Chip's bubble trail again. There are negatives to being a follower instead of a leader, in a diving situation. I pushed myself down, trying to get alongside him for a better view of whatever it was he thought he'd seen, but all I saw was silver swirls of bubbles—could have been anything—and before long I swooped up again, helpless.

I waited for them to come up, treading water and getting more and more gaspy. When Chip finally surfaced his face was purple-red; he shoved his tube aside and pulled his mask up onto the top of his head, and I could see his eyes were wide, like when he'd been electric-shocked in the mud marathon.

"So? Did you see mermaids?" I asked him, in a joking tone. I assumed he'd report a sea turtle, a dolphin or stingray or what have you.

"Deb! There were some goddamn *mermaids* down there!"

Feeling a bit fed up, I snorted and turned to swim back toward the boat, shaking my head. Chip's a fantasist, of course, a fantasy game-player; Chip enjoys the world of make-believe. I think I've made that clear.

I climbed back onto the boat, and when I came out of the head with the wetsuit off and my clothes back on, the captain wordlessly handed me a cold can of beer. Didn't say a word, just handed it over. I was grateful. I sat on one of the white fiberglass benches drinking and taking a breather; before long the other two joined me, climbing the ladder with their faces shining oddly.

"Deb," said Chip breathlessly, shedding his gear, "you thought I was kidding, but I wasn't. Maybe it's a hoax or like that, I'm not saying it isn't, but down there were people with tails. People fully the size of you or me."

"If it's a hoax, how were they breathing underwater?" asked Nancy. "You didn't see any breathing apparatus, did you?"

"Maybe it was a sleight-of-hand trick," said Chip. "Or just like phenomenal timing. I mean, the two of us were down there, right Deb? Nancy and I. And *we* didn't have oxygen tanks."

"But have you seen anyone come up since then? There's nothing but this boat around, as far as the eye can see!" raged Nancy. She turned to me. "Did *you* see anyone come up?"

"Come on, guys," I said, and crumpled my beer can, which was already empty. "Enough, already. You got me. Consider me pranked. OK?"

Nancy glared at me with her eyebrows like angry crawlers. Then she turned back to Chip, as though I hadn't said a thing.

"Maybe they had a submarine to go back to," said Chip. "A submersible. Like in that movie, *The Abyss*. Or even *Titanic*. You know the kind I mean," he said, appealing to me. "For research. Maybe they saw us, then swam back to their submersible. Technically, free-diving for long periods of time is possible. I mean some free-divers can go down two, three hundred meters on one breath. Competitive apnea! Deb, it's an extreme sport! There's one guy who can hold his breath in a pool for eleven minutes. I read it online."

"Be reasonable," said Nancy. "Manned submersibles cost a *mint*. There aren't any commercial ones operating around here or I'd have found out about them. Plus, who'd strap on a tail and swim around in the middle of the Atlantic just for *our* benefit? Nobody."

"You guys," I said, "I'm sure there's an explanation, other than you're both messing with me. Maybe someone rubbed LSD onto your breathing tubes. Or the tubes got toxic mold on it in that box that caused hallucinations. And now I'm ready to go back. Can we please go?"

The boat captain didn't wait on Nancy's command; impatient as any man slighted by underpayment, he throttled up and we motored toward dry land.

THE DAY HAD started well, even gaily. First I'd shaken off the tinge of shame laid on me by the Heartland man; then Chip and I had kissed in a shady grotto, water running around our bodies in pleasing rivulets. We'd been living the American Dream, or the American-Caribbean Dream—call it the American-Caribbean Honeymoon Dream. Whatever you call it, I'd felt clothed in its raiment of sun and sex and booze, lassitude, freedom from opinion. I'd felt a pleasing vacuum of responsibility, filled with trade winds and ocean spray. Washing the salt from our ropy hair as sand, too, swirled down the shower drain. Lying spent and happy on cool white sheets, air on the skin, rustle of fronds in the breeze, the whir of time passing, warm wind of the turning world.

But after the boat trip the dream altered. Within the smooth fabric of the dream a thread of doubt had been picked, and suddenly the weave was unraveling.

The problem, at first, seemed to be Chip. I wanted the old Chip back, the Chip for whom there was real life on the one hand, without mythic creatures, and videogames solidly on the other hand, where mythic creatures cavorted quite abundantly. The new Chip was confusing, even frightening to me, because the new Chip was stubbornly insisting that those worlds weren't separate. That went too far for me. It was a rude jolt. The earth was unstable beneath my feet.

And hadn't even been Chip's *idea*—someone we barely knew had brought the idea to him, and then he'd run with it. There was an arbitrary quality to the mermaid sighting. Yet Chip had signed right up! The honeymoon was supposed to be all about him and me, and instead he'd become a member of a secret society—Chip was affiliated, now, with a disturbed parrotfish expert.

It was as though he'd joined a cult. He was dazed, when we got back to the cabana; there was a look of sheer obliteration on his face. He barely talked to me. And pretty swiftly, there on the island of Virgin Gorda in the British Caribbean, it made me feel terribly lonely, a premonition of the grave. Sitting across the room from Chip as he ignored me—he was scrolling through pages of mermaid lore on the tablet he'd brought with him—I put myself in his shoes. For a second I *was* Chip, *I was Chip,* and *I couldn't help believing.*

As Chip, I had no choice.

But as myself . . .

I made a snap decision. Much as a candidate might flip-flop on abortion when the demographics

113

called for it, I was changing my position. Because the problem, at first, had seemed to be with Chip; but I saw now the problem could equally be seen as mine. And unlike the problem of Chip, that other problem—the problem of me—was one I could solve easily. The plainest solution was the best. Why put up resistance? No need. I bought in. I turned on a dime.

After all, I reasoned, if there *were* mermaids drifting under the glittering waves, mermaids who rose from the sparkling ceiling of their undersea world from time to time, their father someone like Neptune, bearded, big-chested, trident-holding; if there were mermaids who perched on rocks, sunning, who brushed their golden locks and gazed at their reflections in delicately fashioned mother-of-pearl-framed mirrors; if there were mermaids who rode, when the occasion warranted, in giant clamshells pulled by a team of giant seahorses—so much the better for us all.

And if said mermaids *did* turn out to be a figment, there too I sensed no threat to me personally.

"Chip, I'm sorry," I said tenderly, going over to him at our room's long counter, where he was perched on a barstool scrolling. I put my arms around him and rested my chin on his shoulder. "Because if you saw mermaids, you know what? You saw mermaids. I didn't mean to be a buzz-kill, Chip. I *believe* you, honey."

Chip smiled at me, and balance was restored.

That's another saving grace of Chip: he doesn't ask why the politician flip-flopped. He doesn't look a gift horse in the mouth.

ON THE DOMESTIC front, at that point, all was well, but on a practical level there was still the presence of Nancy to contend with—that parrot-fish expert had vim and vigor. As far as she was concerned, as far as Chip was concerned, and therefore as far as I had to be concerned, too, her vacation/our honeymoon had turned from a pleasure trip into a crypto-zoological mission.

First off, she planned a dive session. She made calls, she sent emails, she hit the streets. She visited every dive shop on the island seeking out scuba adepts, fishing enthusiasts, anyone with even the flimsiest of biology credentials who could go underwater as a part of her expeditionary force.

Unlike Chip I hadn't gone diving before; you had to be certified to rent gear from any of the shops in town. Yet again, I suspected, I was going to be left out if I didn't act fast. So while Chip was helping Nancy prepare for the next day's excursion—she would wait for one day maximum, because she feared losing the mermaids if they proved migratory—I went to the dive shop and hired a pro named Jamie. If I took a beginners' class, he'd come with me on the expedition, for a fee.

So I practiced with a rental tank in the hotel swimming pool—it was me and some friendly elderlies—and then I met Chip on the sandy drive that led from the resort's main building to the shop, where he sat waiting in one of the resort golf carts. He drove us back to the cabana while I jiggled inertly.

"We signed on two science teachers," he reported. "That's all there are on the whole *island*. Plus one of them's just a substitute. But he knows *some* biology."

"What did she tell them we'd be looking for?"

"Rare fish. Some kind of huge fish no one has seen for ages. A grouper, I think she said. They weigh four hundred pounds. That's what she's telling everyone. She doesn't want to influence the people who haven't seen anything yet. Observer bias, or something."

"That's smart," I conceded. "Plus there's the fact that, if she said you were looking for mermaids, no one would come but lunatics."

"We signed on one diver who used to be a U.S. Navy SEAL. He bought a house and retired here. We have a bunch of spearfishing dudes—a tourist and a couple of locals. It's looking pretty good; it's coming together. There's a videographer dude, a guy with underwater video equipment, who's staying at another resort, the other end of the island. He's coming too. She had to offer to pay him."

"It'll be worth it," I said supportively. "Although—is there a finder's fee, for something like mermaids?"

Chip had no patience for levity.

The rest of the day rushed past, with Chip functioning as Nancy's assistant and me functioning as Chip's. I called dive shops with equipment orders, dive boats for scheduling; I set up an onboard lunch for twenty (on mine and Chip's credit card, though Nancy claimed she'd cover our expenses. I felt myself doubting that outcome, but hell, it was our honeymoon, we'd said we'd spare no expense). By the time evening was coming on and sun-reddened families were trailing into the resort's restaurants, Chip was pumped for the next day's trip and wanted to throw back a beer. Nancy talked on her cell phone nonstop to what were, according to Chip, some of her colleagues. From what I could discern on our end, they were arguing with her but not dismissing her out of hand, as you might assume they would.

She must have credibility capital to spend, I guessed. A less bold woman would have waited till the sighting was confirmed. That parrotfish expert had some cojones on her.

Chip and I let her conduct her business in peace, for the most part, though she didn't leave our side; it was like a romantic dinner for two where one of the two has a monkey attached to his head. If Chip and I had been a couple of coral outcroppings she would have been the parrotfish, nibbling at our edges and busily expelling grains of sand. She didn't order food herself but perched on a third chair and picked at what was left on our plates when we finished each course—just reached for it and chewed noisily as she said words like *aquatic primate, herbivorous mammals* and *Sirenomelia* into her cheek-parked phone.

"Chip," I said, to cover the sound of her phone patter over our supposedly relaxing dessert coffee, "what did they look like, the ones that you saw? I know it was fast. But can you tell me some details?"

Chip nodded, swallowed some pie. "The one that was the closest to me was the only one whose face I saw at all. And I have to say, she didn't look like you might expect. Not exactly."

"Yellow hair, bare breasts," I said. "Right?"

"Yeah, no," said Chip. "That's true. But she kind of had bad teeth. No dentists in the sea, I guess. No underwater dentistry. The teeth were brownish or yellowish. Like an Englishman."

"No fluoride," I guessed.

"And in the background I saw one that seemed to be a guy. He had big shoulders, you know, a general guy shape? Except for the tail. The tail, I have to be honest, on him it looked a bit girly."

"Maybe it was a butch mermaid."

"Deb. Are you taking this seriously?"

"I am—really. A butch mermaid isn't a joke, Chip."

My husband squinted at me over his fork, sizing me up. Attitudinally. I made my eyes wide. Because I had *meant* it, about the butch mermaid—it wasn't a diss. I've got nothing against a certain butch quality. Plus if there were really mermaids, I hoped they didn't look like Ariel. Honestly, if they turned out to be Disney-style mermaids, I wouldn't like them one little bit. That big-eyed cartoon shit would get on my last nerve.

So I narrowed my own eyes again and lifted the cup containing my decaf, looking past him with what I hoped was a meditative aspect—I was hoping to resemble a person with important, largely abstract concerns. After swallowing my delicate sip, I made my mouth prim. I hoped he got the message.

"Early to bed!" cried the biologist abruptly, snapping her nearly vintage clamshell. She stood up, grabbing a last slice of focaccia from the basket and stuffing it into her mouth, and spoke while chewing. "Got to get up at five to make history! Meet me in the lobby at five-thirty!"

Chip actually whistled as the two of us strode up the Tiki-lit path to the cabin. He held my hand and swung it widely while he whistled a patriotic tune—maybe "La Marseillaise." Possibly "The Battle Hymn of the Republic." Chip, too, believed we might be making history.

I was agnostic where that prospect was

concerned, but open to it, certainly; if we made history, then good. A job well done, I guessed.

I WAS DISPLEASED, the next morning, to find the toe man in our party. People milled in the lobby, when we appeared there blearily at that indecent predawn hour, and he was among them. Adding insult to injury, his wife was *not* among them— I imagined she hadn't been seduced by the prospect of sighting some goliath groupers. And possibly, unlike him, she was also indifferent to the prospect of ogling other divers as they padded naked-footed around the boat or struggled to pull on fins. A person needed tube socks, I felt, with the man from the Heartland free-roaming.

Or fishermen's waders.

I wondered if Chip had invited him and prepared to snap at my newly minted husband for the infraction, but before I could open my mouth he assured me Nancy had issued the invite with no input from him.

I didn't know any of the others, beyond the Bay Areans, though I'd talked to some on the phone; I busied myself carrying a cooler of sandwiches down to the dock, where the dive boat was waiting. I talked to my personal dive pro, Jamie, and then occupied myself with mundane tasks while Chip chatted excitedly with the various divers and fishermen he'd signed on, substituting the word *groupers* into his enthusiastic narrative of the mermaid sighting.

"Them jewfish are real easy to spear," I heard a man drawl. At first the phrase startled me. It turned out, Chip told me later, that groupers used to bear that name before some kind of fish-naming council censored it. "Yeah. Easy pickins. Jewfish will swim right up to you. Fish in a barrel, ha ha. As innocent as babies. I use a Stinger."

"Of course there's no fishing *today*," said Nancy to the spearfisherman, who was sun-wrinkled and had a diamond stud in one ear. "The ban on grouper harvest is respected here."

We all trooped down to the boat—a motley crew loaded with gear and backpacks, some still sucking at their cups of coffee, others munching on remnants of Danish or muffins from their continental breakfasts. The fisherman ambled beside Chip and me. "The jewfish," he said to Chip, "now they're a hermaphrodite, as you may know. Those suckers are born with lady parts."

I sensed a certain degree of puzzlement, among the recruits, at the suppressed excitement evinced by Chip and Nancy. I got the feeling they thought: *Sure, groupers are good, but are groupers as good as all this?* At least one of the party was chalking the vibe up to our vacationer status— "Crazy tourists," I heard him mutter. Someone else nodded sagely.

Nancy focused on the videographer—an

Australian, he sounded like—seeking repeated assurances that he would film constantly, without missing a second, as soon as he hit the water. He shrugged, he seemed confused, but at the same time he was willing. Jamie got stuck in a conversation with the toe man before the boat even weighed anchor. I hadn't asked him to steer clear, of course; I didn't have the stones for that. I only hoped the two of them wouldn't still be fraternizing when I had to approach Jamie physically to get ready for my dive.

Meanwhile Chip was deep in a discussion of unusual wildlife with the retired Navy SEAL, a barrel-chested man who sported a full white beard and a blunt yet bombastic attitude. They talked about giant squid at first, moving on to the Loch Ness monster and a creature called the Orang Pendek, some kind of midget Yeti. The Navy SEAL was a specialist in diving into shipwrecks, and tough enough to impress Chip mightily. I could see Chip wishing the old-salt Navy SEAL was his father, for Chip has always longed for a kindly, tough-love type of father—ideally seafaring. He likes the idea of an oceangoing father, a father who, instead of skipping his child support payments to focus on the deep joy of heroin, merely set sail one day to seek his fortune on the high seas. Called by the sirens and followed by an albatross.

I would have to be careful or the Navy

SEAL/old salt would take over where Nancy left off, commandeering Chip's attention for the rest of our honeymoon.

I WAS NERVOUS about my dive, but when the time came I was even more anxious about being left behind. I made sure I was suited up and ready to go before we dropped anchor; I stuck right by Nancy and Chip, shadowing them as Jamie shadowed me. The videographer was at their other elbow, holding his underwater camera apparatus like it was fashioned of gold filigree.

So we were in the first wave of divers off the boat, scaling a ladder down the side and sinking in backward, tanks first. Once I'd oriented myself in the water my jerk of fear smoothed out, with Jamie on one side of me and Chip on the other, and down we swam toward the sunken, encrusted plane. I felt happy; the water was that bejeweled aquamarine, and nestled in the brilliant coral I spotted skulking eels and other hole-lurkers I hadn't seen before. Mermaids or not, I thought, this was great. For the first time I felt gratified the honeymoon hadn't moved along a normal path. We wouldn't have dived without Nancy, would have settled for snorkeling, probably.

The videographer swam up front with Nancy; then came Chip and I. Behind us swam the second wave, including the Navy SEAL, the high school science teacher and some spearfishermen deprived of spears. A few had tried to bring along their own underwater cameras—cheap deals, not like the videographer's setup. They were trophy-seekers by nature, they hadn't wanted to go down there, spot a monster grouper and have nothing to show for it. But Nancy had made them leave those cameras on the boat, and in return she'd promised them free copies of anything the Australian recorded.

I looked up from the corals and the small, flitting fish at one point to find that Jamie and I had fallen behind the other three just a bit. I kicked hard and scooped with my arms to push up alongside Chip; just as I made it to his side, he snapped out an arm and grabbed my wrist. And that was when I realized that despite my claims of solidarity with Chip I'd no more expected to encounter a bevy of mermaids than the Four Horsemen of the Apocalypse. I'd simply been hoping for an explanation—to find, down there, some natural phenomenon that would help explain the mermaid apparition, some anomalous or physically interesting effect, down there below the waves.

But that wasn't what I got.

What I got was mermaids.

They didn't see us at first, I guess, because they were engaged in a labor of their own, digging around the base of a large rock. Their hair floated in clouds behind them, long weightless-looking swaths like seaweed, as did their tails, which moved up and down slowly as the tails of dolphins move, not side to side like the tails of fish. Those tails were graceful, beautiful muscles, scales shining silver in rows and rows of small coins.

The Australian, I saw, had his camera on them— I couldn't read his facial expression because of the mask. No one's expression was visible under their masks, which is a shame, really, during an event like a mermaid sighting. We hovered there in a kind of frozen surprise, looking down at a cluster of mer-tails, a cloud of mer-hair waving and rippling, their faces hidden from us as they did, industriously, whatever they were doing.

But that tableau lasted only a couple of seconds, and then one of the mer-people turned. She turned her head, looked over her shoulder, and saw us. I saw her face, I saw it full-on—not mythically beautiful, not mythically homely, just a face, its skin sickly white in the water. I saw gills on her neck, their slits opening. I saw a look of surprise.

And I saw her hand: that mermaid was holding some kind of an eel. I had the feeling it was dinner.

Then, like a whip cracking, her tail seemed to buck and all of them were gone, faster than fast, utterly vanished in a turbulence of water.

That was it.

WHAT SHOCKS ME the most, in retrospect, is that within the next few days I would assimilate the mermaids handily. One moment they were impossible, the next they were everyday, in my view of the world. Like moon landings or cell phones. They went from *of course not* to *of course*. By the second day I was not only not *disbelieving* in mermaids but thinking of them as a given. A quirky facet of natural history. Oh the *mermaids,* I would register casually when they were mentioned.

But before the second day, there was the first.

We swam after the blurred wake, but as underwater swimmers, they were way out of our league. There would be discussions, once we surfaced, of radio-tagging opportunities that had been lost, of the possibility of using the sonar equipment so readily available on all kinds of boats, of enlisting local authorities for future coordinated searches; but in the aftermath of first contact we were just frustrated.

Nancy in particular did not wish to yield. That parrotfish expert swam around as rapidly as possible, peering into nooks and crannies in the coral, finding nothing but the usual minor marine life, until her tank was basically empty. The rest of our tanks were emptying too as we followed her around, our adrenaline rush fading. Personally I never held out much hope of seeing the fish-tailed quasi-humans again. There'd been a certain definitive quality to their vanishment, was how it seemed to me. And they knew the territory.

The dive pros urged us back to the boat after about thirty minutes. On the wet decks we milled around stripping off our gear, emitting noises of astonishment and chaotic confusion. Eventually we grabbed up dewy cans of soda and beer—some of us noshed ravenously on bagels or croissants as though we hadn't had breakfast a mere hour and a half before—and settled down to watch the Australian's digital video. He replayed it over and over, with passengers and crew crowding around him as he held up his small monitor. No doubt, no doubt at all, the mermaids were there—their pale backs and shining tails, the weaving, waving cloud/streams of their yellow-green hair.

The mermaids could have been CGI, fully. I mean they looked completely real, but so do the movies about aliens with many tentacles, the movies about talking animals, and the movies about beautiful women. It was only our eye-witness status that made the footage so satisfying, like treasure we'd found whose richness would soon be revealed to the world. We *knew* it was real and there it was, exactly the way we'd seen it, in pixels and HD.

Not, of course, from the selfsame angle—I realized watching it that in real life I'd had the best seat in the house. In the video the mermaid wasn't looking straight at the camera when she turned, but to the side, so that her features were obscured. But under the water she'd seemed to look right at me; I'd gotten a long gander at her features. What had struck me about them was the details: they were the features of an actual person. They weren't generic, they were just eyes, a nose, a mouth, all specific and real. The nose had been a little wide and flat, the lips a little thin.

"She wasn't the same one," said Chip, as the two of us stood near the dive slide, leaning on the boat's slippery gunwale and watching the others gaze at the footage for the umpteenth time. Their faces were the faces of fans or admirers. Light struck the planes of those faces differently: these people were different now, I thought, these people would never be the same. (I wouldn't either, but for me the difference was less a revolution than an adjustment. It's just the way I am, there are some major aspects of the universe I take in stride daily, other small ones don't ever cease to amaze me.) The world had changed for all of us, though. For now, for this moment, it shone with a foreign brightness.

"Pardon?"

"I didn't see the one from before," Chip explained. "The one on the tape is a different one."

"She didn't really have bad teeth," I agreed. "Or not that I noticed."

"And the others, did you get a good look at any of them?"

"Not really," I said. "It was mostly backs and

tails. No other faces. She sounded the alarm. The others never even looked at us, did they?"

"All they did was go," said Chip.

"They really took off," I said.

"You can't blame them. I mean, for all they knew, we could have been bringing smallpox," said Chip. "The black plague. Anything. We could have been hunting them. Right?"

"You really think they haven't met us before?"

"Us?"

"I mean people?"

"They must have! Like Nancy said. That's why we have a word for them!"

The others were talking about mermaid history too, one putting forward the notion that the mermaids were mutations from nuclear tests in the Pacific, Bikini Atoll and all that, who'd moved east after the bombs went off and mutated them. Another suggested they were descendants of an obscure tribe with webbed feet, which subsequently turned into fused legs. The crew, I noticed, who hadn't been down there with us, assumed we were bullshitting—either that or we were connected with the movie industry. And so it went, until Nancy stood up on a cooler of roasted-vegetable-with-arugula sandwiches and addressed the collective.

"This is a great day," she said. "You went out expecting to find grouper—and instead you found mermaids. I'm going to be honest with you, though: the grouper sighting was always a cover. This trip was about mermaids from the start. I discovered them just a day ago, with Mr. Foster over there."

Chip saluted, nodding briefly.

"Of course we knew no one would credit it. So we said grouper. Enough about the past, though. We need to talk about the future. Now on the one hand, I believe in the free sharing of scientific information. But on the other, we don't want a feeding frenzy. We don't want people descending on this island by the thousands and destroying these priceless reefs looking for mythological women with bare breasts."

"Hear hear!" yelled someone behind me.

"As a biologist, that worries me. So we have to have a well-defined, clear strategy for handling this."

"Sell the video!" said one of the spearfishers. "Like to Fox News! This guy could make a million bucks!"

"That kind of thinking is exactly what no one needs," said Nancy sternly.

There were some murmurs then, whose content I couldn't peg.

"But I admit, it's going to be tough to do this one by the book. First thing is, to claim a new species you need a specimen. In formaldehyde, typically. And similar species for comparison. We have none of that here—this is more like a cultural encounter. A meeting with an unknown tribe—what anthropologists call *first contact*. Because let's face it, these guys seem to be an awful lot like *Homo sapiens* from the waist up, though of course we don't have a tissue sample yet. We've never seen a human hybrid. Better safe than sorry, when it comes to human rights. I'm going to call in an anthropologist ASAP. By tomorrow, I guarantee, a colleague from Berkeley will be coming. In the meantime, we can't leak. Is that one hundred percent understood? The find and its location absolutely *cannot be leaked*. Mr. Foster's got some confidentiality agreements I'm going to need you all to sign."

There was a low rumble of dissatisfaction as Chip, who'd pulled out a sheaf of papers, saluted once again.

"Wait. In return—and this is on the forms too—every single one of you gets an equal share in whatever benefits come from this. *Should* they accrue. My motive is research and conservation, not profit, I'm telling you flat out. Still, in the event that any revenues *do* accrue, they will be equally shared. Fair's fair. I'm putting my name on the same contract as you. Finally, we all get joint credit for the find. Keep in mind, though, we don't own anything except this video. These mer-people—well, they own themselves. All we have is a story. But it's an important one. Our story will change the world!"

Nods, respectful signs of assent, a few whispers.

"We're the custodians of a priceless knowledge, a unique piece of *history*. Not grubby profiteers who'll go down in Wikipedia as the destroyers of a race. We don't want to be the conquistadors. We want to be Charles Darwin."

"Charles Barkley?" muttered the Fox News spearfisher.

"So until we get the anthropologist onboard—which should be tomorrow if all goes well—no tweets. No social networking sites. No nothing. Anyone who leaks anything forfeits their share of any proceeds or benefits, as well as their credit. Am I crystal-clear here? And the video is embargoed. *That* contract was signed before we went under at all. OK? Please: Do yourselves a favor. Sign the agreement."

There were grumbles from the Fox spearfisher and maybe the substitute teacher, but it seemed that all the forms got signed, Nancy collecting them and scanning them with brisk efficiency. I had to hand it to that parrotfish expert—she planned ahead. She had the courage of her convictions.

I saw now, despite the purple, owlish rings the mask had made around her eyes, that she didn't necessarily have a derelict/unstable aspect after all. Her look was more take-charge than that of a disordered, rootless individual tragically amputated from society. She was mannish, yes, but now I considered how that mannishness might be helping her, in this new, albeit temporary, leadership role. Those eyebrows, with their insectoid appearance, reminded me of Stalin eyebrows, come to think of it. So many despot eyebrows, in the past, had been untrammeled, left to sprout free, and maybe hers were a bow to this authoritarian eyebrow styling. And the faint mustache on her upper lip, the furry rim, that too could be a nod in the direction of Stalin . . . not that she was a despot. I thought her rule was mostly benevolent.

I'm no expert on the discovery of new species, needless to say, but from my amateur perspective—considering we were in completely uncharted mermaid territory—she had a decent grip.

I BARELY RECALL the rest of the day, which turned into a booze-fest. Because of the embargo we didn't want to celebrate in public, so as the afternoon wore on Chip and I found ourselves letting more and more members of the expedition into our cabana— Nancy's cabana was smaller, since she was on a tighter budget. Before the drinking began, she made calls and confirmed that a first-contact scholar was winging it our way, the Berkeley anthropologist. So there we were, under a gag order, confronted with the existence of beings as improbable as unicorns—hell, more improbable, even.

We waited for the anthropologist.

And while we waited, we blew off some steam. The videographer plugged his camcorder into the cabana's flat-screen TV and our mermaid footage played across it in a loop, repeatedly; after the first few viewings the guests began to treat the bare-breasted fish/woman as scenery, wandering freely in front of the screen, mingling. As the evening wore on the mermaids seemed to swim among us, or we swum among them: they were there and then gone, with the flick of one tail, the flick of many. They were present, the main one's face looking at us, and they were gone again, and again, and again. The flat-screen TV was like a massive fish tank in our midst, with various yellow and orange and spotted fish crossing the field of view, passing corals, passing the sunken plane, before the mermaids entered.

Though I knew it was embargoed, and I didn't plan to share the pic with anyone, I wanted a shot for my records. So I took one, on the sly.

We circulated and talked around the sparse furniture and the dramatic displays of cut flowers, one of us posted as a sentinel at the doorway to make sure the secret video went unseen by others' eyes. No strangers were allowed. We ordered more and more drinks via room service, through happy hour and into the sadder ones; we ordered individual drinks, then later whole bottles, which arrived on the golf carts with a generous surcharge. The servile young men dismounted from the cart and brought trays to our door.

Once or twice there was a scuffle at the threshold, a member of the party who wanted to smuggle in a loved one or friend. The Heartland man, for instance, was turned away by Nancy for trying to sneak in his wife; I think I hid my pleasure quite smoothly. Later a large man stationed himself outside our door, a large man in a flowery shirt. He was a hotel janitor by day, moonlighting for us in a freelance capacity, Chip told me, as a bouncer. That parrotfish expert had outsourced our security.

I can't say my fellow party guests were above average, in terms of charisma, intelligence or conversational ability, but I felt like the mermaid sighting was bringing us together, creating a buzz of enjoyment—until I hit a wall around two in the morning and wanted nothing more than to fall into bed. But that option wasn't available to me; our guests were still milling, tripping, laughing. The bearded old salt had taken up residence in the room's puffiest chair, where he regaled his listeners with stories of diving deep into dangerous shipwrecks to "lay charges." He'd blown up many a vessel in his day, it seemed, ranging from "amphibious assault ships" to "minesweepers." He told stories of diving in Truk Lagoon, where a ghost fleet of Japanese ships lay filled with human skulls.

At that point I happened to glance at the bathroom door and saw the drunken Fox News spearfisherman rummaging in my tampon box. I watched the spearfisher rummage, I took it in stride, and then I cruised over there, casually interrupting him. You don't really get to ask why, when you behold a thing like that, but the politeness vs. curiosity dilemma can be tense.

The spearfisher snatched his hand out of the box when he saw me coming; as I led him out of the bathroom he made small talk about mer-people's gills—claimed he'd once known a guy from Montreal, a regular human who had a vestigial gill himself. Right on his neck, where the mermaids' gills were. It sometimes leaked a clear substance.

"Actually that would most likely have been a pharyngeal slit," said Nancy, appearing with her eyebrows. "Or groove. Not a vestigial gill. A layperson might call it a birth defect."

"I don't get it," said Chip, who'd detached himself from old Navy guy. "Why do those mermaids even *have* gills? I mean wouldn't they be marine mammals? I mean they have breasts, right? And hair. So aren't they, like, mammals? Like sea lions and dolphins? Those guys don't need gills. So why would mermaids?"

"It's very exciting!" cried Nancy. "Of course, gills are far more efficient than lungs at extracting oxygen. They have to be. It's hard to breathe seawater. Less oxygen in water than air. Gills could have been an evolutionary advantage for the mers. Particularly if they have lungs too. They may have both, in fact. It's not impossible."

"The 'mers'?" I asked.

"*Mer-people* could be read as a colonialist term," explained the biologist. "Racist and hegemonic. It'd be my own proposal that, until we learn the culture's own name for itself— assuming the culture *has* language *qua* language, which is a major leap—we shorten our label to *mer,* or *mers,* plural. It's relatively value-neutral. Just the French word for *sea.*"

"Huh?" said the tampon fisherman. "French? Why goddamn French? They should be *flattered* we're calling them people! It's a goddamn compliment!"

"Well, imagine a highly intelligent race of eels . . ." said the biologist.

"No, man," the fisherman interrupted. "I don't *want* to."

". . . and when these intelligent eels discovered

137

our own species," the biologist went on, "they then referred to us as *land eels*. Would that seem like a compliment to you?"

"I wouldn't take it *personally,*" said Chip.

"Makes no sense. We don't look like an eel," said the fisherman.

"My anthro colleague knows this stuff better than I do," admitted Nancy.

I guess the sensitivity racket was mostly for the humanities.

We heard a crash and turned—it was the man from the Heartland, who must have snuck in, without his wife this time, when I wasn't paying attention. Like the spearfisher he'd been nosing around in my business, it looked like, because he was squatting in the open closet, where my clothes were, and as I drew closer I saw an iron from the top shelf had fallen. He was prodding the top of his head with two fingers. Our clock radio lay entwined with the iron on the carpet, two black cords spiraling.

"What the hell?" said Chip, and dashed past me.

Sure enough, I saw from somewhere behind Chip's shoulder, the man was holding one of my shoes. It was a Jimmy Choo. I knew now I wouldn't wear it on this trip; it had a four-inch heel and there wasn't enough pavement.

Chip snatched it away from him.

The man's other hand was bloody from his scalp, which had a bloody dent in it made by the point of the iron. My shoe trembled slightly in midair as Chip looked down at the guy, unsure of his next move.

A thin drip of red trickled its way down the toe man's forehead, so slow it seemed glacial. I had a sense of losing control, of borders fading loosely into fuzziness.

"Uh. You OK, man?" asked Chip, craning his neck to see the gouge.

The toe man nodded dazedly, then abruptly rose and zigzagged around us, through the living room and out the front door.

"Huh," said Chip. "Hope he doesn't have a concussion or something."

I shrugged inwardly. I had no patience for the guy's injuries, incurred during his shoe fondling. He hadn't received them defending our free nation. He didn't deserve a Congressional Medal of Honor.

I turned to the oglers loitering.

"Sorry, but it's time for us to turn in," I announced. The drinking and annoyance had finally emboldened me. "Chip and I are going to hit the sack now. We'll see you again tomorrow. And thanks for coming, though."

IT SHOCKED ME to see, when I struggled out of bed the next morning all headachy to answer a vigorous pounding on our door, that the man who stood there—visible through one of the large picture windows as I tottered out of the bedroom in my skivvies, nothing but a camisole and boy-shorts—was the guy from outside the restaurant men's room, two nights ago, who'd been wearing the Freudian slip T-shirt.

He wasn't wearing the T-shirt now, but still I recognized him.

"What is it?" I asked, opening the door creakily. It felt like five minutes had passed since I collapsed into bed. I couldn't have cared less that the Freud guy was seeing me half-naked and unkempt; all I cared about was sleep.

"I came to tell you, because I think you're friends with—that is, I have some news, the news is bad, you might want to sit down, even? Can I come in?"

"Uh—"

"Thanks," said the guy, whose face was bland, snub-nosed and friendly. It was mournful, too, mournful as an old hound.

He sat right down on our couch himself, quite heavily.

"I'm sorry to tell you this, but I thought you should know they found a body this morning. A— a person died. A woman."

"What woman?" I said, snapping awake.

"The one you've been spending time with. We—I saw you together at the restaurant, with your husband I guess? Her name is Nancy. A Dr. Nancy Simonoff."

I sat down then myself, all the way to the carpet. My knees somehow gave out on me.

Chip stumbled out of our bedroom in even less underwear, rubbing his chin stubble.

"What did you say?" he asked. "Someone is *dead?*"

"Sorry. The resort wasn't sending anyone to let you know—I thought someone should—personally—I was just there, see, I was on the grass near her casita, we're just a couple casitas down and like every morning I was practicing on my yoga mat—"

"Who? *Who?*"

"Nancy," I said robotically.

I wasn't looking at Chip, but he must have sat down too, on the sofa near the Freud guy, and we were silent there, three rocks. Feeling surreal the way you do. In shock, or whatever.

"I don't believe it," mumbled Chip.

"A drowning, is what I heard," said the Freud guy gently. "It's not official yet."

"But she was a great swimmer!" said Chip.

"In her bathtub," said the Freudian. "Because they didn't bring her in from the pool or the ocean, they brought her out of her casita. It's how I even know any of this. I heard an EMT say *drowned.*"

"Drowned in the bathtub? Like . . . suicide?" said Chip.

"No way," I said.

"Never," said Chip.

"I only talked to her a couple times," said the Freudian, "but I'd have to agree it doesn't seem likely. She was very, um, enthusiastic. She wasn't a patient, but still—I'd never have pegged her for suicidal depression."

I realized he might actually *be* a Freudian. Or something like it, in the therapy arena. Beyond the pun on the T-shirt.

"And she barely drank either," said Chip. "She ate a lot but didn't drink. Last night she was stone-cold sober."

We sat.

"I mean. *Murder?*" asked the Freudian.

We sat.

BY THE TIME Chip and I were dressed and hygienic, cold water splashed on our faces and teeth brushed with haste and vigor, the press had arrived. It was a strictly small-time crowd compared to the ravening media hordes back home, but it came on the heels of the police so it felt like a minor invasion—a white van with a satellite dish; two pretty women in pancake makeup who must be reporters; cops teeming. That is, there were a couple of cops in uniform, there was hotel security, and there were some official men in jackets and ties, of unknown identity. And then there were the other guests, passing, standing, gawking—the guests, gathering in small groups, craning their necks, whispering nervously and/or with ghoulishly titillated interest.

The police didn't look like the cops we were used to—these ones had a faintly British, formal look. But the crime scene tape was universal.

We felt ourselves drawn to the Freudian's cabana, as close to the furor as we could be. He'd invited us to go over there, before he cleared out of our own cabana so we could get dressed. Each of us felt disbelief that Nancy had stopped breathing. We couldn't imagine it. We didn't need to use our imaginations, technically—I get that—because apparently it was real, but sometimes you can't imagine the facts.

First there'd been mermaids and now this. We wanted sanity.

Walking across the grass, between the palms, we caught sight of someone from the diving party, the substitute teacher, face stricken, lost as a child. We had nothing to tell him, no words to clear things up, so we just shook our heads at him, our bodies still heavy; he shook his head at us.

Then Chip knocked on the door of the Freudian cabana, and Steve let us in.

"Statistically it's low-crime!" said his partner Janeane, the muumuu woman who was now wearing a tie-dyed sundress. I accepted a cup of in-room coffee gratefully, though I'm an espresso person in real life and knew it would taste like backwash. "I mean, there hasn't been a murder on this island in six years! Before this one. Right, Steve? I know—I have a violent crime phobia. We researched it before we came."

"I didn't know that was a phobia," said Chip, not unkindly. "Old friend of mine has a fear of velocity."

"Interesting," said Steve the Freudian. "Even related, possibly."

"I visualize impacts," added Janeane. "Bludgeoning. Face punches. I took a pill just now. Well, more than one."

"But listen," I said. "Who can we talk to? Who's gonna talk to us? Is someone going to put out a statement? The police? Because the thing is—I mean, we can't talk about it, it's supposed to be embargoed, but Nancy had—she had news. She had information. A major discovery. It was going to break today, maybe."

"She was murdered!" said Janeane dramatically, clasping her hands.

"Uh, I don't know about *that*," said Chip.

"It's not impossible," I ventured.

"She was a fish scientist, wasn't she?" asked Steve. "Did she discover a new kind of fish?"

"Something like that," put in Chip hastily.

We took our mugs of bad coffee outside. By that time Chip was constantly checking his phone, texting back and forth with other members of the diving party, fingers twiddling. The news had leaked out to them all at once—even the vast majority who were residents of the island, not guests at the resort—and they were on Chip for information every minute, they turned to Chip as the premier Nancy authority. Chip had nothing to give, obviously, but promised to keep them informed of any new developments. Sit tight, Chip texted them. The embargo was still on, he assured them; we'd put the Berkeley anthropologist in charge of distributing the digital footage as soon as he arrived.

But of course the anthropologist wasn't here yet. He was due in from Tortola on a late-afternoon ferry.

I watched officials mill around with a growing sense of despair. Chip wasn't available to me, eyes avidly planted on his bright data-cell, attention utterly committed. This was a time of sad aftermath, and I've always hated aftermaths, with their dull, heavy weight of disappointed hope. Nancy's body was already gone, so in fact there was nothing to watch. It was a matter of waiting for someone to speak to us.

And what about the mermaids? It was increasingly clear to me that we were shut out of everything now—the action was closed to us. Just a few hours earlier, with servers at our beck and call, we'd been members of an inner circle: we'd clustered at the nucleus, cleaved to the core.

Now we were far from the core, excluded, floating like weak electrons. Or something.

I worried, I felt queasy at the thought of Nancy, I still disbelieved the story of her demise—I understood it with my brain, possibly, but not the rest of me. The living Nancy, with her bushy eyebrows, was still realer to me than the dead Nancy.

Chip was busily texting when the videographer from Australia came galumphing toward us over the emerald grass, weaving between the spectators, flushed and sweating.

"It's gone!" he said, panting, when he pulled up short. "Oh mate—my footage is gone! And my camera!"

"What do you mean?" asked Chip, looking up from the small screen at long last. "Gone where?"

"Stolen!" said the videographer. "They were both stolen!"

"Slow down there, friend," said Chip. "OK. Let's . . . maybe you left your camera somewhere? Our place, even?"

"I took it back to my hotel room last night," he puffed. "You know—I'm at the Bitter End, about a half-hour drive, I got back to the room in the wee hours. Well, the camera was too big to fit in the bloody room safe, so I stuck just the video chip in there instead, and put the key under the pillow, just to be extra careful. Didn't think I really needed to, but. Woke up this morning and the safe door was wide open. Looked under my pillow, the bloody key was still there! The chip is *gone,* mate! All the footage is lost. Stolen! It's bloody gone!"

"And there weren't any copies," said Chip slowly.

"No copies," said the Australian. "I hadn't uploaded it. I promised her."

Chip and I looked at each other. We had the feeling, I think, people describe as *sinking.*

"Oh," said Chip. "Oh no."

He told the Australian about Nancy. The three of us stood there limply.

We had nothing left. *Poor Nancy,* I found myself thinking, as though she were still alive. But no. We had no mermaids; we had no Nancy. All we had was a deceased parrotfish expert and a story people would laugh at.

And memories.

"We can go out again," said Chip weakly. "We'll find them. We'll go right out again. Tomorrow! She would want us to. She would insist, you know she would. We owe it to her. It doesn't have to be a big group. Maybe a backup camera this time. We'll take the scholar from Berkeley. When we find them again, the scholar will give us credibility."

But we weren't comforted. Not even Chip could crack a smile. Our sadness stood there with us like a fourth person.

When we'd arrived on the island, buffeted by trade winds and cradled by the white sands and all for a few weeks' pay, I'd felt like the American I was. It was a nice feeling, mostly. It had its minuses, sure (passivity, mental blankness), but also its pluses (vague background satisfaction caused by world dominance; non-starvation). When, carried by the white golf cart across the grounds, we'd jiggled inertly, I'd felt American then too—more American than ever, frankly. I'd felt American when we rented a boat and ordered a catered lunch and when we found mermaids. I'd felt American when we had the film of the mermaids in our possession, when we were drinking our fill and eating well and waiting for the anthropologist. I'd felt American when Nancy carried us along in the hubbub of her discovery.

We'd been Americans then, Chip and I; Nancy had too. Now we were spun off to the margins, us and our opinions, our visions, our memories—our singular knowledge. Now we had something to sell that no one would ever buy, we had a secret that cast us out into the wings . . . was it possible we'd stopped being American?

It's like we're not even Americans, I said to myself.

In fact, I thought as I looked around me at the officials milling in their damp costumes, the female reporters in pancake makeup . . . wait, they weren't female reporters at all—they had no microphones! One looked like a secretary, the other someone's girlfriend. Now that I looked more closely, their

148

makeup wasn't heavy enough—they weren't even that self-important.

So where *was* the media? Was there no media after all? The van with the satellite dish—did it not have the call number of a local affiliate on it?

No, I saw now, it was the name of some kind of utility, maybe a cable provider. It wasn't the press at all. There wasn't any press here.

No one was watching us, as it turned out. We weren't the focus of anyone's interest. The death of one of our own seemed, as far as I could tell, to be passing without notice.

I looked around and saw no Americans—no Americans at all.

III.
THE MURDER MYSTERY

*W*e stood on the dock a little while before sunset, Chip and I, with waves lapping quietly onto the sand behind us. I squinted into the distance, trying to make out the faint white dot of the island ferry.

Steve was there too, Steve the Freudian. By then we'd told him about the sighting. With Nancy and the mermaid footage both gone, we'd decided (over a lunch we had no interest in) that our embargo was beside the point. Obviously there couldn't be an embargo without a commodity—in this case the mermaid video. So with me sitting upright next to him on their sofa, Chip had told Steve—Steve and his wife Janeane, who preferred to be called his life partner—about the mermaid sighting.

To my surprise the Freudian didn't mock us. I'd assumed a therapist type would instantly dismiss our claims, but Steve just cocked his head to one side, contemplative.

"Something happened to me, not long ago, that I could never explain either," he offered, nodding.

"What?" asked Chip.

"Enh, I'll tell you the story sometime. But in a

nutshell, I had a strange experience. It made me question things. Question a *lot*."

"It was how we met," said Janeane. "I mean, *after* his *experience*. We both went to this PTSD encounter group."

"For post-traumatic stress?" asked Chip. "Hey. So sorry. I know they say they don't let women in combat, but once you're out in a war zone that line blurs. Doesn't it."

"Oh, she wasn't in the *army,*" said Steve. "Jan*eane?*"

"My practice is around peace," said Janeane. "Sending out empathy for all beings."

"What happened was, a therapist told her the phobia had features in common with PTSD, so she started going to the group. I was helping to moderate that day."

"It was a new horizon," said Janeane, smiling. "Plus I met Steve!"

Now, in the tropical dusk, Janeane was back in their cabana, resting and making all of us a late dinner; she didn't like to eat out much. In the resort's restaurant, she'd said, and the various restaurants off-campus too, there was always the chance of a bludgeoning. Especially now, after this, she was reluctant to emerge. She'd be picking at an overpriced entrée, she'd said, fingering the stem of a goblet, and then suddenly see, in her mind's eye, a machete intruder.

Standing there on the dock, we wondered where

Riley the videographer had gone. We hadn't seen him since he told us the footage had been stolen; he'd said he was going straight to the police, to tell them about his camera. He'd promised to be here to welcome the Berkeley anthropologist, but he was nowhere to be seen and didn't answer Chip's calls or texts.

We worried about the Berkeley anthropologist, too—what he might say, without a video. He'd probably think he'd made the arduous and, let's face it, expensive trip for nothing. It was no joke, flying from California to the Caribbean on a last-minute ticket. And if he turned out to have been close to Nancy, worse yet—for then, of course, there'd also be the grief. We couldn't recall if she'd said they'd been friends or only colleagues.

The three of us watched the white prow of the ferry as it first appeared—it's not a large ferry, really, mid-sized at best—and the lights of the harbor around us twinkled in the gathering dark.

"I like ferries," mused Chip, and squeezed my hand.

"We came in by chopper," said Steve. "I don't do boats. Not anymore. No boats of any kind, not even a rowboat. I'll never set foot on a ship again until the day I die."

"Do you get seasick?" asked Chip.

"Not at all," said Steve.

Chip and I waited politely, but he didn't go on.

The ocean and horizon were dim purple shades,

and the lights on the ferry twinkled—though way more dimly than the lights of the resort at our backs. Then we saw another light, the light of a second, smaller boat as it approached the ferry from one side.

"That's a police boat," said Steve. "The BVI police cutter. Or maybe it's the Coast Guard. I'm not sure the Brits even *have* their own boats."

To our surprise the two ships met. We couldn't tell if the ferry slowed or stopped; it seemed to remain static until the police boat moved away again, off to somewhere we couldn't see. After that it grew nearer steadily.

"I've got a bad feeling," said Chip.

And sure enough, when the ferry reached us at the dock, tourists streamed off—mostly couples, a few singletons with bulging shopping bags, the odd kid holding hands with a tired-looking parent—but there was no Berkeley anthropologist. We thought at first he might have been camouflaged among the day-trip shoppers, and Chip approached one or two, but we got no love from them.

"Do you think," I asked the guys, when the last of the passengers had disembarked and we were still standing there lamely, "that police cutter could have had something to do with it? With the fact that he never arrived?"

Steve looked at me, and I saw it in his eyes: he did.

"I don't get it," said Chip, as we walked slowly back down the dock, slumping. "If the police boat intercepted the ferry to meet the anthropologist— I mean *if;* he could have just missed his plane. But first off, why *would* they? How would they even know he was coming?"

"They have her phone," I suggested. "I'm sure they do. So they can access her voicemail, her texts and her email, no problem. That's my bet. She probably unlocked her phone, since she was using it so much."

"But why would they *want* to intercept him? I mean he's not a suspect or anything."

"And the cops around here are kind of a joke," said Steve. "I researched it, you know—because of the phobia. Our assumption was, in this kind of tourist economy, good cops would actually be a bad sign, in terms of the likelihood of violent crime. The Virgin Gorda cops have to call in the troops from other islands when something serious goes down. I can't see them doing anything they didn't have to do."

"Who *does* have the power on the islands?" I asked Steve. "Do you know?"

Steve shook his head.

"*Is* there power?" he asked naïvely.

"There's always power," I said. You'd think a Freudian would know that better than anyone, but I kept my mouth shut on that point. "The question is who has it."

"Whoever has the money," shrugged Chip. "Right?"

We stepped off the dock and onto the white sand; we looked up at the buildings of the resort in front of us, stretching far out to the sides, along the beach, and quite a ways back, to where the soft hill of the park began to rise. We felt the comforting shape of their well-designed spaces, their welcoming lights.

BACK AT THE Steve/Janeane cabana, the two men and I sat on the back porch and Janeane brought out a brownish pile of hippie-style grain, mounded low and flat on the serving plate like a dormant volcano. We all felt worried and restless, so the mood wasn't great; soon after she sat down and we all began to eat, we were interrupted by a crisp knock on the cabana's front door. I flashed back to that morning, when Steve had knocked on our own door and brought me news of death. Then I abandoned my fork and ran to answer the summons, admittedly relieved to be clear of my quinoa mountain.

There stood someone I'd never seen before, a young guy dressed in business casual—I'd almost say dapper, except his tan was a few shades too deep. It crossed the fine line between handsome and pleather.

"Hey there—Mike Jantz," he said, or it might have been Jans or Jams, the exact name was one of those small slivers of knowledge that slips through your fingers forever. "I'm with Paradise Bay Guest Services. Good evening!"

"What's this about?" said Chip, coming up behind me—he too, I think, was eager to escape the quinoa.

"You must be our newlyweds in the Star Coral Cabana, am I right?"

At Paradise Bay all the cabanas have names; ours was Star Coral, the Freudian's was Pearl Diver.

"That's us," said Chip, and cocked his head. "How did you know?"

"We try to give all our guests a caring, very personal service. I make sure I always know who's who."

"That's nice," said Chip, putting a hand on my shoulder.

"I apologize for interrupting your dinner," said the tanned man. "It's delicate, but we at Paradise Bay want to bring together all those who were associated with Dr. Simonoff, who, as you know, has passed away. We want to make sure the guests who were associated with Dr. Simonoff are kept in the loop—that everything is done, from our end, to make sure your needs are met at this upsetting time."

"We were associated too!" called Janeane, hovering at the sliding doors to the back patio. "We ate at the breakfast buffet together! Twice!"

"Talked about aphids," said Steve modestly. "Pea aphids. These bugs self-detonate. Whole suicide bomber thing, they self-explode. To take out ladybugs."

"Uh, sure," said the tanned man. His tie, I noticed, seemed to depict fireworks on a maroon background. "That's good to learn. Please join us, in that case. We're gathering in the Damselfish Room in twenty minutes. We'll send a buggy for you. I should go—doing my best to locate all the guests with a, you know, acquaintance or relationship. With the deceased."

After I shut the door on him I couldn't move for a minute. It was like I was paralyzed.

"Deb? Deb?" Chip was saying. "You OK there, honey?"

I didn't like the way the pleathery man had said *deceased*. The texture of it was greasy, smarmy. Death was trivial, in that mouth. I felt dizzy.

Then I snapped out of it and nodded.

"Fine. Yeah. We should go."

"Hmm—Damselfish Room," said Steve, who'd also come in from the patio. He unfolded a dog-eared map that lay on the bar counter. "I'm pretty sure that's—yeah. It's way over on a far corner of the property. See? It's where they do the nature slideshows no one signs up for, the natural history talks. I went to one. A guy talked about lizards that jump like frogs. It's in one of those futuristic hippie domes. What are they called?"

"Hydroponic?" said Janeane.

"Geodesic," said Steve, nodding like they agreed.

"I've always wanted to see inside a dome like that," said Chip.

THERE WASN'T ROOM in the golf cart for all four of us so Chip volunteered to run beside the cart while Steve sat up front, squeezed in next to the buggy's driver. This one wasn't acting servile, I noticed—more casual. A relief. He and the Freudian started chatting about trivia; the driver couldn't act fully servile, I guess, all thigh-to-thigh with Steve up there. The servile dynamic didn't work smoothly, with two guys rubbing thighs.

At that point, with manly thighs rubbing—at that point even a servility professional has to throw in the towel.

It was just Janeane and me on the passenger bench in the back, left there to jiggle inertly. Janeane jiggled a good amount. What was it, I asked myself, about the jiggle that so captivated me? Then it occurred to me: this was a Gina thing, the small Gina that always traveled with me. Because Gina talked about fat quite a bit, in her career as an academic failure. She'd written an article once, which, she said, was published in a journal six people read, two of them exclusively while defecating. It was called "Death and the Fat

American." I remembered her telling me about it over beers. Or maybe that was her ironic wine spritzer phase, where she ordered cantaloupe spritzers, sometimes pomegranate/honeydew.

Of course, I didn't remember exactly what she'd said. The bar scene stayed with me more than the details of Gina's monologue. That often happens. She did say there was the phenomenon of morbid obesity and then, as a separate matter of study, our cultural and individual responses to it, the response of the non-obese as well as the actual obesity victims. Obesity was a piece of death we carried constantly, she announced to me as she scanned the jukebox lists for "Don't Stop Believing."

Not only physically, she rambled on in front of the jukebox—in terms of heart disease, the liquids pooling in the vast, giant bodies, the wrongness of any human being possessing ankles that could brush along the floor—but also spiritually/symbolically. Our fat was obviously our death, entombing us prematurely. But that's not all, she said, there's more! The passive, consumer posture of fatness was a perfect embodiment of our "object status," I think that's what she mumbled out, though I may have got it wrong.

Our life of abundance, our tragic lack of agency, our infinite foregone conclusion of abject uselessness—our fat was a death that went beyond death, Gina orated (as nearby men, with some belligerence, began to stare).

Fleetingly angry because the Journey song was not available, she settled for "Urgent." A drunk guy stumbled over to us and asked Gina to give him some sugar, please. She said *Fuck off* and he asked if her sister was less of a bitch than she was (leering at me).

I tried to cheer myself up, after these unpleasant ruminations, by watching Chip's lean, muscled ass as he jogged effortlessly alongside (Janeane did too, I noticed). It was a solemn time, an anxious time, but we still had eyes and there was still Chip's ass, running. His beige cotton slacks showed it off—the grounds of Paradise were dark by then, of course, but the golf cart had headlights and there were footlights at intervals along the path.

When I turned to Janeane to talk to her, after a minute, she moved her eyes away in a small, shifty motion, like they'd alighted on my husband's ass purely by chance, and purely by chance were moving off that ass again.

"We're going into a rainforest," she announced. It was a couple of scraggly bushes. "Look! Thick vegetation, big, waxy leaves, giant, bulging flowers like penises, gonads, flowers are sex organs, you know that, right?" Her voice was rising in pitch and volume. "In the tropics they're huge—what does that mean? They threaten you! Tropical flowers are rapists! It's a *jungle!* Giant rapist flowers!"

"Are you worried about, uh . . ."

I trailed off. I didn't know where to start.

". . . flowers?" I struggled on. "Hey. Don't worry about them. You know—no legs. They can't run after you. To get raped by a flower you'd have to, like, *put* yourself on it. But by accident. But then how could—no. Plants can't be rapists, I don't think."

I was getting a little obscure, a little nitpicking, thinking about it. The day had been bad—man. So bad. I felt delirious.

But it didn't matter. Janeane had already moved on.

"She was murdered. I know it!" she squeaked. "I'm *sure* she was murdered. Alone in her bathroom. Naked! In the tub! He burst in and he murdered her. He probably had a knife! Or gun! He wanted to shoot her face off! That poor, poor, poor woman. So full of life! Like we are now! Alive!"

I nodded. Nancy *had* been alive.

"The murderer could still be nearby. Concealed. He could be lurking in the bushes!"

By this time she was rubbing her hands together anxiously—wringing them, I guess you could call it. But the cart was already slowing down; we'd passed through the bushes and come out into a small parking lot, at the end of which was a dome-shaped building, gleaming gray. The cart stopped.

Chip was instantly pleased by the dome. He

pulled up short. He hadn't broken a sweat, and he hadn't had to listen to Janeane, either.

"Deb, we should get a dome home," he enthused.

I sprang out of the cart, leaving phobic Janeane behind; I wasn't equipped to comfort her. There were lights shining out from the dome's windows onto the parking lot's pavement, making it look blackly wet. Light fell on the clumps of red flowers Janeane had talked about (admittedly they *were* large, roughly the size and shape of butternut squashes). Chip and I passed them, with Steve and Janeane lagging, and went through the door into a room with yellowing botanical drawings on the walls. It had to be some kind of disused educational facility. There was a small fleet of schoolroom desks near the back of the dome-shaped room, where the ceiling was low—wood, ink-stained children's desks with chairs attached to them.

Some of the other members of our expedition were already sitting, legs awkwardly folded beneath the miniature desks. Some of them stood; some grazed along a foldout table against the wall. It bore a vat of coffee, a stack of plastic cups, and a couple of plates of cookies. I don't know what I'd expected—a PowerPoint? Wreaths? There was a nondescript woman with a plastic name tag pinned to her lapel, wearing a long, Mormonish skirt and standing near the front of the room with her hands clasped.

"The gang's mostly here," said Chip. "Though I don't see Riley the videographer. Still AWOL, I guess."

"I hope he's OK," I said uncertainly.

". . . glad you could make it tonight," the Mormonish woman was saying. We'd already missed part of her spiel.

". . . doesn't feel like a safe space!" Janeane stage-whispered to Steve, nearly into our ears. She seemed to be gearing up to a panic attack. "How many bars does your cell have? Steve? Steve! How many *bars?*"

"We at Paradise Bay want to be sure that you, both our guests and members of our larger community, feel supported in this time of bereavement," said the Mormonish woman.

It was her skirt, really, that made her a Mormon, an ankle-length floral thing a Mormon wife might wear; I couldn't make out her name tag from where I stood.

"Here's the thing," said the old Navy SEAL, whose broad back I was looking at since he'd sat down in the front row. "We're not buying the bathtub story."

"Sir, my personal area is guest relations and community outreach," said the Mormon. "Anything legal or technical—of course, you'd have to take that up with the police."

"Don't kid a kidder," said the old salt. "I've been around the block. And back."

"I'm sure you have!"

"I *live* here," he went on. "The island cops? You're joking, right? Those kids only take the job so they can dress up in the outfits. Not a man jack among them with half the sense God gave a Guinea baboon."

"This is a time to come together," said the Mormon. "Offer each other our mutual support. The healing can only really begin when we let go of the anger."

"Shit on a stick," said the old salt, and pushed himself out of his chair.

"It's so important to us that our guests feel supported!" said the woman.

"Can you just tell us what happened to Nancy?" said Chip, becoming impatient. "That's what we want to know. What the hell happened to Nancy?"

"We understand she had asthma," said the woman. "There was, maybe, a breathing issue while she was in the bath, with the asthma, and then the bathwater, that situation in the bath, and so eventually, what we're surmising, is what happened was, unfortunately, that."

"What?" asked Steve, under his breath.

"What?" asked Janeane, loudly.

"Bathtub asthma drowning?" said Chip. "Is that even a *thing?*"

"In that scenario," I said directly to the Mormonish woman, summoning my resentment, "she had an asthma attack while she was in the bath, is that what you're saying? But then, instead of reaching for her inhaler, which she always kept close, she just, as an alternative solution, did a face plunge? Just stuck her face right under the bathwater to cleverly fix her major breathing problem?"

"Unorthodox," conceded Steve.

"We don't have the official forensic report at this time, yet," said the woman.

"Bathtub asthma drowning?" repeated Chip.

"So then according to you," said Janeane, her voice rising unsteadily, wobble-screeching, "no one came *in?* Snuck in with shadows disguising him and crept up behind while she relaxed in the soft bubbles, maybe with earphones in? Some peaceful music playing, like Zamfir flute? And then this guy never grabbed her and forced her under by the head? Burst in, strong and hulking, and murdered this poor, naked woman, meanwhile his dick raping?"

"Oh. My."

"Rape-*rape!* Rape-*rape!* Rape-*rape!*"

Janeane's brow was furrowed as she said that, her face red; one of her hands was clenched into a fist, her arm moving in a curious rigid, pumping motion.

"Oh dear," said the Mormon woman.

"You know what, let's head back to our cabana, why don't we," said Steve soothingly, his hand on her upper arm, rubbing, trying to slow the arm down. It was a raping arm. That much was clear. People were really embarrassed. "We're maybe ruffling a few feathers here. And we're all so tired, aren't we? So exhausted. What a stressful day it's been. Let me help you, honey."

Chip felt bad for both of them, plain to see, and I felt restless, so in solidarity we followed them, filing toward the door. I figured the Mormonish woman wasn't going to say much anyway. There was no point to her. At least from our POV, the woman had no reason for being. Sheerly from an outside perspective. I've noticed that can happen pretty easily: you look at a person from just about every side there is—except for from the inside, obviously—and there just doesn't seem to be a good reason for them.

It's frowned upon to say so, but if we're being honest, come on—please. There are currently billions of humans. Even allowing for some repetition, are there billions of reasons for being?

"Before you go, though, would you sign in? Please? We really need to get *everyone's* full contact info, emails, cell phone—"

She was cut off as we retreated.

OUTSIDE THE DOME, the golf cart wasn't there. Those massive red flowers bulged under the building's outdoor lights; our fairy-tale coach had turned into a butternut squash.

"Jesus!" shrilled Janeane, and stood still. "Now

we're supposed to *walk?* Across the whole grounds in the *dark?*"

Steve talked her down, holding her wrists gently.

"We're perfectly secure," he said. "Take a deep breath. In, out. That's it. Good. In, out. In, out. *You, are, safe, here*. Now breathe again. Pranayama."

"We can go back and ask the name-tag chick," said Chip. "Or, hey, I'll just run up and get a cart. You guys wait here, I'll go get it. I need the exercise. It's no problem."

"No! No! We can't split up!" cried Janeane, interrupting her breathing. "Disemboweling!"

"Sorry, she means that's what'll happen next," explained Steve over her shoulder, still holding and patting her. "Like in the slasher movies."

"OK, listen, I'll call up to the front desk, then," said Chip. "They'll send a driver down, I'm sure. It's no big deal."

Chip's a master of smartphone usage; he'd set up a Listserv for the dive group, which he used to communicate with everyone. He'd been messaging the Bay Areans, the foot fetishist, the divers and spearfishers all day.

Once he'd made the call, while we were waiting for the golf cart, the two of us left Steve to work his Freudian/yoga magic. We stepped back from the others, under the overhang of a big old tree with feathery leaves.

"Maybe she watched too *many* of those slasher

movies," said Chip quietly. "Maybe she saw it happen one too many times—where everyone gets picked off one by one."

Hatcheted, I thought, and then de-limbed. Their arms and legs tossed here and there like rice after a wedding.

"I was thinking this was a single-murder scenario," I said to him. "Hoping, at least. And then they solve it. But—you really think it might be more of a slasher deal?"

Chip cocked his head, considering.

"Wait! Think before you answer, Chip. It just occurred to me: if it turns out this *is* a slasher movie, and we act all dismissive—if for example you look too smug right now and shrug your shoulders, disdainful and smirking—then for certain we'll be the next to turn up all murdered."

"OK. So, for the record, I'm considering carefully. No one's dismissing the slasher possibility out of hand," said Chip. He looked around respectfully, reassuring the hidden camera. "But, having considered, I think it's fairly unlikely, on balance. It's not really a slasher *format*. Because Nancy, Nancy was great, I mean—"

He looked a little choked up for a second so I drew near and laid my cheek against his chest.

"—*Nancy,* man. I still can't—believe . . ."

We stood there in silence till Chip felt able to speak again. A few feet away Steve and Janeane were not dissimilarly clenched. Among the squash-sized flowers the four of us made up two couple-units, each standing close.

"What I was saying," he said after a minute. "So. The slashers usually start with a beautiful, slutty woman getting the ax. Or cleaver. Butcher's knife. Sword. Stiletto. Anyway, blade. There has to be a slice, a gouge, or a full-on carving. Often the sacrificial non-virgin is wearing white, right? She's really young, too, maybe a teenager even. That isn't anything *like* Nancy."

I thought of the eyebrows and I agreed; if this was a slasher movie, it was the weakest possible knockoff. Like a Mickey Mouse doll fashioned of dirty straw in someplace like Guangdong.

The box office would be a bust.

"I hope you're right," I said.

We heard the whir of a golf cart and shuffled out of the shadows to greet it.

THE NEXT TIME we saw Riley was at breakfast.

Only he wasn't Riley, or not exactly the Riley with whom we'd briefly had an acquaintance. He was the "after" photo in a before-and-after pair. He carried himself with more of a swagger; his hair seemed blonder. That he was actually blonder seemed pretty unlikely—a dye job performed so quickly and out of the blue—yet it was true: *he seemed blonder*. Even Chip noticed it.

More to the point, he'd turned against us. That's the best way I can put it.

When Chip saw him and dashed over to his table we'd been loading up at the buffet, so Chip was hefting a huge plate of waffles, strawberries and whipped cream, scrambled-egg mounds, bacon, and green and orange melon balls that threatened to fall off and roll willy-nilly. Chip, with his happy, golden-retriever attitude, waxed joyful that Riley was in one piece, holding his heaping plate awkwardly all the while as he stood at Riley's solo table with the videographer looking up at him impatiently.

But instead of thanking Chip for his concern, Riley brushed off Chip's worry like it was girlish. He came off superior and breezy, with a grin from shampoo commercials.

I was standing a few feet away, holding a table open for Chip and me in the busy all-you-can-eat buffet scenario, so I didn't hear all that Riley said. I just saw what I saw.

"Huh," said Chip, coming over to me and sitting down.

His golden-retriever light was dimmed.

"That guy's kind of douchey," I said. "Isn't he."

"He said that Nancy drowned and I should just get over it," said Chip, staring down at his cooling plate of buffet bounty.

I waited a second until I was sure: Chip had a tear in his eye—one at least, possibly two. I took his hand. "You know what, Chip?" I asked gently. "Someone just bought him off. That's what it is."

171

Chip met my eyes, touched his teary one with the back of a hand, then said gruffly, "Bought him—?"

"I'm in the business world, remember? I hear when money talks. Yesterday he was average or below, finance-wise—in terms of people who can afford to take Caribbean vacations in the first place, that is. But today he's coasting. Today he feels rich. I can tell by looking at him."

"His hair does seem yellower," Chip mused, slowly returning to his baseline mood.

"And how come he's *here?* He's not a hotel guest."

"He said he's taking a meeting."

Riley got up and strolled out then, leaving only a coffee cup behind. Wherever he was taking a meeting, it wasn't in the buffet zone.

WE WENT DOWN to the shore later to forget our troubles, swim and snorkel off some buffet calories; Steve came with us, dressed in a cruel Speedo. We saw it when he shucked his oversize Pink Freud T-shirt. Janeane was recuperating in their cabana: she was much better, he said, he'd dosed her with sedatives the night before and at sunrise they'd done yoga and meditation.

It was while we were stretched out on some cotton-padded lounge chairs between snorkels— Chip scrolling and tapping, Steve touching his toes and grunting, me reading a dog-eared paperback from the resort's library of exuberantly stupid books—that I noticed the crowds. Down the beach at the marina, out on the docks, there was a flurry of activity. There were more boats than usual; there was more movement.

"Huh," said Chip, frowning down at his phone. "People are unsubscribing from my list! The fishermen, the guy with the foot fetish, a bunch of them . . . they're leaving the Listserv, sending me messages saying they want to be taken off. It was down to eleven when we got up. And now it's down to *six!*"

I studied Chip's bemused face; I swiveled and studied the scene at the marina, its far-off hustle and bustle.

"Let's take a walk," I said. "I need to stretch my legs. Shut off your phone for fifteen minutes, Chip, won't you? Try to relax. Think of this as our honeymoon."

We ambled along the sand toward the marina, me acting casual and leisurely on purpose, Chip trying to pretend he wasn't hurt by the defection of his Listserv and speculating, to distract himself from those feelings, about Nancy's family and what they had or had not been told. Steve, a relentless exerciser whose physique completely, utterly failed to reflect this apparent fitness obsession, was executing, as we walked, some arm-and-chest movements that resembled a slow chicken dance.

"We have to keep after the resort manage-ment," said Chip. "At any time there could be brand-new information."

"Mmm," said Steve noncommittally.

"Mmm what?" asked Chip.

A pelican flapped slowly along the shore beside us and I felt a stir of fondness for the foolish-looking yet steadily graceful creature. I thought about how it must be inside the pelican's throat pouch, the stench of bile and rotting fish. Nameless debris.

Steve and the pelican, each with their own flapping, made a nice parallel/contrast.

"I'm just not sure we'll be told more than we know now," said Steve. "That's my feeling."

"But that's not *right*," said Chip, agitated. "You know it isn't. This isn't right, none of it is. It's like no one else *cares*. And someone's dead who *shouldn't* be! A good person, a person who has tenure at a major U.S. university!"

"Believe me, I agree," said Steve.

"Deb," said Chip, turning to me. "Please, honey. Can't we call someone and give them a bunch of money to solve this? Aren't there police you can just *hire?* Who figure out the crime and catch the bad guys? And make sure justice is done?"

"They call them private detectives," I said. "I don't think they handle the justice part, though."

"I didn't know if those existed anymore," said Chip. "I thought maybe they went out with black-

and-white movies, or maybe when Columbo died."

Steve nodded sympathetically, did some neck rolls.

"I'm serious, Deb," said Chip. "We can't just let this go."

I nodded too, wondering why the hard-boiled sleuth of the 1940s and '50s had morphed into crime procedurals. People didn't believe in a lone sleuth these days; they didn't believe one man could solve a crime. Or one woman, either. Miss Marple was a joke, same with the *Murder, She Wrote* lady.

Deductive reasoning? Get the fuck out, was what Americans said to the obsolete sleuths of yesteryear. Even in the heyday of sleuthing, American detectives relied mainly on guns, not brains like the unmanly English. (I'd hardly thought of Gina since the mermaids, I realized then, Gina and Ellis in their love nest of Union Jacks and irony.) The gun is mightier than the pen, was our true opinion, and the RPG is mightier still.

Gina had discussed this subject with me too; Gina used me as a sounding board now and then. She said she liked to talk about her work to people outside the academy, people who weren't constantly baffled about how she got tenure in the first place.

The sleuths who went solo, looking cool,

smoking cigarettes, etc., had been replaced by highly efficient teams of police officers with integrity, brilliant forensics specialists, earnest lawyers, and superefficient computers. It doesn't matter to the TV-watching public that in real life America has basically none of the above, Gina says, due to the fact that we stoutly refuse to cough up taxes to pay for it. Gina studies what she calls the formulas/standard deviations of TV, along with junk food and pop song lyrics. On our TVs, she says, we like to see the governmental institutions functioning perfectly. People don't want a lone man armed with nothing but a snarky wit and a lame analog peashooter. They just can't take that seriously.

That was my train of thought, walking along the beach in the British Virgin Islands while only partly attending to Chip's worries over memorial-service protocol.

". . . want to send something ourselves, maybe a flower arrangement? Or maybe a donation to a charity?" he was saying as we came up to the marina, where the dock's pilings, in front of us, stretched barnacle-encrusted above the lacework of the tide.

"Whoa," said Steve, finally noticing the traffic. "I don't like this. I don't like being so close to boats."

"What the—? What's going on up there?" asked Chip.

I'd been walking a few steps ahead of them, and now I turned around. I was wearing a creamy sarong over my bikini, albeit a flowing sarong with pouchy pockets for my cell phone and room-key card, strands of my shining hair floating around my face and neck in the ocean breeze. I like to think I looked attractive at that particular moment—as well as authoritative and trust-worthy.

To Chip, anyway. Along with being a universal ear, a spouse is a universal eye. A spouse is watching your biopic at all times, much as you're watching theirs. And even if you don't admit it you want both those biopics to be well filmed, in warm, nostalgic colors. Plus heart-achingly scored.

"I think you *know* what it is, Chip," I said gently.

CHIP TOOK IT hard. I'd known he would, I'd feared he would take it hard and I was right: he did.

We got up on top of the docks, though Steve stayed down below. He didn't do ship, boats, anything seafaring, he said, a matter of personal policy. Chip and I found ourselves among the slips, among the boats, within the throng rushing to and fro and readying vessels for excursions. Small boats but mostly larger boats, soaring white yachts you might almost feel comfortable calling *ships*—all manner of watergoing vehicle was being fitted out. Gorda's the yachtiest of the Virgin Islands: yacht people swarm daily off their boats into the restaurants, onto the beaches, looking for terra firma and their share of landlubber food and sport. This was one of several marinas on the island, and it was white with yachts.

Also there was an overwhelming vibe of haste, mission, even urgency: a vital enterprise under way. We couldn't get an answer out of anyone because they were ignoring us, in their furor and commotion. They wouldn't stop to explain; they didn't even look at us in passing. We moved among them like shadows or ghosts.

Presently, as we stood there being buffeted by hurrying people—a little dazzled, a little lost, now and then jostled by a passing workatron—Chip located someone from our dive group and grabbed his shoulder, stopped him mid-rush. It was a recent Listserv defector I hadn't ever paid attention to, a thin guy with bulging eyes.

"They're paying time and a half," he told us, sweating from the exertion of hefting a sack. It wavered on his shoulder. "Plus open bar tonight."

"What for? What's going on?" urged Chip.

"We have to cordon off the area, these boats here are kind of the support system for those other ships we're using, these big ships with fishing nets—trawlers, I think that's what they are. Or maybe it's purse seine. They're going to drop the nets around where the marvels are so that they can't escape," said the guy.

"The marvels?" said Chip.

"The marvels, *you* know, the attraction. The *fish* people," said the guy, and then he got a stressed look on his face, glancing past us at someone, I guess, who needed either his sack or his presence. He quickly turned to leave. "Gotta bounce."

Chip looked at me, stricken.

"They're going after them," he said.

I saw a face I recognized, then, up on the deck of one of the nearer yachts: Mike Jans or Chance or whatever, the too-tanned resort employee from Guest Services who'd come to the door of Steve and Janeane's cabana. He wasn't wearing his maroon tie anymore; now he was clad in what I guessed was modern sailor gear, a windbreaker and a cap, a pair of mirrored sunglasses. Approaching him from the gangplank—another face I recognized!—was our other Guest Services rep, the name-tag woman who'd been Mormonish the night before.

Well, in daylight she wasn't Mormonish at all. She wore flipflops and shorts, and her bare legs were strong and muscular as a carthorse's, plus clearly waxed. I'm not sure, but I don't think waxing's much of a Latter-Day Saints habit. *She's not a Mormon,* I couldn't help thinking a little disappointedly; I couldn't help feeling just the tiniest bit betrayed. Sure, she'd never directly claimed to be LDS, but the ankle-length, floral, asexual dress had made the claim for her, and now she was renouncing it without so much as a by-your-leave. It came to me then that dressing badly could be seen, in a way, as a form of disinformation, a form, almost, of psychological weapon.

But I didn't have time to go down that road. Chip was upset.

"Deb," he said quietly, standing close to me. His hands were actually trembling. "They're going out there to hunt them, is that it? Hunt the mermaids?"

"Oh, I don't think so," I said. "I really don't think that's it."

"Then what *is* it?"

I pointed at a banner flapping behind Mike and his coworker. And that was our introduction to the new mermaid tourism company—incorporated, as it turned out, with mysterious rapidity as a wholly owned subsidiary of the multinational chain that also owned our resort—that called itself the *Venture of Marvels*.

Beside the words, a logo of a fishtail sticking out of a frothy, stylized wave.

"They're going out there to market them," I said.

THERE'S NOT A lot of anger in Chip, really; I'd say he's well below average on the anger meter, for his demographic. He's white, he's male, and he's quite young, but he's got no serial killer in him—none at all. No tendencies to violence that I've ever seen. Or if he does have them they channel completely into the gaming, sex, and athletics.

And yet, when he looked up at those words and that logo and then looked down at the Guest Services team standing beneath it, their tans glowing against the white of the yacht like twin beacons, I saw blood rush to his face. His face, all of a sudden, looked lightly mottled, and I actually caught the movement of his jaw clenching. I thought I heard his molars grinding, even amidst the pandemonium on the docks.

"No," said Chip. "No. No. No. No. No!"

"Hey," I said, "hey, there." But as I reached out to comfort him I reminded myself of Steve the Freudian wrangling Janeane, which made me jerk back my hand from his arm. It wasn't that I didn't want him to be comforted, just that I didn't want to act like a *life partner,* exactly. I figured the process would have a neutering effect.

"They can't do this," he said, shaking his head. "It's just like Nancy said! They're going to wreck *everything!*"

I didn't doubt what he said, which made it hard to come back with a soothing remark.

"The others from the dive are *working* for them! For these people. The Venture of Marvels, whatever that is."

"I suspect it's the same people who run the resort. Or at least their parent company," I said, inclining my head toward the tanned people astride their yacht, above us.

Chip's brow knit.

"That's why they left my Listserv, I bet they felt guilty," he said. "They felt *guilty* because they were cashing in. They were betraying Nancy and everything she stood for! *And* violating our contract! They're getting paid to sell out the mermaids!"

"Yes," I said. "I think that's a pretty fair assumption."

"Deb," he said, "you're the strategist. What can we *do?*"

I looked around for a place to sit; all I saw was the top of a piling, a sawed-off stumpy thing spattered with seagull white. Any port in a storm, I said to myself, but then I disagreed.

"First," I said, "who's still on your Listserv, Chip? Who hasn't defected yet?"

He lifted his phone, tapped a few times, studied the screen. "Thompson," he said. "Rick. Ronnie . . ."

"Thompson? Who's that?"

"The retired wreck diver, you know, the ex-Navy guy with all the great stories. You called him *the old salt*. Then Rick and Ronnie from San Francisco that we had dinner with. And then— just—no way! Another unsubscribe. Right now!"

"And?"

"There's only one other person left, I guess, Miyoko. Young, Asian, some kind of big-wave surfer but she came here just to dive. She wanted to see the reefs. Dolphin tattoo on her ankle. Remember?"

I vaguely did. She was quiet and self-possessed, with excellent skin; we hadn't spoken much.

"OK, Chip. We've got to call a meeting."

AFTER WE SAW the banner for the so-called Venture of Marvels I didn't know whether to feel invisible or paranoid. On the one hand, we were afraid that Nancy had been murdered for her mermaid discovery, in which case we *should* be paranoid because we, too, could be killed if we didn't toe the line.

On the other hand, it was in fact possible that Nancy had died a natural, if unlikely, death and that our mermaids had been discovered by the resort only *after* her death, basically *because* of her death—from Nancy's cell phone records, which led them to Riley's video.

In that case we'd invented the cover-up, invented the idea that the resort had murdered her in order to profit off the mermaids; in that case we didn't need to be paranoid, possibly, because although the resort's parent company, if that was true, had been repulsively quick to leap into a niche—had leapt into that niche unethically, cynically, and with the most craven of motives— it wasn't per se criminal, necessarily. Or it was more a form of white-collar crime or maybe just moral turpitude (a favorite phrase of Gina's). So maybe the parent company didn't care what we thought or even what we did.

But of course, we didn't know which it was, theft or murder. We had to err on the paranoid side, ultimately. Should we operate covertly, sneaking around like spies, or in the wide-open spaces?

In the end I opted to start with wide-open spaces, figuring that our best insurance might be obviousness. Or it might not. It was a risk. Anyway we gathered, the seven of us, in the gazebo of a palm garden (Janeane was still in the Pearl Diver Cabana, building her confidence). There was Steve, Thompson, Rick, Ronnie, Miyoko, Chip, and me. That was all that remained of our catered excursion force, our motley crew of spearfishermen, dive pros, vacationers, and parrotfish experts—all that was left of the boatload that had, for the first time in human history, videotaped mermaids.

Around us the palms were planted in a geometric pattern around the colorful tiled patio, creating a sense that we were on the grounds of some raja's palace and might at any moment see a line of elephants lumber into sight, caparisoned in finery and bearing howdahs for some Indian royals. Of course we saw no elephants, only the golf carts, loaded with tourists like ourselves. There were also human-size statues of knights, kings, queens, and pawns, arrayed along opposite edges of the patio beside our gazebo. A couple lay on their sides, fallen. The patio was a giant chessboard.

"I guess my question is," Chip said, when we were all sitting, "what's our first priority? Justice for Nancy? Or helping the mermaids?"

"We gotta go where we can get shit done," said the old salt Thompson, with his usual gruffness.

"Nancy would want us to help the mer-people," put in Rick, the independent film guy.

"That's right, she would," agreed Ronnie, his boyfriend the designer. "That's what Nancy would want. Definitely."

Miyoko gave the slightest of nods.

"Makes sense to me," said Steve.

"So the next question," said Thompson,

twiddling the knobs on his elaborate wristwatch, "is how far are we willing to go? To save these critters? Where do we draw the line?"

"Nonviolent protest?" offered Ronnie.

Thompson barked out a laugh.

"No, seriously though," he said, turning to Chip. "One thing. I've got experience with explosives. Another thing. I've *got* explosives."

"Jesus," said Rick.

"What kind of explosives?" asked Chip curiously.

"Need-to-know basis. Just saying."

"A middle ground, maybe," said Steve. "Between the sign-waving and the bombing?"

"What's the specific goal, Chip?" I asked. "If we're trying to stop this hotel chain from destroying the mermaids, OK, but what's the deliverable? What's the actual outcome that we'd like to see?"

"It's Terriault-Smith, right?" mused Rick. "The parent company? They also have a pharmaceutical arm, I think. And maybe frozen foods."

"I know what Nancy *really* wanted," said Chip. "She wanted, like, a mermaid *park*. That was her vision, a national park in the ocean, but for mermaids. Like with the Channel Islands, remember that trip, Deb? It's set aside for nature, and then you're not allowed to fish for them."

"So how do we do that?" asked Thompson. "That's a political deal. Got nothing to do with us."

"A petition!" said Ronnie.

"Feh," said Thompson, shaking his head, and started to roll a cigarette, pinching tobacco from a leather pouch.

"Well, we're in a British territory," said Rick. "So yeah, no. It's kind of out of our hands. You live here, don't you, Thompson—would you happen to be a British citizen?"

"Yeah right," said Thompson.

Finally we decided the first step was to stop the parent company from dropping its long nets. The mermaids (none of us ever called them "mers," no matter what Nancy had said) didn't deserve to be imprisoned, we decided, whether we could do anything else for them or not. There was no call for imprisonment—it just didn't seem fair. The nets might catch and hurt them; there could be sharp hooks on those things. I pictured them struggling in those nets like dolphins, asphyxiating, possibly. I saw their half-human blood dispersing cloud-like in the sea. It would be our fault: we would have brought those hooks to them. Not on purpose, but still.

We all agreed we didn't like the idea.

"Time to monkey-wrench," said Thompson. "The hour of sabotage is here."

"We can't stop the boats from sailing," objected Rick. "Some are already out there."

"The nets?" said Thompson. "Blast holes in them? Cover of night?"

"With terrorism going on, and that, we probably shouldn't blow stuff up. I say we talk to the folks in charge, you know?" said Chip earnestly. "Just set up a meeting with whoever's in charge and plead our case—plead on the mermaids' behalf. Maybe we're underrating them, maybe they'll listen to reason."

"A poodle pissin' on a wildfire," said Thompson. "Come *on,* Chip. And you too, what's your name, the smaller homosexual—Lonnie?"

"Uh, Ronnie."

"Boys, put some lead in your peckers. Sit-ins, writing letters, corporate-office chitchat, it's for wussbags. Poltroons and pantywaists."

The rest of us were momentarily silenced by this. Then, for the very first time since we'd gathered, Miyoko spoke. English wasn't her first language; I hadn't been sure how fluent she was, up till then. Her voice was small but firm.

"TV."

IT TURNED OUT Miyoko was some kind of personality on Japanese television. She wasn't a reporter, exactly—more of a VJ type. She talked to teenage girls about fashion crazes and middle-aged office ladies about weird fetishes; she interviewed pop stars and other brainless celebrities.

Millions of people watched her show, she said. She stated the figure offhandedly. She'd come here on vacation, she had no broadcasting equipment with her, per se, but she did have her ultra-powerful laptop with its various capabilities, and we could get our hands on whatever else was needed, she assured us.

"You think people will care about the mermaids, in Japan?" asked Chip.

Rick chimed in.

"Your, uh, Japan's a whaling country, pretending to kill whales for scientific purposes, then eating them?" he asked. "Not exactly eco-freaks. Plus they do those dolphin slaughters on the beach."

Miyoko didn't take offense.

"The mermaids are very special," was all she said. "My viewers will love them."

Two prongs were needed, we determined; ours would be a two-pronged campaign. Thompson wouldn't relinquish the idea of stealth; as a former Navy SEAL, he insisted on it. And he was right, we decided: there *was* a place for stealth, if not for heavy-duty weaponry. (At this stage in our discussions, we dispatched Chip and Rick, alternately, to walk the perimeter of the chess patio, checking for both skulking resort employees and security equipment; we couldn't risk having our new plans overheard.) The place of stealth was this: we wanted to steal back our mermaid video. The chance of us finding the mermaids again anytime soon, under conditions ideal for recording, was virtually nil. And for those millions of Japanese viewers, we needed evidence. We needed the visuals. We figured that, by now, the parent company must have made copies; there'd be a few in existence, by this time, we guessed, and all we had to do was lay our hands on one of them.

Thompson and Chip and Ronnie, who was a decent diver, would make up the stealth team; Rick really wanted to go, I could tell—get in on the man-of-action deal. But with his filmmaking expertise he was needed for AV stuff on the media team, which included Miyoko, Steve and me. We split into our teams to plan, with media retiring to the Pearl Diver Cabana, where Steve made us vegan sandwiches and Miyoko discreetly checked the room for bugs. (We didn't want to frighten Janeane.) She knew her way around a micro-phone, she said, even a small one; luckily, she didn't find any.

Janeane was doing a lot better, I was glad to see, though her hair was flattened on one side of her head. Also she was wearing a housecoat garment that gave her an invalid/shut-in aspect. But she was smiling now and then and speaking normally, not screeching or gibbering. With her Steve tried to downplay the enterprise a bit, didn't let on how sizable the allied forces were, the forces of the parent company. He didn't mention the armada of yachts and fishing boats arrayed at the docks, the trawlers, the droves of eager, commandeered labor earning overtime pay and, afterward, free liquor. He didn't tell Janeane how most of our own diving party members had defected to the other side. He didn't mention the stealth prong, the fact that Thompson had advocated for the use of powerful incendiary devices, which he apparently had the means to produce and deploy. Janeane would ideate nonstop if she knew that.

While we sat around their bamboo table and ate our chunky sandwiches—which combined hummus, beansprouts, and diced cucumber into a substance neatly devoid of flavor—Miyoko typed out a few texts on her cell phone (it looked like a handheld, razor-thin spaceship). She had a quick conversation in Japanese, holding her phone in front of her so she could see the other person's face and they could see hers too. I peered over, inquisitive: another Japanese person, this one with spiky hair. Probably male, either quite young or with skin as smooth as Miyoko's. Hard to tell more.

"They're ready when we are," she said when she hung up. "For optimal quality, we need a portable satellite dish."

"On it as soon as I'm done eating," said Rick, his lips daubed in beige hummus-paste. I was gratified by the media team's efficiency, though I personally had failed to contribute one iota.

We'd have a waiting game to play, when our tech ducks were in a row, until the other team fulfilled its own mission—which wouldn't happen until dark. We planned to fill the time setting up social media, under Miyoko's direction. Rick and Steve would be tracking down equipment while Miyoko and I labored to put together a mini-presentation on the reefs and islands, to go along with our mermaid story.

I needed Chip's tablet for the task—I hadn't brought my own on the honeymoon—so after lunch I headed back to our cabana to fetch it. I said I'd be back in ten minutes.

But on my way out of our cabana again, tablet in hand, I was met at the door. Of all five men standing there, blocking my free egress, I recognized only two: the bouncer from our party and the blond Riley.

"Ma'am," said the man at the front, who wore a suit and no name tag at all, "we'd like you to come with us, please."

I DIDN'T CAVE right away. I didn't like the man-huddle. I felt their eyes burning into me, as I stood there in only my bikini and sarong. On the other hand, there were enough of them hulking there that I was in a bind. (Riley avoided my eyes, I noticed, looking pointedly off to one side like he had better things to stare at.) I protested, first asking why—they shook their heads and shrugged as if that was an irrelevant question—and then saying I had to tell my friends where I was going.

Where *was* I going, by the way? A meeting in Conference Room B, said one of them. Can my friends come too, then? I said, but the man at the front said they were already there. Really? I said, because I'd just left them. In that case I'd stop at the Pearl Diver Cabana, I said, just to make sure my friends were all included in the meeting.

They nodded grudgingly, but a couple of minutes later—as we walked along the path that passed Steve's cabana—I found myself jostled and forced away from it, surrounded by a wall of men.

At that point I considered making a scene, even yelling/screaming. But that's where my personality got in the way, my personality that, especially as I got older, I hadn't worried about so much. I'm not a screamer, never have been, and it turned out this situation was no exception to the rule. The idea of screaming seemed foolish. Here we were in a Caribbean resort. What was the worst that could happen? Then I caught sight of Nancy's cabana and thought of her bathtub, but still the scream stuck in my throat.

So I didn't do anything except call out Steve's name a couple times, then Miyoko's—probably not loud enough to be heard from inside. And for once there was no one around, not even a single golf cart transporting its inert, jiggling cargo.

We went through a side door into the main building, the building with the lobby and most of the restaurants, and then we were in a service elevator, and then a narrow corridor, and then we were in a room that, if it *was* the famed Conference Room B, was certainly a small one. It'd be your two-, your three-person conferences that took place in that baby.

There was barely room for the man-huddle; they pressed me in, then hovered at the threshold. The room had a table with two chairs, a TV, another door and one window—a picture window overlooking the beach and the sea.

A picture window that, of course, didn't open.

At the door of the room they looked around at each other for a second, and then, abruptly, without saying a single thing, the one who'd stood at the front leaned out and just grabbed Chip's tablet, which I was still holding. Just like that he took it from me. And then every one of them left. They sluiced out the door fast as liquid.

I was alone.

I stood there for a second, kind of in disbelief, and then stepped toward the door they'd sluiced through and rattled the knob hopelessly. Locked, of course. I crossed the room and opened the other door; there was a toilet, a sink and a pink plug-in air freshener shaped like a butterfly.

I walked back to the middle of the room—we're talking maybe a twelve-foot room, so it wasn't far—and stared out the picture window. I was in a bad situation, and really the person I had to blame it on was me, me and my personality, which, as a prisoner with nothing at all to do, I was now free to worry about. Who the hell wouldn't scream, being kidnapped like that? I'd been abducted in broad daylight and I hadn't even put up a fight. There was something wrong with me, and now I had plenty of time to ponder that. For all I knew Steve, Miyoko, and Rick were also in rooms like this, just stuck in idiotic rooms, like me. For all I knew it was the same with Chip, Thompson, and Ronnie. I hoped that wasn't the case. I hoped, for the mermaids' sake, that they had better personalities.

I blamed myself, standing there in my bikini and skirt, utterly powerless. Then I remembered something. I touched my loose, flowing sarong and felt a hard thing against my fingers and my bare leg. I said the word *yes*.

I glanced around me to see if there was a camera in evidence, a little electronic eye. Could I be sure? I investigated the TV. I looked at the electrical outlets. I even looked under the table, where a camera would be no use. There was one floor lamp, and I checked that. I stood on a chair and touched the sides of the fluorescent light fixture. But I still wasn't a hundred percent sure. These days, who knew how small and camouflaged a camera could be? So I stepped into the bathroom and closed the door. There were no cameras there, unless they'd made cameras completely invisible, with their technology.

I slid my hand down into my pocket, standing there next to the toilet, and I took out my phone. There it was. They hadn't seen I had pockets. They hadn't seen that at all. I smiled. My kidnappers were even less competent than I was.

I felt slightly better about my personality—compared to theirs, anyway. I turned it on. Three bars.

I said the word again, somewhat triumphantly. *Yes*.

THE FIRST THING I texted Chip was an SOS. I let him know where I was, locked in a room with a picture window. I told him the elevator had taken us to Floor 3; I told him I didn't fear bodily harm, though maybe I should. But I didn't want to stop the mermaids from being saved, with my stupid predicament. On the other hand, I texted, I *was* locked up against my will.

It took him a few minutes to text back. During that time, I found out later, he was visibly upset. But then he gathered his wits and texted me back, asking what door we'd come through and could I take a picture out the picture window, just in case it helped them to locate me.

So Chip wasn't also locked in a room, and that encouraged me. I emerged from the bathroom, throwing caution to the winds; I snapped said photo with my phone and sent it off.

I sent a text describing the path we'd walked along, the part of the building we'd come into. I wondered in passing how humankind had existed before the advent of cell phones—my own life, before cell phones, was often a featureless blur. I sent off a picture of the door, too, although I didn't think it'd be particularly useful. From the outside it probably looked like every other door along that narrow corridor. Next I considered whether the men, watching me via a camera I hadn't found, would come back in and try to grab my phone from me. I retreated to the bathroom. But there was no lock on its door, anyway, so I slunk out again.

I didn't want to keep texting Chip, but I knew someone else who wouldn't mind hearing from me. So, staring out at the empty beach and the sea, I went ahead and texted Gina. She prefers text to voice.

Kidnapped, I wrote. *Locked in a room in our resort. Chip coming to save me (hope). Saw real mermaids. Even got video, but video stolen. Someone died. Possibly murdered.*

That should pique her interest, I thought smugly. For once I'd be the one to shock Gina, instead of the other way around.

Gina's never far from her cell, love nest or no. So I knew it wouldn't be long before she texted back. Indeed: five seconds.

Fuck off! she wrote.

Of course, Gina would never credit such a fanciful-sounding tale. Her irony was far too bulletproof for a mermaid sighting; her irony was a Kevlar of the mind.

Then I remembered our code. The words we used to show we weren't joking, that we were hardcore, that we meant every word. We'd used those words since we were kids, but only a handful of times and always in deadly earnest. Those words were not ironic. Those words, once spoken, could never be doubted and could never be taken back.

On your mother's life, I typed. *On the life of your mother.*

Because Gina had lost her mother not long after we met. Ninth grade. Cancer, long and drawn-out. I was there for her from then on; I'll never forget the depth of her grief. It changed her forever. It's fair to say she never recovered.

For once there was a text silence.

Finally, broken.

Do you need me? she typed.

Just that.

It's OK, I typed. *You'd never get here in time. I'll be OK. Chip's coming to bust me out.*

Mermaids, typed Gina, after a few moments. *I'll be goddamned.*

I THINK PART of me expected, when I sent my SOS to Chip, that he'd show up in fifteen minutes.

Maybe thirty. I thought Thompson might be in tow, possibly packing a sidearm.

But this was not reasonable. Also it was not the case.

I heard occasional footsteps outside the room; each time I did I got excited, all prepared to leave. But each time the footsteps faded. My texts to Chip came back unanswered, creating anxiety. I knew I couldn't call the island cops; Thompson had said they were fully in the pocket of the parent company. I didn't want to use my phone much, because I didn't have a charger with me, and the battery was in the red. That phone was my life-line; besides the toilet and sink, that phone was all I had. The TV, on its metal trolley, didn't seem to get reception—when I turned it on there was nothing but gray static.

So I drank some water from the bathroom sink, splashing it into my mouth; then I sat and stared out the picture window. It was blocked on one side by the building itself, which stretched out to my right; ahead was a strip of beach and ocean, which stretched out to the left until some palm trees blocked the rest of the view.

After a while I saw boats on the ocean. First one, then many. White dots of varying sizes. It had to be the Venture of Marvels: the armada was going out, I guessed. The mermaid site must be within my field of view—too distant for me to see any-thing, though.

I got frustrated, without any response from Chip; I imagined scenarios, and those scenarios were not pleasant. I'd be like Janeane, I thought, if I let my imagination have free rein. That road was a bad road. I wouldn't go down that road. I'd leave here, I'd get out, I vowed, and I'd be none the worse for wear, either.

In fact, I decided, I wasn't going to sit around waiting to be rescued. My country didn't have princesses—or if it did, they weren't the kind you bowed down to. They weren't the kind that got saved by princes, certainly.

I'd made my first mistake not screaming; I wasn't going to make a second. I felt around for my key card, the plastic key to my room, remembering when Gina had taken a lock-picking course because she was pissed off that she had to pay a locksmith every time she locked herself out of her car. That was back in the days when cars had actual keys, obviously. Gina's always been prone to losing keys, as well as phones, credit cards, and cash money. Back then she'd tried to convey her newfound knowledge of locks to me. I lost interest fast, regrettably, but I had a couple of the basics and it seemed to me there was quiet outside the door now. So I decided to give it a whirl.

My bet was they hadn't planted a sentry; from the rare footstep sounds it seemed they were content to check on my locked door periodically. So I listened to make sure it was silent, and then I slipped the card between the door and the jamb and tried to get somewhere. I got nowhere, was where I got, with that flimsy rectangle—it simply didn't have the thickness and quality of credit.

Then I noticed the knob was the kind with a hole in it; it wasn't made to be secure, really. All I needed was something to fit in that hole. What did I have? I had a wedding ring. I had flip-flops. I had a pink butterfly air freshener. There had to be a thin piece of metal here somewhere. The TV was all plastic, nothing to break off there . . .

Eureka. I'd put my hair up before we went to the beach; the bun in its elastic was falling now, wispy tendrils on my neck, but yes—a bobby pin. In fact I had two of them.

Gina had said you needed the curved end. The curved end could hook around the lock button inside the knob.

So I slid the bobby pin into that small hole. At

first I jiggled, but then I thought that movement wasn't right, too hasty, too chaotic. I pushed the knob in with the other hand as I moved the bobby pin slowly around. Now and then I got discouraged, my wrists aching a bit from the pushing and the turning, and took a break, and then I started up again, always listening for footsteps. Sometimes crying a bit, that weird dry-crying you do when there aren't any actual tears, mostly from frustration. A few times I stood up, walked around, shook out my hands and aching wrists, gave myself a pep talk like a madwoman. Twice I thought I almost had it, I felt the pin catch, but then I lost it again.

The third time I thought I almost had it, and then I did. I turned the knob.

HOOKING MY FLIP-FLOPS from a couple of fingers, I bolted from that room like a bat out of hell. I ran, skin tingling, vision bleary with fear, to the service elevator. Then I didn't want to be in another tight space, so I kept going right past it to the stairs, down the stairs on my bare feet, one flight, two flights, three flights and four—there was the door to the outside. It was a great feeling, coming out into the breeze and sunlight. I'd freed myself. I felt proud.

And from there I kept running, just ran and ran on those paved paths all the way back to the Pearl Diver Cabana. *Now* there were golf carts around, now when I didn't have any use for them at all there were plenty of hotel guests moving to and fro, but I didn't stop, just ran, smiling to be free, my phone hitting against my leg until I grabbed it in the non-shoe hand; I ran, not worrying about the sharp pebbles I stepped on, the stray leaves and grains of sand and flower petals that stuck to my heels and gathered between my toes.

It was the best I'd felt since we arrived, with the exception of a few seconds of sex on the first day. (Maybe.) Then I was banging on Steve's door, breathing heavily, shooting worried glances over my shoulder.

It was Janeane who opened it, Janeane who said, "Good Goddess! I heard from Chip they kidnapped you—are you all *right?*" She pulled me in and shut the door, then bolted it. "We're safe here. You poor thing!"

She was alone; the others had gone out before Chip called her about me; he'd told her not to worry them, that he and the stealth team had me covered, to just let them get the AV equipment.

We called Chip on Janeane's cell, not wanting to use the hotel phone in case the bad guys might be listening in; I told him what had happened. Chip, whose voice cut out and in again, said they'd been on the brink of finding me, he was certain, but he'd tell me later about the obstacles they'd encountered. For now Janeane and I were in what she called a "safe space," though I wasn't so sure. But the doors to the patio locked too, and I figured that was probably the best we could do. Coasting on the high of my lock-picking self-liberation, I felt newly powerful.

Full steam ahead, damn it, said Chip, and I concurred. Those hotel-running, abductor bastards weren't going to get us down.

I picked a lock, I texted Gina after plugging my phone in with Steve's charger. *Rock on,* she texted me.

It was late by now, well into the waning afternoon, and before long Janeane and I were joined by Miyoko and Rick and Steve. They were loaded down with equipment, even a satellite dish, which Steve was manfully struggling to carry. There were no big-box electronics stores in the vicinity, so I was pretty amazed, but I didn't have time to ask where they'd got the stuff, because Janeane was too busy squeaking out my kidnapping story.

"Jesus," said Steve. "You actually escaped? Picking a lock with a bobby pin?"

"Must have been a cheap lock," I conceded.

"Very *good,*" said Miyoko, but her composure wasn't affected. She gave me a small, pleased smile. It'd take more than an amateurish kidnapping to faze Miyoko; I saw that now.

"Why you?" asked Rick. "Why bother with just one of us, wouldn't they need to put all of us out of commission?"

"Maybe I was just the first," I said. "I was the only one alone, anyway."

"Phase one?" said Steve.

"Well, you *were* a sitting duck, going off by yourself like that," nodded Rick.

"Blaming the victim!" said Janeane.

"So we have to stay in groups from now on," I said. "I guess that's the lesson here. No solo travelers."

"Right," said Rick. "I wonder what the situation is, litigation-wise. The parent company's U.S.-based, you know. You should be able to suc these guys."

"Instead *we're* paying *them,*" I said. "I paid these people good money to stay here, and they go ahead and kidnap me."

I found I could make light of the abduction, now that it was over.

We busied ourselves getting the tech set up—or at least Rick and Miyoko did, while Steve and Janeane and I offered moral support. Miyoko had brought her laptop in; she charged me with finding open-source video of the island that we could use. That was more up my alley than the AV end, so I set myself to the task.

It was almost dusk by the time Chip and Ronnie showed up—Chip and Ronnie, but no Thompson. They looked sub-bleached and waterlogged, with salt crusted on their skin and in their hair. When Chip and I were done with our reunion—not tearful, but a tad private, so we withdrew to the bedroom for a few minutes—he told me Thompson had stowed away. After they'd done some homework to identify the armada's flagship yacht, and Thompson had equipped himself with a duffel bag of night-diving gear brought up from his condo down the beach, Thompson had snuck aboard the flagship while Chip and Ronnie created a diversion.

"What *kind* of diversion?" I asked.

"You're going to be pissed at me."

"What? *Why?*"

"So it probably wasn't the best alternative. But we didn't have many choices, was how we saw it. How Thompson saw it, anyway. With the time pressure and all."

"Chip. Oh no. Chip! Did you guys . . . blow up something?"

"It was just small, though, Deb. Just minor. *Believe* me."

"Chip! You could have blown your arm off! Or someone else's! You could have gotten arrested by Homeland Security! You *still* could! Jesus, Chip!"

"We're not at home, though, is one positive. I don't think they have DHS agents here."

"Chip! Explosives? Who knows what file your little prank could end up in? You think I want to be married to some kind of PATRIOT Act jailbird? Seriously!"

"It was a broken-down part of the dock that was

already wrecked, a couple of pilings off in the ocean there, not holding up anything at all. Just a small explosion. Deb, it was just a minor dynamiting. Hell, construction crews do way bigger things all the time. It wasn't even that loud."

He sounded a little disappointed, frankly.

"You're missing my point completely."

I'd been spot-on, I was thinking, to worry about Thompson's powerful influence on Chip. Show Chip an ex-Navy father figure with a bomb, I'll show you a bomb-exploding Chip. We were lucky it hadn't gone terribly wrong, that no one had been injured. There'd be some serious work to do, when we got home, I told myself, on my better half's daddy issues. Chip needed a personal Freudian.

"But it worked, Deb. It worked like a charm. They got so freaked out, running around and panicking, that they weren't even *watching* when Thompson boarded her. Not a single one of them. Then they saw it wasn't even anything and it all went back to business. No cops even showed up. None at all, Deb, not a single one! Mission completely accomplished."

"Was this before or after I called you all kidnapped?"

"Deb. How can you even ask that?" Chip looked pained. "It was after you *escaped*. Of course."

"Chip. I know you look up to Thompson, although, as far as I can tell, he's a certified, wing-nut paramilitary freak. But from now on, acts of terrorism and violence are family decisions. OK, Chip?"

"Fair enough, honey," said Chip. "I promise, though, there were no people anywhere near."

"A boat could have passed," I said. "Anything, Chip. Once the bombing starts, all safety bets are off. Look. I don't want to argue about it now. But promise me."

"Done," said Chip, overwhelmingly relieved. "Done and done."

"Thompson didn't take more explosives with him, did he? That wasn't part of his little kit?"

"No, no," said Chip hastily. "None at all. The next phase is the robbery, that's all. He's just going to get the tape. And then he'll swim back, in the dark, in his diving gear."

"He must be a very strong swimmer. Those boats are pretty far out."

"He's super strong," said Chip. "He once competed. Distance."

"How about guns, Chip? Did he take a weapon with him?"

"Of course not. Guns can't get *wet,* Deb."

"He's doing the robbing before he's doing the diving, right? I could see that guy sacrificing a gun. If he got a chance to wave it around first. Plus which—you ever hear of *dry bags,* Chip? Maybe he just took a gun in a dry bag. I mean surely he took his cell with him, right, to communicate with you? That's got to be in a dry bag. Maybe, while he was packing it, he also stuck in a gun."

I didn't put it past Thompson to go rogue. With the so-called *minor dynamiting,* he already pretty much had.

"But Thompson's not a *criminal.* He used to be a Navy SEAL! He fought for our nation, Deb! Or dove, at least. He dove for our great nation."

"Uh-huh," I said, unconvinced.

Finally we hashed it out, as much as we could without a therapy session, and emerged into the main room, where the others were running an equipment test. We wouldn't use it till morning—that was the plan, at least—when we'd likely be broadcasting from the beach.

"Pretty soon now the first boats are due back," said Chip, checking his phone. "The flagship's staying out there, from what we overheard, staying out tonight watching the nets, which will have been set by now. But a lot of the smaller boats are coming back in. We've got a man on the inside, Deb, did I tell you?"

Turned out they'd bribed the Fox News spear-fisher, the one who'd rummaged in my tampon box. He claimed to be acting as a double agent, undercover in the armada. He had no allegiance to the parent company, much as he'd had no allegiance to Nancy or to Chip and me, but for a

hundred bucks he'd agreed to tell Chip everything he'd seen, out there on the sparkling waves.
And possibly beneath them. He'd promised to
make his first report in the evening; Chip had an
assignation with him behind the restaurant-bar
where the other turncoats would be helping
themselves to free libations.

I found myself wishing we were doing some
sleuthing, that we had the manpower and the chops
to figure out exactly what had led to Nancy's
untimely death. I discovered it was nagging at
me, the unresolved question of whether our
scientist had died through simple misadventure or
someone's evil intent. It nagged at me. It really
did.

But for now, at least, the murder mystery
remained unsolved. We had to fortify ourselves,
sooner or later, and that was what we did; at a
certain point I realized my brush with kidnapping
had left me hungry. When dinnertime came we ate
Janeane's vegan fare, we drank, and periodically
Chip received cryptic email bulletins from
Thompson, whose cell phone was apparently
hooking into the yacht's WiFi. He was hiding in a
closet full of mops, pine oil, and bags of scented
kitty litter. Whoever the yacht belonged to liked to
keep cats aboard, but Thompson hated cats,
claiming their shit could make you schizophrenic.
(Chip showed me his email: *Cats> civilization>
toxoplasmosis> people schiz out OR their brains*

swell/burst.) The smell of the scented kitty litter was making him, as he wrote Chip, "want to upchuck."

There was the matter of sleeping arrangements, next, complicated by the fact that we didn't want to split up. The more of us there were, in one locked space, the stronger our chances—who was to say another contingent of hotel employees wouldn't show up, this time with firearms and greater powers of coercion? So we decided to camp out on sofas and the floor, posting sentries throughout the night. We'd take shifts, two at a time, one at the front window and one at the sliders; we kept the outside lights on. As Rick pointed out, if they had real brains they'd cut the power to our cabana, but it hadn't occurred to them to do that, I guess—and here again their incompetence, as adversaries, was helpful.

But before we could sleep there was the problem of Chip's appointment with the under-cover spearfisher. He couldn't keep it alone, since we didn't do solo travel. We decided that Rick, Chip, and I would do the sortie.

It seems a little poignant, in retrospect, to think how we armed ourselves with kitchen knives—mine in particular, since it was a bread knife with a rounded end. I didn't feel comfortable carrying a butcher's knife, figured I'd slice myself to ribbons. So I took up arms with the bread knife, meaning the worst I could have done to an

attacker was scrape him, kind of broadside—
cause an abrasion of some kind.

But night served us well as we crept along the
backs of buildings. Chip had mapped our route out
in his head; he had orienteering skills gained
while gaming in made-up lands. We didn't use
flashlights, though Thompson had lent us some,
but relied on our eyes and Chip's sense of
direction, and whenever we heard the electric
whir of a golf cart in the near distance we'd dodge
behind a clump of trees, taking cover.

By and by we fetched up behind the main
building, near the bar's patio, where we were
screened from view by an oleander hedge. It was
five minutes till the meet time. We stood there
wordless, waiting. The tampon spearfisher was
late, of course, punctuality wasn't his strong suit.
When he finally stumbled out onto the patio, beer
in hand, I could see right away he was a few
sheets to the wind.

"Psst!" said Chip. "Over here!"

It took the fisherman a minute to make us out,
shadowy figures behind the screen of foliage. He
fought his way through branches, swearing; he
dropped his beer bottle on the flagstones, making
noise, and then complained it had been almost
full.

"I have your cash," said Chip. "But first we
need the goods."

"This is some sneaky shit," said the fisherman,

and actually belched. "So what's your angle, man? Still trying to keep the mermaids for yourselves?"

"Not for ourselves," said Chip. "That's not the point at all."

"Enough with the chitchat," said Rick. "You're here to make a buck, right? What've you got? Was there another sighting?"

"Nah," said the fisherman. "They dropped the nets, though, and those nets are massive, man. We're talking goddamn miles of them. Saw tons of dolphins."

It was good, I thought, they hadn't seen any mermaids, but I felt a pang about those long, long nets. I wondered if they were the kind that scrape along the floor of the ocean, wrecking and killing everything. I'd seen a documentary. They probably were, I cogitated gloomily. Otherwise how could they be sure of sealing it all off?

"Then what's the plan?" said Chip. "What's next?"

"Tomorrow we search the grid. They've got it all mapped out, you know, into these squares. And as we search, they move the nets. We basically search the area, square by square, right? And as we exclude the squares, we bring the nets closer in."

"I see," said Chip. "How about leadership? Who's in charge of this operation?"

"Shit, I don't know. They brought in suits from Florida. Plus there's this geeky professor dude."

Chip and I exchanged glances.

"An anthropologist? From Berkeley?" I said.

"Yeah, right," said the spearfisher. "An anthrocologist. Yeah, he's advising the suits. On *search logistics*."

I could barely believe it. Nancy's old colleague was a turncoat too. You couldn't trust anyone, in this world we inhabited. Or was he just a stooge? Had they even told this guy what happened to Nancy? Did they secure his help under false pretenses?

My mind has cogs, and they were spinning.

"So what's their endgame?" prodded Chip. "They want to, what? Sell tickets? To this Venture of Marvels? Sell tickets to see the mermaids?"

"Biggest tourist destination in the world," slurred the fisherman. "It'll be like Disneyland. You kidding me?"

"They already do fine with tourism," demurred Rick.

"But see, the reefs, man," slurred the fisherman. "Everyone knows they're bleaching. Everyone knows they're dying out. Shit. You can *see* it with the naked eye. *Every* reef man knows. I'm a reef man, see? But it's some dying shit, those reefs. The reefs are done, dude. Done like a dinner. Global-ass warming. Acid oceans. Hey. Can I go in, get me another brew? I'll come out again."

"No, man," said Chip. "Come on. Talk to us first. *Then* get your beer."

"Killjoy," said the fisherman. "Listen. It's too bad, but the reefs are over. This is the next big thing, my dudes. Without the coral reefs, out here, we don't have *shit*. Sand, water, you can get that boring crap in *Flo*rida. Hell, even in Jersey. This is the next big meal ticket. Man, this is *it*. I mean this is all we've *got*."

And with that he held out his hand for the cash.

IT'S FAIR TO say we felt downcast, as we walked back to the cabana. I was remembering the first dinner with Nancy, when she'd said the same thing—except for the part about mermaids and meal tickets, of course. I know all about economic incentives; it's my job. This was a big machine, I thought. A big machine you couldn't stop. Once it was started, it kept moving. And who were we? We were honeymooners, tourists. We didn't even *live* here.

"But they're overlooking something," said Rick suddenly, just as we reached the Pearl Diver. We were going in from the back, the way we'd come out, fighting our way through more flowering hedges to get to the patio. "That's what Nancy would say. They're overlooking one major aspect, if that's their plan."

"What's that, Rick," said Chip wearily.

"The likelihood that the mermaids *also* depend on the reefs," said Rick.

215

We stood there, on the patio, Chip and Rick and I.

"Exactly!" said Chip.

"That's where we saw them," said Rick. "It's probably their home. Just like so many other fish-type animals, right? Sure, we don't know their biology yet, Nancy'd be the first to admit it. But chances are, the reefs are probably a major food source for them. Their hunting grounds, as it were."

We nodded slowly, all three of us, like so many bobbleheads on my coworker's computer.

"Then, to have the mermaids to show off for tourists, they'd *have* to save the reefs," I said. "Right?"

"Easier said than done," said Rick.

"But that has to be part of our message," I urged. "What we broadcast with Miyoko. That they're wrong, these mermaid hucksters have it totally wrong. They *can't* use mermaids as their meal ticket when all the reefs are gone. It's not either/or—it's both."

"I bet they plan to feed the mermaids," said Chip. "They'll make, like, kind of a zoo for them, I bet. Like, artificial reefs."

Then we all felt discouraged again. A mermaid zoo. Yep: we could see that happening in a heartbeat.

It was a rollercoaster for us, the hope followed by the disappointment.

MIYOKO, I THINK, stayed up most of the night working on footage for the "B-roll," as she put it. I slept a total of four hours, tossing and turning on my blanket on the narrow couch when I wasn't on sentry duty. Chip slept even less; he finally settled down at three only to wake up again at five, when he received a text from Thompson: Santa Claus was coming down the chimney.

Chip didn't wake me up right then—he was worried about me getting enough sleep after what Janeane called the *psychic trauma of the kidnapping*—but when dawn came I was woken by the soughing, restless trade winds rattling the palm fronds.

And then he told me right away.

I think it was the first time I'd seen him crack a real smile since Nancy.

I donned some fresh clothes borrowed from Janeane, since I didn't want to wear my bikini for another day running, so I was dressed like a bona fide hippie, in a flowing, brightly colored dress that looked to me like maternity wear, when Thompson knocked on the sliding doors. And when I pulled the curtain back he raised two fingers in the V of victory.

I FOUND I warmed to Thompson quite a bit, after that. I appreciate a person who can get things done. And though his methods are sketchy, i.e.

illegal, unsafe, and destructive, Thompson simply *is* such a person.

For here was our tape—now in the form of a shining silver unmarked DVD—and there, right on the screen when we popped that disc into the drive on the side of Miyoko's laptop, were the mermaids, just as I remembered them. As soon as I saw that familiar footage, I had a renewed appreciation for the cunning and expertise of our nation's armed forces, and in particular the Navy. A sigh of delight ushered from us—a sigh, some whoops, a couple of happily uttered swear words. Thompson was embraced, clapped on the back, heartily congratulated and thanked.

Had he been discovered? asked Chip. Had he met with any resistance?

Thompson shook his head. Surgical strike. He'd actually encountered people a few times, he said, as he made his rounds of the yacht, rummaging in strangers' rooms and belongings; but he'd played it cool, like his presence was completely authorized, and no one ever questioned him.

"Well, not quite true," he admitted. "A drunk woman asked me what my star sign was. A lady of a certain age. But I told it to her straight: I don't give a shit about star signs, and I like my ladies young."

"You're a hard case," said Chip.

"Huh. Not *too* young, I hope," said I.

We drank some coffee and planned the logistics

of our media strike. Go time was 8 a.m., the hour of Miyoko's program in Japan, I guess, which came on at night, around the same time as the news. We wouldn't be able to hide, once we were broadcasting, so the stealth team was going to be retasked: their new job was security. We'd make a circle around Miyoko, except for Rick, who would be filming her, and me and Chip, who would be guarding Rick. (Janeane would stay in the cabana, to guard it, as she said, though frankly Janeane couldn't guard a hamster. She didn't like to be alone there, she conceded, but she'd done it the day before and she could do it again.) Miyoko had to send the mermaid footage first—she swore her producers were trustworthy—and that would take a while to upload to their server, along with her B-roll, so we were on a tight schedule. She bent over her computer, focused, industrious.

"No guns, right?" I asked Thompson. "No guns."

"Agreed," he said. "Guns would attract undue attention. Give the rent-a-cops an obvious excuse. However, we *will* have other weapons. From my martial-arts collection. I stashed them in my jeep. Mostly nunchucks. Correctly known as *nunchaku*."

"No way," said Chip, gleeful. "That's pretty rad."

"You'll need a brief tutorial," said Thompson. "It's an ancient art form. No hope you kids will master it. We're shooting to look credible, that's it. A fifteen-minute tutorial will have to do."

So the security team set off for the jeep, while we women, and Rick, stayed in the Pearl Diver, Miyoko typing away, Rick fiddling with his camera obscurely. Before I knew it Miyoko was done with her script-typing—she'd put in what we asked her to about the mermaids likely depending on the reefs; she'd reviewed and even memorized it—and moved on to her makeup. She didn't have her professional kit with her, she said, but she had some odds and ends; before long, with the aid of some hair gel, eyeliner and fake eyelashes, she was a hipster Tokyo VJ again. She even stuck a small jewel to the side of her nose, to look like a piercing, I guess.

When our security detail returned—Chip swinging his nunchucks happily like a man who'd been born to them, Ronnie carrying the things with what I can only describe as distaste—we loaded up our tech and, after a cringe-inducing breathing exercise mandated and led by Janeane, set out across campus. We were passing the side of the main building, trying to keep a low profile (the nunchucks, at that point, were largely out of view) when a group of new arrivals filed into the lobby lugging their suitcases. We turned our faces away, avoiding eye contact studiously until I heard, behind my back, a British-accented voice call out, "What ho!"

I feared—all of us feared—an obstruction to our progress toward the beach from the minions of the parent company. And so I turned slightly, a wary, even hostile look upon my face, no doubt.

And there I saw not minions of said parent company but two highly familiar faces and forms. Standing in front of the lobby, smiling widely, were none other than my friends Ellis. And Gina.

IV.
GLORIOUS REVOLUTION

*J*esus," said Gina disgustedly, before she said anything else. "What the hell are you wearing, Deb? You look like a hangover from Woodstock. I mean, you look really bad."

We ushered them to us hastily, decamping to a small clump of trees behind a stucco half-wall where we weren't in full view.

"We're in a hurry, G.," I said. I was suddenly seeing myself the way Gina saw me, clad in Janeane's hippie hand-me-downs, my hair like a cheap fright wig from Walmart. I tried to shake it off. "We've got to keep moving. My God. I can't believe you're here!"

She and Ellis stashed their roller bags in an oleander and we kept going. Miyoko had a broadcast appointment to keep; we'd timed our walk to the minute because we hadn't wanted to hang out, waiting, in the open. We hoped that, once we were broadcasting live, we'd have a little more protective cover.

As we hurried down to the beach in our group, heavily laden with AV equipment and nunchucks, Gina explained she'd had to come. It was a moral imperative. Honeymoon or no honeymoon, she had to be in on the mermaids. It hadn't sounded like we had much privacy anyway, right? "I'm being obviously euphemistic," she added, "what I mean is, no time for sex." (Chip and I acknowledged that reality with mournful head bows.) And once she decided to book her ticket Ellis had flatly refused to stay behind—the British Virgin Islands being, of course, Her Majesty's territory.

I gave Gina the plot summary as we hastened along, breathless and no doubt confusing. She wanted to see the footage, couldn't wait, but she also yearned to tangle with the parent company. She'd flirted with the law once, Gina had, I mean, not flirted with a cop—though she's also done that, almost serially. I mean she flirted with the idea of becoming a lawyer, before she decided academia was more her speed (the law being, as she put it, a little too much real work). Still, she had a few law courses beneath her belt, as well as a brother who's a hotshot litigator in D.C., and she was foaming at the mouth to threaten litigation.

Then we were there, on the sand, vigilant and purposeful, on the lookout for minions. At first the only people nearby were some early-morning beachgoers, who ogled us curiously, their eyes asking: *Is that pretty young Asian woman a celebrity?* Yes, I answered those curious oglers in my mind, quite a celebrity, well known to millions but not to you. Or me. Then we were setting up;

then Miyoko was smiling and smiling and speaking in Japanese, while Rick filmed her and Steve held the small-but-heavy satellite dish. Her small black mic was on her small black collar and behind her stretched the blue-turquoise expanse of ocean, upon which, in the distance, the white dots of the armada could be seen.

But sure enough, before long we had company.

THEY MARCHED TOWARD us across the sand, parallel to the water, from the direction of the marina—men in formation, dressed as soldiers. Yes: *soldiers,* said their camouflage uniforms, and *soldiers,* said the long guns they were carrying. They wore berets, I saw as they got closer, which gave them an effeminate quality, or French at least. But then they chose the long guns for accessories, which lent a tone of seriousness to the outfits. They made you hesitate to laugh at the berets—the laugh impulse was certainly silenced. And the soldiers had tucked their pants into their boots; I wondered what Gina was thinking of that, the pants tucked into chunky combat boots. I couldn't ask, while Miyoko was recording, but I did wonder.

It wasn't only foot soldiers, either. From behind their ranks appeared some vehicles, and the vehicles soon overtook them. The vehicles were jeeps, and those jeeps, as far as I could see, were chock-full of soldiers, those jeeps without tops on them, those open-air jeeps bouncing over the creamy white sand.

Where had the soldiers come from? They looked like UN peacekeeping forces, with those berets—the guys that got sent out to deal with Somalia, the Sudan, war-torn, distant countries where their job was to resemble soldiers but not do anything. Here we'd thought it was only a few policemen, only the resort's pathetic rent-a-cops, as Thompson had put it, but now we had soldiers on our hands. To go with the armada, there was now an army.

By this time, luckily, Miyoko was wrapping up her speech. The next part of our broadcast was to be the mermaid footage, safe in the computers in Tokyo. I was so grateful, in that moment, for those Tokyo computers, so grateful for the TV producers Miyoko implicitly trusted. I was so grateful for technology, for social networking even, and also for our Thompson, that Navy

SEAL Santa, with his distracting incendiary devices and surprising skills of stealth.

We looked to Thompson now, all of us did. Chip did, I did, and even Gina did. We expected great things of him.

"Outmanned and outgunned," was what he said, shrugging.

Miyoko was the one who told us what to do.

"Don't stop filming," she said. "Rick. Turn the camera. Film the soldiers. Keep it rolling. No matter what. We're still *live*. We're still *broadcasting*."

And then she said something, I guess to her viewers, in Japanese, and Rick swung the camera around and pointed it right at the soldiers.

On they came till they were right beside us. Maybe twenty soldiers on foot, and more in the jeeps. Some soldiers jumped out of the jeeps. Among them were a couple of civilians—a man in a suit and the woman who'd pretended to be Mormonish, then fully reneged on it.

"I'm sorry," said the non-Mormon, but her tone wasn't apologetic. Not one bit. "Do you have a permit for whatever it is that you're doing?"

"We're hotel guests," said Gina. "We have a perfect right to be here. Or do you tell all your guests they can't set foot on your beach? Is that your policy?"

"You should know we're broadcasting live," added Chip. "Millions of Japanese viewers are watching this."

The soldiers unhooked their guns from their shoulders and, in an unhurried way, lifted and more or less pointed them. At us.

I'd never had a gun pointed at me, other than a paint gun at a corporate retreat, and I have to say it felt more personal than you might think. It seemed it'd be far too easy for one of those guys to pull the trigger. Glocks, I'd heard, had hair triggers on them, cops shot themselves in the foot with those things, just taking them out of the holsters. These weren't Glocks, though, I told myself—Glocks were mostly handguns. Weren't they?

Words were what we had, I told myself. Words were the only weapons that we had, since the nunchucks hadn't come in handy, and this was the time to deploy them.

"You should also know," I said, maybe a little shakily, "that we've sent them the video footage. A major TV station in Japan. They have it and they're showing it. The Japanese are seeing the mermaids, too. The Japanese *know*."

"You'll have to stop what you're doing and come along with us," said the man in the suit.

He did look paler, didn't he? Now that we'd told him about the people of Japan?

"This is how you want to be introduced to the world?" said Gina. "Really, Mr. Corporate Asshole? Does the term *Facebook* mean anything to you? The term *Twitter?* To say nothing of the lawsuits your company will be facing. We have a litigator lined up already, in D.C. Meyers & Finkelstein. Kidnapping of a U.S. citizen, just for starters. And trust me, that's only the very tip of *that* iceberg."

Miyoko spoke in Japanese. She was talking about the soldiers and the suits and who paid their bills, she told me later, and though what she said was pretty damning she smiled brightly throughout.

"You think people will come to see your mermaid zoo once they know how you started it? Like this?" asked Chip. "Kidnappings? Guns? They'll boycott it. You'll be notorious. And how about Nancy? *She* was the one who found them. And she wanted the mermaids to be like Darwin's finches. Not—not Barnum & Bailey's poor old elephants. These mermaids were *her* discovery."

I felt proud of Chip, then, for his eloquence.

Miyoko translated for her audience, keeping up a rapid patter while the suit leaned close to the woman, whispering something.

"Stand down," said Thompson loudly, in the direction of the soldiers. He had his balls back, suddenly. "You're on the wrong side here. I am an officer of the United States Navy."

One or two of the soldiers looked at each other insecurely.

"Then you've got exactly *no* jurisdiction here," said the man in the suit.

"He's just a retiree," sneered the woman.

"You think I don't have strings to pull, lady?" said Thompson. "I've got some strings. Don't force me to pull them."

"You don't have strings," she said. "You've got no strings at all. Now who's the bullshitter."

"That far out isn't territorial waters," said Thompson. "It's still in the Exclusive Economic Zone, sure, but it's contiguous zone, where those coral heads are. I measured it."

I turned and stared at him, then back at the corporates. I wasn't sure what Thompson was talking about. But the suit looked like maybe he knew.

"Last night," he went on. "I measured it last night. It's only inside the territorial zone, see, that they have a crystal-clear right to tell everyone else what to do. Assuming they're in cahoots with the cops, a.k.a. what passes for government in the BVI. In the contiguous zone the law's not so clear. So they're trying to cordon the mermaids off with those nets, bring them closer in. So then they can claim the rights to them absolutely. No wiggle room, they figure, if they can just bring them closer in."

That would have been good information to have earlier. The suit/non-Mormon looked shifty.

"The mermaids don't belong to you," said Chip. "They're not a fish stock. They're half-human! They don't belong to anyone!"

"Look, people," said the man, after a long pause. "What we have here is essentially a misunderstanding."

"Then tell your toy soldiers to lower their guns," said Thompson. "Remember you're on live TV. Come on, Mr. Money. Give the order."

The suit conferred with the non-Mormon again. After a while she nodded, and he gestured at the soldiers. Guns were lowered.

We all stood there, silent except for the sound of Miyoko, still talking in her native tongue.

"And how about Nancy?" asked Chip. "Dr. Nancy Simonoff? We want justice for her. You're still claiming she drowned in her bathtub? A first-rate swimmer and diver?"

"The woman was an asthmatic," said the woman. "Her accidental passing is regrettable."

"Deeply regrettable. Yes, very sad. And also, no comment," added the suit.

"I demand an autopsy," said Chip. "By someone other than the locals. Say, for instance, the FBI."

"We're not prepared to discuss any of that, other than with her family," said the suit. He whispered to the woman and gestured to the army again.

"Have they even been *notified?*" yelled Chip, as the soldiers executed a snappy about-face and began marching away. The suits, then the jeep soldiers hopped into the jeeps. "Release her cell phone! You have no right to it!"

"Neither do we," pointed out Rick from behind his camera. "Technically."

"We can talk to her family," said Gina. "She was an academic, right? Look, there are avenues. I'll do research. Just lead me to a laptop. Forget these ass clowns. We've got them on the run."

As quickly as it had appeared, the convoy made a wide turn and drove off, foot soldiers bringing up the rear. Marching away, they looked almost foolish.

Miyoko finished her broadcast and signed off; now, she told us, the mermaid footage was running. We'd have to spread the word to other countries, send out our press release to as many places as we could—basically make sure that the mermaid footage went viral. That'd be no problem, Miyoko assured us. It took a lot less than the world's first mermaid video to generate a viral scenario.

"I'm thinking we should stay somewhere else," said Chip, as we walked up the beach toward the cabanas. "Another hotel. Another part of the island."

"No kidding," said Gina. "Let's get the hell outta Dodge."

WE THREW OUR clothes and toiletries into bags and drove down the road, some of us in Rick and Ronnie's rental car, the rest in Thompson's "jeep," which turned out to be a Hummer, a car Gina admired with particularly hard-edged irony. She congratulated Thompson when she saw it, told him owning a Hummer was the most antisocial act a person could commit without breaking the law.

The sticking point was Janeane, who had a little trouble leaving her safe space despite the fact that it really wasn't safe anymore. In the end Steve gave her a couple of horse tranquilizers and called it good. We practically carried her out.

A lot of the places were booked up, so we landed at a cheap motel in the end—probably just as well, we figured, since it wouldn't have corporate ties. It wasn't a chain and it wasn't directly on the beach, either, though it was within walking distance. We had thin-walled rooms but there were enough for all of us; we needed to maintain our safety-in-numbers policy. (We'd thought of Thompson's house, but we'd be too easy to find there if the company decided to come after us.) The pool had leaves floating in it, even a toad, and the clerk had to be enticed out of his back room with impatient shouts to check us in. He wasn't a go-getter.

On the upside, it had WiFi and cable and it wasn't too far from our previous location. Chip and I crossed the road and walked down to the ocean just after we checked in: we could still make out the dots of the armada.

Someone got the apathetic clerk to unlock the door between the two biggest rooms and we set up shop with our modest tech array and Janeane's surprisingly large supply of groceries, sadly lacking in meat, dairy and refined sugar. We convened what Chip called a "leadership conference" to decide on our next steps. We'd broadcasted, we'd faced them down for now, evaded capture; but what was our next goal? There'd be a horde, Miyoko'd warned, descending on the island soon; that was the other big risk we'd run. Now that the mermaids were public knowledge, first in Japan, soon virally, there were new challenges.

We'd done what we had to do, but we'd also opened up a world-size can of worms.

"Not everyone who comes will be on our side, either," piped up Ronnie. "We can depend on that. Half of them will probably just want to pay the price of admission to the Venture of Marvels."

"More than half," grumped Thompson.

"We need to call in some people who'll be on our side, then," said Chip.

"Like, who?" said Rick. "Animal rights people? Environmentalists?"

"No, people with power," said Gina. "Shit. First off, we need some celebrity spokespeople. Like Miyoko. But more so. And American."

"And scientists," said Rick. "We have to get some of them. You need at least one famous scientist, in a situation like this."

"At least one major politician," put in Steve. "And a rich guy, someone famous for being extremely rich. Say a Bill Gates, a Warren Buffett."

We brainstormed like that, as Miyoko slaved away on social media and did some phone interviews. Gina took a break to watch the footage, which was posted on YouTube; it already had six figures' worth of hits, mostly from people in Japan, Miyoko said, but people in other countries were starting to catch on. Before long the hits would be in the millions, she told us confidently. Plenty of people thought it was a hoax, pure Hollywood—good, said Miyoko, that was just fine with her, maybe it'd keep some of the riffraff out.

"More likely it's the riffraff that'll *come,*" said Thompson. "Your alien abductees, your Bigfoot believers, your New Age freaks that go to Sedona to find the vortexes."

Janeane looked startled at that last one, like maybe she'd made some trips to Sedona herself, but said nothing.

The rest of us thought he had a point.

"Jesus," said Rick. "Maybe *we're* the bad guys here. Maybe we shouldn't have done this."

We all felt the panic of that possibility, for a long moment. We saw the hordes, in our mind's eyes, overrunning the island and the mermaids, and we didn't like it.

"It was our only play," said Chip finally. "This was our *only* play. We have to make it work."

"I'm going to find a number for Nancy's

family," said Gina. "We need to get them on board, then reach out to the scientists she worked with. Science will give us our legitimacy. Who's got a spare laptop? Or iPad?"

Chip's was still in the possession of the parent company, but Rick had one and he set Gina up. Ellis claimed he'd get in touch with a British embassy or consulate—there had to be one nearby, and maybe, since he was a citizen, they could be of some help.

"Ellis," I said, in a private aside, "really, man. Listen. I'm always on your side, with the English thing. You're free to be you. Completely. But you might have to, like, *prove* you're a citizen, dealing with a consulate."

Ellis gave me a hurt look. "Well-w, Deb-rah," he said, "wot d'ya fink *dis* is?" (He goes cockney when he's feeling confronted.)

And damned if he didn't reach into a zip compartment on his roller bag and pull out a UK passport. The thing was red, with a gold crown on it and a couple of royal-looking animals standing up on hind legs. Seemed like the real deal. I've known Ellis a long time, and I still have no idea how he got his hands on it.

Anyway, we figured there was no harm letting him waste his time with embassies or whatnot. There were none on the island, that was for sure.

The group had decided no one should use words like *murder* or *homicide,* when one of us talked to Nancy's family. Those words were not comforting words, and the truth was, without any cops to talk to, without having even seen the body (except for Steve, who'd seen it covered in a sheet) we didn't actually know shit. Once Gina had a number for Nancy's parents, which she accomplished with a speed that impressed me ("Failed academics run in families. Turns out her old man's a professor too"), we decided Chip would make the call. He'd been the closest to Nancy by far, and Chip, when he wants to, can be tactful.

He needed privacy for the call, he said, so we let him out onto the balcony, where he fortified himself with a few swigs from a dewy beer before connecting.

Meanwhile Miyoko had started getting Tokyo celebrities on board; she also had ties to some American actors and rock stars, she told us, a lot of them did lucrative commercials in Japan, for perfume and jewelry and clothing, and she'd interviewed some of our A-listers now and then. Still, they weren't her best buds so getting through their handlers would take some time, she said. But she was up for it. She didn't have many ins with scientists or government officials, but pop-culture famous people were her stock in trade.

Gina and Chip would handle the scientist angle, Gina being in the academy herself and Chip having had Nancy's ear. Rick would try to schmooze the wealthy, since, as an independent filmmaker, he knew quite a few of them. Plus his money contacts had friends among the nationally prominent Democrats, since many made sizable contributions to political campaigns. He'd handle that angle, and Ronnie would help him. Thompson insisted he could pull strings, that he'd call on some old friends still on active duty; he'd try to put together some military might for us, he said, though what he meant we weren't entirely sure.

There they were, all on cell phones, all frantically dialing and talking. And then there were the rest of us, with no contacts at all. The best Steve could do were some astronomers in Palo Alto, who wouldn't be much help. They were preoccupied, he said, didn't have an interest in marine biology: their eyes were fixed on the heavens.

Janeane and I also had nothing.

So Steve, as a therapist (though apparently he didn't practice anymore) and therefore a de facto interpersonal specialist, would try to do some coalition-building, visit some places of business and government locally, trying to reach out to the year-round community. He'd be armed only with a tablet and our footage, and he'd try to garner local support for a mermaid sanctuary.

We didn't have high hopes for that part of the outreach, but it was a nice time-killer for Steve, who, like Chip, enjoyed meeting people, whoever they might be. He didn't feel great about going out alone, but Thompson said he could drive the

Hummer and I think the novelty may have encouraged Steve a bit.

Janeane and I were relegated to the menial jobs: Janeane was in charge of keeping us fed and watered, and I—well, I had the lowest task of all. I had to tweet.

Miyoko had several million followers, but they followed her in Japanese. So we established a mermaid-group handle linked to the Facebook page she'd set up, plus the footage of us on the beach, and I tweeted from that. I'd never tweeted before, but it's not rocket science and I'm a quick study. At first the tweeting was slow-going, but soon enough, with Miyoko's input, I gained a following for us. Re-tweets were everywhere.

We saw the TV tape on YouTube, our confrontation with the suits and the soldiers, the Japanese TV broadcast. I didn't like the feeling of watching myself on TV—the shapeless garment I sported was a blot on the landscape. A lifetime of good dressing went out the window; now I was immortalized wearing Janeane's floral quasi-muumuu.

Gina took my hand, the first time we saw that footage, and squeezed it in terrible sympathy. I would have cried, if I'd had the time and energy. But there was no pause to allow for tears, and the milk was already spilt. The world now knew me as a muumuu woman. I looked like Janeane.

Before long the personal calls and texts started

rolling in to my cell phone. I ignored them all—people from work, friends, even B-school people I hadn't heard from in years. There were three calls from Chip's mother alone.

Chip ignored his calls too; the long conversation with the Simonoff family—Nancy's mother, to be specific—was draining. As it turned out, the family had known something was terribly wrong, because someone unfamiliar had answered Nancy's cell phone when her mother called to check in. That person had said Nancy wasn't available and not to call again, then promptly hung up. When the father called back (by then the mother was too distraught), no one picked up, so they called the resort and were put through to Guest Services, where they were given the run-around. As a result, the father was already en route to us. Worried sick about Nancy, he'd simply gotten on a plane.

When Chip broke the news to Nancy's mother about what seemed to have happened, the woman went into shock. It took a while to get her back on the phone, at which time, without prompting from Chip, she brought up the possibility of foul play. Nancy'd had her inhaler since she was in preschool and there was no way, her mother said, she would have failed to use it. She always had extras, too: she was always stocked to the gills.

The family had heard about the mermaids from Nancy before they ever saw the video—they'd been the first ones she called. Nancy had never been a liar or one whit fanciful, they said, on the contrary, she'd always been painfully literal. She had no interest in movies, except for documentaries on marine life; she never played non-educational games or read make-believe stories, and she abominated the frivolity of novels. When other girls dressed up as princesses for Halloween, she put on a snorkel mask and went as Jacques Cousteau. (And once as a blowfish, her mother admitted, which set off a bout of weeping that called for a phone handoff to a neighbor and delayed the conversation another twenty minutes.)

The parents had retired to Florida when the father went emeritus, so it was a short flight and Prof. Simonoff was due in shortly. Chip's new directive was to keep *him* from falling into the clutches of the parent company. He'd meet him at the ferry, and this time there'd be no interception from the marine police: we were the only ones who knew he was coming. And not only was the Prof. coming, Nancy's mother had told Chip, but he was bringing some medical expertise with him—a doctor friend from their retirement community. You never knew when that might come in handy.

The problem was, the armada was still out there. As far as we knew, they were moving full steam ahead with their plan to cordon off the mermaids and "bring them in." The way we saw it, none of our activities, no part of our energetic bustle was going to bear fruit in time to stop it. We needed an injunction, a court order that would make them cease and desist their mermaid-corralling activities. And that was something we didn't have.

Time flew that day, with many of us doing video interviews as well as phone—I made sure to shed the muumuu, now that I had access to my own clothes again—and a couple of meltdowns, like when Janeane first saw (against Steve's explicit wishes) the beach footage, complete with soldiers/guns. She barricaded herself into the bathroom and we had to call in Steve, who was making his rounds in the Hummer, to lure her out again.

There was also an altercation between Thompson and Rick when Thompson referred to him and Ronnie as "the two fairies"; it ended with Rick getting First Aid from Steve for a small cut above his right eye, while Ronnie prepared an ice pack. Thompson refused to say he was sorry, claiming that *fairy* was a purely descriptive term having nothing to do with homophobia/hate crimes/being a giant bigot. Also, Thompson maintained, when he'd inquired whether Ronnie was "the gayer one" he'd just been honestly trying to understand their deal. They didn't have to be so touchy about it.

Gina attempted to show solidarity with Rick by dumping a whole bottle of cayenne pepper from Janeane's travel-size spice rack into Thompson's whiskey flask when Thompson wasn't looking, then admitting it openly after Thompson spit whiskey all over the motel bedspread and complained the skin was peeling off his gums. Thompson wouldn't hit a woman, that was as much a part of his code as calling gay men fairies, so Gina was protected from brute-force retaliation. Still, she hid the other spices just to be safe, and watched her own food and drinks like a hawk subsequently. From then on she'd only drink beers she opened herself, and no cocktails at all, she vowed.

For there was some drinking going on, no harm in admitting it; the stress, the pressure was getting to us, plus we were all on vacation. Those of us who normally had five o'clock rules suspended them (save for Janeane, a teetotaler), and those of us with no such rules, such as Thompson, proceeded all the more vigorously.

Chip, in his cups by 2 p.m., needed a designated driver to pick up Prof. Simonoff, so I, who at that time had only had two light beers, volunteered. I didn't like going out just the two of us, so Thompson got the Hummer back from Steve—who'd met with rudeness and disbelief, for the most part, in his outreach activities and wanted to spend some time with the fraught Janeane—and we set out for the marina as a threesome. Thompson was a sight, by then, wearing some rolls of gauze in his mouth, soaked in hydrogen peroxide, that covered up his teeth. I glanced back at one point from the driver's seat to see him loading shells into what looked to me like a high-powered rifle.

"Thompson," I said, "you're not packing that thing. You're drunk, for one. Put it away right now. That violates every rule of gun safety."

"Lock and load in my sleep," mumbled Thompson through his gauze. A piece of it fell out as he spoke; he fumbled the rifle as he tried to shove it back in.

"No way, man," said Chip. "You know how much I respect you. But we have to be cool here. You'll scare Nancy's father half to death. He's already gonna have a personal tragedy to deal with. He'll think we're a bunch of crackpots."

Thompson grudgingly put the gun aside, harrumphing through his gauze, and contented himself with donning some kind of camouflage cargo or fishing vest, with multiple bulging pockets in it, that held knives and sundry other objects of utility and aggression. I saw him sneak something that looked like a grenade into one of the compartments, but right then we passed a convoy of jeeps that alarmed me and I forgot about his doings, too busy watching the rearview mirror to see if any of the jeeps turned back around and followed us. (They didn't.)

Then we were at the parking lot near the marina, where we waited until the ferry was pulling up to the dock, Thompson scouting all around, first with the naked eye, next with binoculars, for other gun-wielders. Finally they jumped out and walked, as calmly as they could, I guess, toward the disembarking passengers. I waited in the car, doors stoutly locked, gas-guzzling engine running noisily and doing its part for runaway climate change, for the two of them to come back with our distinguished visitors.

PROF. SIMONOFF WAS an elfin man, smaller than Nancy had been; his wife must be a giant, I thought, for Nancy to have come from the two of them. He looked the part of the emeritus he was, balding on the top of his head with a monk-like fringe of white hair, and wore glasses. His doctor friend was on the portly side, black, and might have had a jovial way about him, I sensed, in happier times. They both wore suits and ties, and carried briefcases and laptops. No roller bags at all. I was glad of that. It lent them a certain gravitas none of us had in our tourist playgear.

The Prof. had talked to his wife when he got off the plane, and she'd delivered the bad news. But that emeritus seemed to be in denial—he was pale, he was wan, but he wasn't weeping. He wasn't conceding anything.

Chip gave them the rundown as we drove, Prof. Simonoff up front with me. He left out certain parts, including the minor bombing and the gay-bashing scuffle that had led to Thompson wearing gauze rolls in his mouth—"His gums are bothering him," was all he said on that.

Thompson seemed to be on good behavior now; he'd even kicked the rifle beneath the backseats. It was as though, faced with two educated men of his own vintage, he finally had peers and wished to impress them. He even took the gauze rolls out, after a few minutes, and stashed the bloody pieces in one of his many pockets. I winced when I saw that. He hadn't been exaggerating, I guess, when he said his gum-skin had been peeling off in strips. Also he took a call from someone who purported to be military, and while he talked gave a quite passable impression of not being drunk at all.

But things weren't rosy back at the motel.

"What the hell," said Chip, as we drew near. "Deb, don't turn in, just keep driving! Don't stop!"

For it seemed the parent company hadn't given up on us. The motel parking lot was full of jeeps—the same ones, I warranted, that had passed us on our trip out; the same ones from the beach.

"Shit," said Chip. "Damn. How'd they find us?"

He lost no time in putting in a call to Rick, hitting his speakerphone button so we could all hear it.

"They just got here," said Rick. "We wouldn't let them in. It's been quiet for a minute, after we refused to unlock the doors, but it won't be for long. We think they're going to get the clerk or something. We've got the chains on the doors."

"That won't stop them for a second," said Thompson. "They're just maybe warning the clerk they're busting in."

"Unacceptable," said Simonoff calmly.

We'd passed the motel by then; with no destination anymore I drove aimlessly down the coast road.

"We can't abandon them," said Chip. "We have to go back, Deb."

"I'll talk to them," said Simonoff.

"You don't know who you're dealing with," said Thompson, shaking his head. "They won't listen to reason."

"It's not reason," said Simonoff. "I'm going to threaten them."

He was such a tiny emeritus, sitting there next to me in his glasses, light glinting off his pate. I felt like patting him.

"We already mentioned litigation," said Chip.

"You better find a place to turn the car around," said Simonoff to me.

"But we were trying to *save* you from them," said Chip, a little plaintively. "They have guns, sir. They have soldiers."

"And I'm an old man with no daughter anymore," said Simonoff. "I've got nothing left to lose."

"Except your freedom," said Chip, worried.

"I do have *weapons,*" offered Thompson modestly.

"Are private citizens allowed to keep guns here?" asked Simonoff, surprised, I guess, into a general knowledge question.

"Not to carry," conceded Thompson. "For display only. I have special permits. It's a historical collection. But all in excellent working order. They happen to be in the vehicle here, currently."

"I see," said Simonoff, almost gently. "Still, guns or no guns, they have an advantage, when it comes to brute force, I'm sure. Unwise to sink to their level. No, I'm a grieving father; I have the moral high ground, and I'm prepared to use it."

I noticed, in my rearview mirror, Thompson fingering his grenade wistfully. The doctor, seated on Chip's other side, was not in a position to glimpse it, but I could.

"You heard the man, Thompson," I said sharply. He tucked it away, a bit downcast.

"OK," I said, once I'd pulled off onto the dirt. "Back to the motel, then?"

"We need a plan," said Chip.

"What plan?" I said. "It's an army. And there's no back door."

"Leave it to me," said Simonoff. "Just let me do the talking."

As I drove us back, I thought of being in jail. I

didn't want to. I thought of those long guns pointed at me. I parked with fear in my heart. I wanted to stay in the Hummer; I wished to exhibit cowardice.

The first thing I noticed, dismounting reluctantly from that large, possibly armored vehicle—because Thompson's wasn't some glossy poseur H2 or H3; it was a battered, old-school original—was that a couple of soldiers were leaning against their jeeps relaxedly. One smoked a cigarette while another nodded to me, then smiled almost flirtatiously. Flirtatious smiles were what I could look forward to, when I was thrown in jail, I guessed. And worse.

But as we made our way along the catwalk to our rooms, more soldiers seemed to be loitering. Instead of pointing any guns at us, they stepped aside to let us through. We reached the door to our room: it stood open, but wasn't bashed in. And from inside the room, I heard laughter issue.

Miyoko was sitting on one of the beds, an open laptop on her lap, showing two soldiers the footage from the beach. One of the soldiers held a beer; the other pointed delightedly at the screen.

"That's me!" he said.

"Oh man," said the beer soldier. "You looking *fierce,* Jerry. I hope Annette saw that, she won't be holding out on you now. No way."

More laughter.

A couple of soldiers were talking earnestly to Rick and Ronnie; another stood in the kitchenette with Steve and Janeane, munching on one of her soy-chicken taquitos. "Not bad at all," I heard him say, and Janeane offered him another. In a corner, Gina appeared to be showing a handsome soldier her lower-back tattoo, pulling up her shirt while Ellis eyed her uncertainly/jealously.

Was it some kind of trick? I looked at Chip; his mouth was hanging open just a little.

The ones talking to Rick and Ronnie seemed to be the most serious, from which I deduced they might also be the ones in charge. So I took a deep breath and stepped near.

". . . end of the day, we don't take orders from them. Not if we don't have to. And what I thought was, hell. We *don't* have to. As long as we don't hear to the contrary from the higher-ups, that is. And so far I haven't heard squat from them," said one of the soldiers.

He had some flair above his pocket, a couple of badges or something.

"It's a goddamn relief," said Rick. "I'm not going to lie to you."

"Thanks, man," said Ronnie. "Yeah. *Big* relief."

"Hey," said the CO, noticing me. "What's *your* name, honey?"

"This is my wife, Deb," said Chip.

"Gotcha," said the CO, and winked.

"No harm done," said I.

"Whatever she says," said Chip, and put out his hand to shake. "I'm Chip."

"Chip's the one who found the mermaids," said Rick. "With Nancy."

"So anyway," said the CO's wingman, "until the order comes down—*if* it does—we thought we'd swing by, see if there's anything we can do. To help out. We don't want to see this place turned into Disneyland either."

"We already got a Disneyland," said the CO.

"And Disney World," said his second.

"Lots o' Disney," agreed the CO.

"You sound American," I said to him.

"Grew up on St. John. Sam here did too. I'm Raleigh. Virgin Islands National Guards. The Brits have bupkes here, armed forces-wise. We lend a hand. But hey. Tell you my life story over a beer?"

"He doesn't give up easy, does he," said Chip, and put an arm around me. "But seriously, this is awesome, guys. Having you on board. It really is. Kicks ass."

"Let's put our heads together," said Rick. "Right, Chip? See what we can come up with."

"My troops'll have to keep a low profile," said Raleigh. "Far as the suits know, we're out on a drill. We can't get in their faces. Other than that, though, we're here for you."

The six of us stood around the small table in the room, though we really didn't fit. Raleigh said he

251

had some information, first off, which was that the armada still hadn't spotted any mermaids, even with their dozens of divers.

They were painstakingly crossing quadrants off their grid and moving the nets in, but there was low morale, out there, with a growing majority of skeptics. The parent company had shown the mermaid footage to the searchers, but many still didn't believe it was genuine, said they'd seen better CGI mermaids in kids' movies. With each fruitless search there were more divers who thought the video was simply a hoax.

Raleigh thought the best move would be to "take ownership," as he put it, and come out and admit it was a hoax—our hoax, that *we* were the hoaxers. We'd buy ourselves some time that way, he claimed, although the parent company wouldn't be swayed; they claimed to have had the footage "authenticated" by "experts" before they took action in the first place. If we pulled back, he said, in essence pulled a hoax now, claiming to have hoaxed before, they'd lose a lot of manpower. They'd lose logistical support, and it would set back their project, at least temporarily.

Miyoko wouldn't like that at all, said Chip, she'd staked her reputation on this being real, she'd gone the whole nine yards for us.

Rick nodded. We didn't even want to bring it up with her.

"We don't need to go public with it," said Raleigh. "Losing face *here,* with the teams they're depending on to find the mermaids for them, that could do it. Without their divers, see, they're screwed, and the divers are already pissed and impatient, chomping at the bit."

"How would we do that, though?" said Chip. "We don't have access to their divers. Do we?"

We knew a few of them, of course; Chip had emails for the ones who'd been in our group before they defected.

"They won't believe the hoax angle," said Chip. "I mean, some of these people were with us. They *saw* the mermaids. Personally."

"You'd say it was all a setup," suggested Sam. "Some kind of elaborate publicity stunt. Say you *put* the mermaids there."

"Like, they were free divers," said Chip. He'd always liked that angle. "Wearing fake tails."

"Maybe it was a gambit to protect the reefs all along," said Rick. "Nancy's gambit! To save her parrotfish!"

"Hold it," came a voice from behind us. "What's this?"

Prof. Simonoff was hovering.

"You'd make my daughter out a liar?" he went on. "Is that what I'm hearing?"

"We're just tossing out ideas," said Chip, apologetic.

"It wouldn't be public," I added. "We're just

trying to think how we could undermine the parent company."

"I can't support any scheme that would tarnish my daughter's reputation," said Simonoff. "I'm sorry, but I couldn't allow it."

I did a glance-around to cover my feeling of embarrassment. Janeane and Steve were talking intently to the soldier who liked soy taquitos; Miyoko was doing another phone interview, pacing and talking as the bed filled with soldiers, piled up there practically on top of each other, watching themselves on her laptop. It was like a clown car, only the car was a bed and the clowns were wearing camo. Thompson and the doctor were examining Thompson's array of what he called "folders," a.k.a. folding knives, in a corner.

I had to turn back to Simonoff eventually, who stood there, humble in his demeanor but with a resolve I can only call steely.

"You understand," said Raleigh after the silence, "this would be temporary. We could spread a rumor, in effect, just among the divers working for the company."

"Rumors have more life than fact, in our economy," said Simonoff. "I'm sorry, but I can't risk it. Even afterward, once you set the facts straight—if you were able to—some of her colleagues would think of her as a purveyor of hoaxes, if it got out. And it would. Everything gets out, nowadays. You know I'm right on this. To some people, she'd always be the person who committed fraud. No, the risk is too great. I'm very sorry."

"What if she were the victim?" offered Chip. "I mean she was. She *is*. We could make me the villain of the piece, say the scam was my doing, that I roped her in—"

"No," said Simonoff. "That makes her look foolish. My Nancy was not a gullible woman."

We'd thought, for a moment, that we had an idea with maybe some traction, but now we had nowhere to go.

"So the disinformation campaign is off the table," said Raleigh, with difficulty.

"We have to see my daughter's . . . remains," said Simonoff. "If this wasn't a drowning, or if it was and there are any signs of a struggle, well, that'd be a game-changer. Wouldn't it."

"Then you'll need to go straight to the . . ." began Chip.

"Mortuary," said Simonoff solemnly.

That guy was really keeping it together.

"The trick will be the local police," said Raleigh. "These guys aren't serious. They do what the corporates tell them. So we need to get Mr. Simonoff here—"

"Professor Simonoff," corrected Chip, deferential.

"—I'm sorry, yes of course, Professor Simonoff—to where his daughter's remains are located, and make sure we get him and the doctor out again after that examination without the parent company interrupting us."

"They've got no business interfering," said Simonoff. "I have a right to privacy. Anyway, the mortuary's just a private institution. We couldn't get a hold of anyone at the police station or the resort, but they must have moved her—they don't have the right facilities at the police station. There's no . . . er . . . refrigeration."

He could barely say it.

"Still, we'd be more comfortable if these gentlemen had a couple of your guys with them," Rick told Raleigh. "An escort, as it were. Possible? Or is that too obvious?"

"Sam and I will supply the escort," said Raleigh to Simonoff. "As long as it's not all of us, we may not raise any red flags. We'll keep a lookout, is all, when you go in."

So they went off, Simonoff and the doctor, Raleigh and Sam.

"MAN," SAID CHIP, after they'd left. (The rest of the soldiers were still with us. They loved Miyoko; they clustered around her wherever she went. Which wasn't far, in our connected rooms.) "I really liked that hoax idea. Too bad."

"I see his point, though," said Ronnie.

"Yeah," said Rick. "Still. Nancy would have wanted to do whatever it took, for her mermaid sanctuary."

We sat around the small table, meditative. Nancy would have done whatever it took. She wouldn't have worried about posterity. We knew that. But then, she'd been alive back then. Like all of us.

We felt the ridiculous sadness of her being dead—worse, then, than it had ever been.

To take our minds off the waiting, we busied ourselves with tasks. I did some more tweeting, responding to other tweets, updating our status on Facebook. It was tedium, all the social networking, it was Boring Central, plus I got agitated thinking about Simonoff and the doctor looking at Nancy's body—I thought of how Simonoff must be feeling, the punched-in-the-gut devastation. My eyes glazed over as rows and rows of comments rolled in, each one less interesting than the last. I drank an extra beer, lamented its weak impact to Gina, and thought fondly of the days, back in college, when I used to put anything I felt like in my body. Kids think they're immortal, I mused, giddy. Then, before they know it, they're no longer good-looking.

Chip, using Miyoko's laptop while she talked on the phone, immersed himself in aggregators and quickly discovered an anti-mermaid backlash. It seemed the mermaid tapes had enraged a highly vocal contingent.

"I think it's some folks in the Heartland," worried Chip.

He peered in close at the screen, scrolling through comment lists. The defection of the toe fetishist had been nagging at him—he'd wanted for so long to craft new friendships among the fellow citizens he doesn't understand, the ones from the vast unknown. With the Heartland couple he'd made a special effort at outreach, an effort dating from that very first dinner, but he had failed; the Heartland couple had turned on him.

"It *is!* Deb! It's Middle Americans!"

Chip knows his Internet research, he knows how to trace trends and memes and what have you, and so I didn't doubt his opinion.

The Heartland had spoken. The mermaids were against God, the people of the Heartland said: the mermaids were unholy.

Some said the mermaids were descendants of Lucifer: when he'd fallen from grace he'd grown a tail and been condemned to swim the deep. Couldn't the ocean's depths be hell? Others said mermaids were the hybrid spawn of ancient hippie-pagans. The long-ago hippies had loved animals more than humans, much like their current-day equivalents, the mermaid haters said. And it had driven them crazy. Therefore they mated with some fish.

There was confusion there, I guess, because, though most of the threads Chip found were staunchly creationist, there was some chatter about mutations that looked a little science-y to me. We tried to imagine olden-time people mating with fish, Chip and I did, as we hovered over the screen, but we couldn't muster it, not a single obscene mental picture could we call up on the blank walls of our brains.

Some of the haters claimed God had just stuck those fish tails on people suddenly—a penalty for a heinous crime against the Bible's teachings. One day the mermaid ancestors had been walking around free and clear, on two fine, dandy legs; the next, flop, swish, legs gone and hello tails. Then, probably embarrassed, they had to slide all snakelike to the nearest body of water. "Wriggle on their bellies like unto the Serpent that tempted Eve!" posted a Churchgoer from Tuscaloosa in a newspaper's op-ed comments.

These people had convictions, no one could argue against that. They didn't agree on how the tails and gills had happened, on that point they were all over the map, but as to *why* the tails/gills had happened—on that front they were perfectly united. It was the bestiality aspect. The crime was loving animals, whichever way you sliced it, they said. For it was clear as day, to all these hundreds, then thousands of commenters—as the movement gathered steam across the web and reportedly on right-wing radio—that the punishment had been tailored, by none other than God, to fit the crime.

"If a woman approaches any animal and lies with it, you shall kill the woman *and* the animal!"

posted an irate blogger called No Monkeys Here. "Leviticus!" He thought God had been too lenient, electing not to obliterate the first mermaids. God had been too liberal. If he weren't so deeply respectful of God, so deeply pious, personally, the blogger wrote, he'd almost be tempted to voice a suspicion that God had been, in a word, *weak*. He wanted to say right out that God had been a fuckin' pussy, said Chip, but he didn't have the stones.

"One man's weakness is another man's mercy," said Ronnie.

By that time the others had joined us; every screen was tuned to the groundswell of mermaid hatred.

"What did the mermaids ever do to *them?*" asked Janeane. "It's unloving."

WE WERE STILL huddled like that, scrolling and scrolling, peering and peering, when a knock came on the door: Simonoff, the doctor, Raleigh, and Sam.

"She wasn't there!" said Simonoff.

You'd think he'd be distressed by this fact, his inability to locate the physical evidence of his only daughter, but his face was glowing with energy, a fine sheen of sweat. I saw a glint in his eyes.

"What do you mean?" said Chip. "It's the only facility on the island. With, um, the necessary—cold storage."

"Exactly," said Simonoff. "The attendant said they never saw a body. Not only that, they never *heard* of a body. No one ever called to make any arrangements. No one got notified. We talked to everyone there. Literally every single person on staff."

He took his glasses off and wiped the lenses on his tie. Scrubbed them, more like, scrubbed furiously.

We looked around at each other, mystified. There was a feeling of being dumb, a feeling of stupidity.

"But here's the kicker," said the doctor. "They didn't know about any death certificate."

"It's a small place," said Raleigh, nodding. He had a hearty quality to him, Raleigh, an admirable meat-and-potatoes attitude a person might find almost attractive, if they were unmarried. "Usually they know right away, pretty much, when to expect business. The news gets out. But this time, nothing leaked. None of the local doctors signed a certificate. No one in an official capacity."

Simonoff put his glasses back on, poked them up onto the bridge of his nose with the tip of a finger. He did a quick tic of a half-smile, nervous, almost imperceptible.

I saw where he was going: our emeritus was getting his hopes up. I didn't want it to happen; it was like a slow-motion roadkill, and I couldn't stand to watch.

"Well," I said, in a measured tone I meant to sound matter-of-fact, "she could still be at the resort. They may not have ever released her. Although that'd make them look pretty guilty."

"I wouldn't put it past them," said Chip, shaking his head. "Keeping her."

"Did you call?" Rick asked Simonoff. "I mean, they'd have to know where the—where she got moved to, wouldn't they?"

"I put in the calls myself," said Raleigh. "Just to make sure management didn't get its hooks in the professor, I went ahead and handled the inquiries."

"And?" asked Chip.

"And nothing," said Raleigh. "I got passed down along the admin chain, and in the end they sent me to the cops. And the cops passed the buck back to the funeral home."

"But I saw them!" protested Steve. "The cops were the ones who rolled out the gurney."

"You know," said Thompson, cleaning a folding knife with a handle made of bone, maybe antler—sort of a dirty, white-brown color, narrowly ridged like corduroy. "The place has big restaurants. Restaurants that serve hundreds of people at a time. Big restaurants have big freezers."

Gina put her hand on Simonoff's arm, like Thompson's bluntness might injure him. Normally G. doesn't give a shit about bluntness/offending, if anything she aims straight for it, but after the homophobic name-calling episode she'd appointed herself a general anti-Thompson deputy, an anti-Thompson missile defense shield with broad jurisdiction.

Thompson flicked his antler knife open and closed, open and closed. With the pinkie of the other hand he rooted around in his ear.

"Looks like we need to send a contingent over there," said Raleigh to Sam. "Doesn't it."

With Gina guiding him, Simonoff turned away, followed by the doctor; they needed refreshment, maybe some rest. The doctor opened the door of the mini-fridge and bent over, rummaging.

"But like, undercover," said Rick. "We need access to the kitchens. To the . . . to all the storage facilities connected to the kitchen areas."

"Whoa," said a soldier standing behind me, and yelled over his shoulder. "Jerry! You hear that? They need someone with restaurant access at the Big House." Then, turning back to us: "Jerry can get you a backstage pass for sure. His girlfriend waits tables up there."

Raleigh signed on the girlfriend, Annette, with lightning speed. Her ringing, strident voice on the other end of the speakerphone reminded me uncannily of Chip's mother, that same combo of raw power and fingernails on a blackboard. Jerry had to promise to pay some bills if Annette lost her job as a result of the spying—her own mother had racked up a sizable debt to a psychic hotline.

He got a bit sheepish when she brought that up, with all of us listening. But Annette couldn't have cared less about Jerry's embarrassment: that much was abundantly clear. She was slaving to pay off her mother's credit cards, she reminded him. "This is serious shit, Jer," she shrilled. "Serious shit."

We had no doubt of it.

Simonoff was restless, as the late afternoon wore on, impatient for Annette to begin her shift. He had a flicker of hope now, he wasn't as defeated as before; he stood up slightly taller, though it kept threatening to break my heart— there's nothing more piercing than seeing hope lighten the face of a devastated person, that futile, doomed, and lovely bird of hope with its bright wings and round, dark eyes. First rising over a warm nest, wings softly spread, sheltering tiny chicks—then struck and flattened.

But there was no denying it, he and the doctor both looked better than they had an hour or two earlier. They'd been invigorated by the missing corpse. In my view, a missing corpse isn't something to rejoice about. The absence of a corpse, well, it doesn't mean there's no such thing as one.

I tried to ignore their hopefulness, the easiest way to deal with it. Meanwhile Steve, I noticed, trotted out references to Nancy's body at regular intervals, speaking about it with an attitude of clinical firmness. Our Freudian was on the c

All of us had turned off our phones by then, Miyoko and Chip who were doing interviews, because we couldn't handle the call volume. Rick and Ronnie were obsessing over the mermaid haters, who had their own social media pages now—even their own funding. Their cause had been embraced by undisclosed sponsors. These sponsors, Chip opined between phone calls, seemed to be paying for rapid dissemination of the anti-mermaid message on screens across the world. *Hunt them,* they said, *and put them down. This is a test of faith!*

That lust for blood worried me; it even seemed to worry Gina, though her ironic distance prevents her from showing too much concern, typically. As she and I stood there, shoulder to shoulder at the counter of the kitchenette, and studied the chatter on the screen, I had a feeling of compression. I felt those lines and lines of speech pressing me down and overpowering me—the weight of all the haters out there, a juggernaut of loathing. What was their problem? Our problem, as a race? (I was woozy on beer and lack of sleep.) We started out soft and warm, trusting. I'd seen babies—held a couple, even.

It seemed to me the virtual world was even worse than the real one, when it came to humanity. To look at screens like these, you'd think there was nothing left of us but a pile of pixilated ash. We were a roiling mass of opinion, most of it mean. Here we sat at civilization's technological peak, and what we chose to do on that shining pinnacle was hate each other's guts.

First I'd been excited about the social networking; now it seemed, like nuclear weapons, to be one of the worst ideas ever.

"Where are the nice people?" I asked Gina. "Seriously?"

She patted my hand.

"The meek shall inherit the earth," she said.

"Uh huh. The meek with six legs," said Thompson.

Gina hadn't been heavily ironic, it occurred to me, since she got to the island—but this was evidence, wasn't it, that her approach had merit. This mass of humanity that hated the mermaids demonstrated how right Gina had been, our whole lives, to divide and separate, to detach herself from any earnest passion, to preemptively give up on the ideas of goodness and of meaning. People would disappoint you every time.

Rick, on another computer, was fixated on some ugly animations that were proliferating on the web—crude images of mermaids with tridents that morphed into Satans with pitchforks. There was a clean version and an X-rated one, with oversize sexual characteristics.

He had to be pulled away, finally, for spending his time and energy on fruitless anger—much as he'd tired himself, over our first dinner, unleashing a torrent of anti-climate-denier rage on the hapless toe fetishist. I couldn't help recalling the toe man as he'd been that evening, first claiming with a smirk that the Arctic would be a nice vacation spot once all the ice and polar bears were gone; then feeling the accidental, stroking touch of *my own foot* upon his hairy calf; then saying in his juicy voice *toe-genital intimacy*.

Yep, Rick was rising to the bait, joining the fray, and we couldn't let him go there, so in the end Ronnie shut him down with some kind of appetizer tray Janeane brought out involving caramelized onions.

Tired of the hater opinions, Gina and I turned away too. We turned our faces away.

WE'D FORMED THREE teams by then, adding to our media and stealth divisions a Simonoff department—devoted, obviously, to the question of justice for Nancy. I wanted to switch off the media team, I wanted someone to change places with me, and to that end I persuaded Ronnie. He'd be with Rick, once they were both media, and he'd enjoy that; meanwhile, I'd be with Chip.

So Ronnie officially took over my tweeting duties and I joined Chip, Thompson, Gina, and Ellis on stealth detail. While the Simonoff team waited for bulletins from Annette, we'd spy on the parent company's mermaid search. That would be our gig, as soon as the sun finished setting and darkness took over: we'd be investigators.

Thompson had borrowed a friend's powerboat, which was waiting for us at a slipway down the beach road. We walked out of the motel smelling the sweetness of jasmine, hearing the faint splashes of kids in the motel pool (which I idly hoped had been divested of toad corpses). It was a balmy evening. Thompson had his own rig for fishing, he said, as we drove over in the Hummer, but it was an old rust-bucket. This one, I saw when he parked the Hummer, was sleek and high-end. We got out and approached: the vessel was black with red detailing and looked like it went fast. A monster pickup was towing it, and backed down the ramp as we walked over; someone ran down and set up a stepladder deal.

"Not too shabby. I feel like 007," said Ellis, busting out a gleeful, preteen grin at Chip as we clambered aboard.

Gina was sour-faced.

Inside it looked swank, with modern leather appointments and polished surfaces. We arranged ourselves near the front—bow?—and hovered behind Thompson as, above a futuristic-looking display, he flicked toggles and turned on head-lights.

"Hold on," he said, after a minute or two, and I grabbed the back of a seat as he prodded a couple more buttons. Chip and the others did the same—

just in time as the engine roared to life. We reared, bucked, and set off bumping across the incoming waves.

"How are we supposed to sneak up on anyone in this small-dick cockboat?" said Gina.

Thompson pretended to be deafened by the din.

From the beach I'd briefly made out the lights of the armada, a scattering of yellow pinpricks on the horizon where dark met dark, but now those far-off twinkles were lost in the bright foreground of the boat's headlights. It was surprisingly hard to see, at night, with the glares and shadows, confused by speed. I'd let Thompson be in charge of our fate, I determined, at least while it depended on this flashing dart of fiberglass. If I closed my eyes I felt queasy, so I kept them open and stared out through the speedboat's moonroof—a thick, tinted Plexiglas sheath. Once my eyes adjusted I thought I could see a raft of stars, the blurry Milky Way, though my neck ached from craning. Being inside an enclosed cabin was a negative; I would have enjoyed fresh air, salt spray.

Neither Chip nor I wanted to sit, we wanted to stand with our feet planted firmly, holding on to something, feeling the bumps and the insane freedom of fastness. Still, after a while our necks hurt from standing/craning and we were forced to sit down. Our posture went from triumphant to vanquished then as we slumped into each other on the seats, his arm around me, my head in the crook of his neck. Across from us, on the opposite bench, Gina and Ellis took up a similar position, with Ellis doing his best to execute a familiar, possessive arm-over-shoulder maneuver and Gina ignoring the draped appendage, trying to yell across to me over the engine roar.

Chip and I were reminded, in our physical proximity, of how our tropical honeymoon concept had been derailed—of how, despite not choosing the Tibetan monastery trip, we'd ended up monk-like and sexless after all.

FINALLY THOMPSON CUT the engines; our boat slowed down and bobbed a bit, quietly. Then he cut the lights too. I was queasier, with the slow rocking motion, than I had been when we were going fast. (Would I vomit? When that's the question you're asking, you don't have time for others.) I fixed my eyes on a small, thin door at the back where the toilet must be.

Thompson fiddled with some controls. I drew a couple of deep breaths and felt slightly less inclined to empty out my stomach.

"What's happening, Johnson?" asked Gina.

She'd taken to calling him by the wrong name whenever she addressed him, each time a different one.

"Fishfinder," he muttered. "Sonar."

We got up and gathered behind him, looking

270

over the console at a screen with some numbers in the corners, some scraggly fields of color. A radio emitted staticky voices, but the codes and terms meant nothing to me: it was a drone of noise. Through the acutely slanted windshield I could tell the armada rose up ahead of us, its lights the tall geometry of cities, buildings. I couldn't see the shapes of the ships, only their clusters of brightness.

"The bad guys have these toys too, don't they?" asked Gina.

"A buttload," said Thompson.

"With all that gear, those greedy cretins haven't found the mermaids yet?" said Ellis.

"Maybe the mermaids have burrows," suggested Chip. "Some *fish* do, Nancy told me. They camouflage themselves beneath the sand. Those flat ones, kind of ugly. I mean, no offense. The sonar wouldn't show them there, would it? Maybe the mermaids are hiding."

Thompson went *hmph*.

"Hey, can't the other boats see us?" asked Chip. "Aren't we too near?"

"Nothing on the channels I checked," said Thompson. "There was a window, sure. Where someone might have noticed. Don't think they did. I woulda heard the hail. Believe me. These morons couldn't find their asses in a shit tornado."

"A shit *tornado*," savored Gina. "You're a wordsmith, Swanson."

271

"No training, is the problem. *Morons*," he said, turning and glaring at Gina, "with no *training*."

"We need people like you, Dobson," said Gina. "In academia, where I work. Man, do we ever need people like you. People who *have* been trained. To do the high-level work. Such as killing."

She smiled, of course, when she said that. Gina tends to.

"Whoa," said Chip. "What's that?"

On the fishfinder, a formless mass appeared.

"School of bait," said Thompson.

"So what are you looking for?" asked Chip. "The mermaids? The divers?"

"This right here is the edge of one of the nets, where they've set it. Between that ship over there"—he inclined his head to the left—"and a ways off to the south-southeast is where this net stretches. I propose to cruise the perimeter of the nets, sounding and scanning. I'll tune the radio to the frequency they're probably using, see if we hear some shit. Meanwhile we'll keep a lookout on the screen. See what we can see."

"And if they notice us?" asked Gina.

"What do *you* think? We'll book it out of here. Their boats'll start up slow."

So Ellis and Gina got tasked to radio, while Chip and I gazed at the fishfinder's screen, with its frizzy fields of color. It was interesting enough for a while; Thompson pointed out fish, reefs, and the lines of nets as he steered us along, the engine putt-putting at a low murmur, running lights shining on the waves. He showed us what undersea objects looked like, in those blazes of false hue. Fishes were fish-shaped, long crescents, mostly; bait schools moved by in slow blobs. I thought of how it really must look down there, the darkness of the depths, the warmth of the water. Waving seagrass, maybe, bulbous long whips of kelp.

It was peaceful and black out there, peaceful and nauseating; I wished I'd taken some Dramamine, cursed my poor planning. I kept hoping to see the shape of a human torso on the sonar, the shape not of a diver but of a person with a tail—I stared and stared, while Gina and Ellis listened to the radio. But the minutes soon ran together, my eyelids felt heavy, and elements of the scene blended. There were no mermaids; the closest we came was spotting a few night divers, which Thompson had to point out to me. But they had no tails, and so they didn't hold my interest.

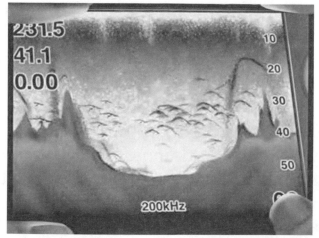

Thompson muttered to Chip, describing features, using lingo: *honeyholes,* he said several times, as my attention drifted. I heard it quite distinctly. *Honeyholes.*

After a while—it must have been past midnight, and I'd given up on watching and dozed off atop one of the leather benches, imagining myself in the electronic purples and blues of the sonar images, my own body, its legs like scissors, then fused in a long, graceful triangle, tranquilly sinking down into the waving eelgrass beds—

"Shut up," said Thompson.

I vaguely registered Gina retorting—he must have been talking to her—and heard the radio squawk. I struggled to sit up. The boat's satellite phone was lighting up and ringing. Thompson hovered over the radio, turned up the volume, and reached out to pick up the sat phone receiver, I guess to stop the racket—I personally couldn't parse the radio exchanges, a mere patchwork of sounds. We waited anxiously, not knowing what was going on, until Thompson handed the sat phone to Chip and nodded at him to deal with it, while he leaned in close over the radio.

Chip had to talk low so Thompson could hear the radio chatter; I couldn't tell who was calling about what until he dropped the phone and was leaping around oddly, a raw nerve of excitement, trying to contain himself.

"What *is* it, Chip? What *is* it?"

"We have to go back," said Chip, after he grabbed the receiver again and hung up, beaming. "We have to go *back!*"

"Not yet," said Thompson, who was rummaging in a heap of duffel bag on the floor. Holding a padded case in one hand, he used the other to steer the boat this way, that way, around the glare of lights. "Gotta see what's going on. U.S. Coast Guard cutter is almost here. Boarding the flagship. They're taking someone into custody."

"Custody?" echoed Chip. "You mean, arresting them?"

"Not us, I hope," said Ellis.

"These binoculars are night-vision," said Thompson, and waved the case in my direction. "Get 'em out, wouldja?"

"Sure," I said, but as I did it I whispered to Chip, "Tell me!"

He shook his head stubbornly, still wearing that grin.

I handed Thompson the binoculars as he throttled down, as we took up a position near a much larger vessel, maneuvering around a bit, this way and that. It was one of the soaring white yachts. Sure enough, another boat was pulling up alongside, the small police boat we'd seen once or twice before; then there was a gangway-type deal, a walkway was being lowered. We didn't need the night-vision goggles, as it turned out: the scene was flooded with halogen-white lights, and there were crowds on the decks of the yacht, looking down. My problem was I couldn't get a good angle on the scene, Gina and Chip were blocking my line of sight. I tried to peer between their heads, around and over them, but it wasn't working out for me.

"Well bugger me," said Ellis, "it's the bird from the beach," and at first I thought he meant a waterfowl—a seagull, possibly a tern.

"The woman from the parent company," crowed Chip. "Look, Deb. And the guy with the spray-on tan!"

I got a good, solid five-second glimpse, between the heads of my companions. They were walking across the gangplank: the previous Mormon and her coworker, Mike Chantz, Janz or Djanz. They wore polo shirts and shorts, dressed for leisure, I guess, but there were plastic twist-ties around their wrists, and their wrists were behind their backs, and they were walking a little awkwardly.

"What's the game now," growled Thompson.

But Chip nodded. "I think I know, I think I know," he said. "Thompson, you have to get us back!"

I stayed frustrated with Chip as the boat sped toward the shoreline, Thompson talking sometimes on the radio, other times hunkered down over the controls. I was frustrated because Chip wouldn't tell me what the good news was: Chip was flat out convinced his information-withholding was in my own best interest, a point on which I flat out disagreed. He was like a small child on Christmas morning, during that trip back—the nearer we got to terra firma, the more excited he became.

I tried some tactics: I tried to freeze him out, completely stonewalling him, my face shut tight and bitchy, my eyes dead like a shark's. I wished, by signaling my coldness, to force him into confession. But it did no good.

Long story short, we achieved the shore without anything surprising happening. Next we scrambled out of the boat and trudged/hastened up the beach, each according to his mood. Thompson exchanged a series of grunts with the boat's owner, who sat in the small parking lot idling his truck. Finally, when Chip had almost expired of pent-up energy and boiling impatience, Thompson hauled himself into the driver's seat and drove us back to the motel.

There, in our room, surrounded by a raucous crowd, was Nancy.

Not dead at all. *Au* contrary.

I DON'T KNOW if you've ever been sure someone was dead, then found out you were wrong. It's not really a standard experience—there's no card section for it.

Prof. Simonoff, for obvious reasons, was the hub of startlement/amazement; we were bowled over and stupefied, but the professor was in a different category. That guy's whole self was *completely transformed,* his bearing, his voice, even his face looked new to me. Although, in any of these arenas, I couldn't have told you exactly why. The instant change taught me a lesson about mood or affect or what have you—not quite sure what the lesson was, per se, but it was in there somewhere. Something about the spirit animating the body. Or not animating it.

My point is, there was Nancy, a smidgeon paler but alive and well, not decomposing in the least—except insofar as we all are, dying as we live, or living as we die, taking that opportunity. Depends if you're a glass half-full type or a glass half-empty, I guess.

Nancy was full color, animated, and life-size.

We charged up to embrace her, plowing through the cluster of others, Chip just ahead of me—though Nancy was never much of a hugger, if I'm being honest. Even at that moment, appearing among us like Lazarus from the tomb, the risen Christ, etc., she wasn't big on hugging. She's more the kind of person who stands there stiffly, passively enfolded. When she gets hugged her cardboard form sends out a signal of awkward unresponsiveness, with her plainly wondering when the "display" of "affection" will be completed. In that realm she has a maybe autistic quality.

Imagine my shiver of recognition, then indignation when she told us she'd been kidnapped. My kidnapping was extremely small potatoes, next to hers; mine was a casual, throwaway kidnapping where hers was serious (though also highly incompetent). I felt embarrassed by the inadequacy of my personal kidnapping. I was in the bush leagues, as a kidnapping victim.

Unlike me, Nancy had been stuck with a syringe, covered in a sheet, and rolled out of her cabana and across the grounds on a gurney, dressed up as a corpse. Then they'd stowed that expert in a windowless room, a room off the hallways behind the main restaurant, where she'd been found an hour before, while we were on the boat. Annette had been passing the door on her way to a walk-in freezer and heard Nancy's thin wail of *help, help* through the wall; she used a key off the ring she'd snatched from the staff pegboard and *voilà*, set her free.

Not one of the refrigerators, no—the place had simply been a disused storeroom, standard room temp, but they kept Nancy on a cot, shot up with drugs to make her sleep. ("Benzodiazepine, I'd guess," she said.)

Periodically a man would come in and hustle her to a small bathroom down the hall or give her a tray of restaurant vittles; he wouldn't talk much at those times, she said, no one had deigned to tell her what she was doing there until she got it out of a second guy, who subbed in with the food one time. The Venture of Marvels needed a certain number of days, he said, to put its claim in place, to establish its rights. Until then, she was stuck.

"No one told me they faked my *death,*" she said, as her father stood close beside her and gazed fondly at her living face, with its many-legged eyebrows (Homely virtue! I thought. How good to have her back). He kept a hand posed quasi-formally on her shoulder, as though to indicate to himself that his daughter was there, actual, real and independently breathing— without, however, showing excessive affection: like daughter, like father.

"They *never* mentioned that," went on Nancy.

"Why would they," said Thompson. "No advantage in it. A female; possible hysterics."

"I don't get this," said Simonoff. "Why do that? Why tell everyone she—she had drowned? Good God! I mean! It almost gave her poor mother a myocardial infarction!"

"Probably thought it would shut us up," said Chip. "Shut us down, right? Keep us from going after the mermaids. Plus we'd stop asking annoying questions about her whereabouts sooner or later, if we thought she was done for. Right?"

"They took my cell records, my email, contact info, the signed paperwork from the excursion," said Nancy. "And Riley's digital video? Listen to this. See, Riley was my only visitor, other than the food guys. He felt a little guilty so he asked to see me, but his conscience didn't go too deep. He talked to me, though, so I do know what happened. He *sold* it to them. Just outright sold it."

"He had a contract with us!" said Chip. "With you!"

Nancy shrugged. "He sold it."

"I thought they stole it," I said.

"First," said Nancy. "But then they actually watched it. And decided they needed to own it. So they just made him an offer."

"We still don't know who they even *are*," said Rick slowly. "Do we, Nancy?"

She shook her head.

"We know who *some* of them are," added Raleigh. "But we don't know how far up the chain it goes."

"They just arrested two of them," I said. "We saw it! On the ship. The woman and the guy with the really dark tan. Arrested. The cops came in a police cutter and arrested them."

"Scapegoats," said Thompson solemnly.

"Sacrificial lambs," agreed Rick.

"Thrown under the bus," said Chip.

I thought how much I disliked the non-Mormon and the Mike Chance guy: I felt an instinctive distaste for both of them, and had from the get-go. Still, distaste or not, they hadn't seemed like criminal masterminds. They seemed more like consultants, maybe sales reps.

"Were they acting alone?" I asked no one in

particular. "Or was management pulling the strings?"

"I think the point is we can't know," said Rick. "Kidnapping Nancy—and you too, Deb, for sure—*that,* for one, they're going to want to pin on the PR people. At least, that's what I'm suspecting."

"Our orders, which they called a 'request for emergency assistance,' came from the suit on the beach," said Raleigh. "He's the GM who runs the resort. Reports to the regional veep. I'm gonna make a call, find out what's going down."

As he turned away the rest of us fell upon Nancy like a flock of chattering parakeets, trying to pull out strings of explanation with our curved little beaks. How could it even *be* that Annette had just walked up and unlocked the door, patrolling on her fifteen-minute break, using a ring of keys from the pegboard in the staff break room? (Ronnie.) Why didn't the company guard its prisoners? (Rick.) Especially when I'd escaped, too? (Me.) Wasn't she pissed that Riley had turned out to be a Judas? (Thompson.) He'd seemed so cool at first, hadn't he? (Chip.) And (closely related) how much had they paid him? (Ellis.) Was she starving? (Janeane.) Didn't she need a shower? (Janeane.) Where were her belongings? (Janeane.) Did she want to go back to her cabana and try to get them? (Janeane.)

Wait. Very important. Did she have legal counsel yet? (Gina.)

Prof. Simonoff, the doctor and Thompson announced their intention to make a sortie to Paradise Bay to reclaim Nancy's personal items. Thompson, I could tell, was spoiling for a fight, even if it had to be over nothing more epic than a biologist's toiletries. The three of them, all men of a certain age, went out to the Hummer and roar/chugged away. Gina wanted to debrief her brother on the litigation possibilities, and Ellis wanted to cloyingly massage her shoulders while she did so. Miyoko assented to yet another video interview, Janeane made a midnight snack, etc.

But Nancy had only one objective, amid the hustle and bustle. Grass didn't grow beneath her feet, the solid feet of that kidnapped parrotfish expert; she waved away the questions, she splashed cold water on her face, she shoved handfuls of salted peanuts into her mouth without even taking a seat. Then she ushered a bunch of us outside, so she could breathe the tradewind breeze in more limited company. The rooms had gotten claustrophobic.

Once out there, standing beneath some rustling fronds beside the pool, she asked Raleigh for a full report on the status of the Venture of Marvels.

"Here's what I'm being told," said Raleigh. "The general manager's claiming he had no knowledge of your kidnapping. He says he, too, was told you'd drowned. That he wasn't in on that bullshit. He's helming up the Venture, of course, that much he's copped to—he's taking ownership of that part of it. But where the backstory's concerned, his version is: Mike and Liza brought him the mermaid video. He had no idea they'd taken it from Riley, he thought you'd just drowned and the tape and other mermaid-related texts, excursion records, and all that shit was in your personal effects. In a nutshell, he's doing his best to avoid criminal liability over what happened to you, Nancy."

"Why'd they bother with that meeting? Where we first met, uh, Liza?" I asked.

"That was to get everyone's contact info," said Raleigh. "That was part of our briefing a couple days ago. They had a manifest from the boat trip, that's how they knew some of the people to invite, but they needed *everyone's names,* emails, and cells. Hadda make sure *everyone* came under their umbrella, ideally came over to work for them. At that point they only had Riley on board."

"Sleazebags," said Chip.

"But they never got you guys signed up, so the plan was, instead, to round you up, lock you up, and shut you up. Like with Nancy," said Raleigh, looking at me. "Mostly, I get the feeling, they screwed up. They had some miscommunications. There were a couple power struggles, with them and the Keystone cops—a lack of unity, some confusion. So honestly? You lucked out."

"How about the search?" asked Nancy. "And my

colleague from Berkeley, what's happening with him?"

While Chip talked to her I ran inside, went through my clothes and threw on a swimsuit. (I'd lost the bikini by then, but I had reinforcements.) I was unkempt and I needed liquid immersion, so I listened to the conversation from down in the water, clinging to the concrete lip of the pool. Occasionally I'd reach for a cocktail Janeane brought out to me, a tepid, mojito-like beverage in a flimsy plastic cup. I listened as Chip and Raleigh told stories, occasionally interjecting an anecdote of my own, and watched velvety bats flit under the patio overhang of a vacant room.

I floated in the pool throughout the planning session, in fact, dipping my head occasionally, smoothing back my wet hair. Periodically I'd hold a mouthful of mojito in my cheek pouches, just see how long I could keep it there. After a while Gina joined me, and we hung side by side, our arms adrift in the chlorinated water, our fingers pruney. A soldier would pass by, now and then, stopping to refill our cups. We felt strangely content. ("Here we are," said Gina, "in a swimming pool in the tropics, and at regular intervals young, muscular men in uniforms supply us with intoxicants.")

She'd already shelved her vow to drink no cocktails, in fear of Thompson, and I didn't remind her of it.

It was so satisfying, such a relief to watch Nancy sitting, talking, every bit as alive as a person can reasonably be. A reassurance of comforting proportions—almost enough to dispel the fear I'd been nursing earlier of loathing, of all the loathing crowds, the mermaid haters descending.

And I could consign them to the screen, almost, for a brief time: I could believe they only lived in that small, glowing rectangle. When I was a child and got scared by a TV show or movie, my mother used to say to me, "It's not real, darling. It's just pretend." I'd loved it when she said that. I willingly believed everything bad was made up only for entertainment—nothing terrifying was real, nothing real was terrifying. Only in stories did the witches cackle, their mouths gaping open to show yellow, razor-sharp teeth; only on Hollywood sets were there wars, cruelty, the tragic deaths of unspeakably beautiful and innocent creatures. In life there were none of these.

I said that to myself when I thought of the screen, full of the angry words of people who had never seen the mermaids but nonetheless hated them.

How small it was, that screen. Irrelevant, maybe. A triviality.

Anyway, Nancy was determined to go out again first thing in the morning. We'd line up some boats, we'd motor out to where the armada had dropped anchor, and we'd boldly confront it. Nancy said she didn't even know if it was legal to drop those commercial fishing nets where they were dropping them, near the reefs—in fact, she strenuously doubted it. She'd like to hire a local attorney, she said, but that would have to wait—at least till businesses opened on Tortola, maybe even the U.S. islands, St. Croix, there had to be some lawyers familiar with the local situation.

In the meantime, we'd go out onto the ocean and board the armada, take on its leaders. Why, we'd defy them openly.

I swear, that parrotfish expert seemed to have no fear. She'd been far less affected by her death than we had.

In her experience, she'd been kidnapped; she'd been locked in a storeroom for a few days, treated with casual rudeness and brought paper plates of cold French fries to eat. There hadn't been a microwave, plus the ketchup was watery. And they'd unlawfully injected narcotics. But still, she hadn't particularly feared an escalation of the violence (Janeane could barely believe this, thought Nancy was the bravest woman ever to walk the earth). She'd fallen asleep fully clothed after the party in Chip's and my cabana; next thing she knew she woke up on a cot in a store-room that smelled of disinfectant and onions.

So that's what Nancy had endured, but meanwhile, *we'd* endured her death—possibly even her murder!

Later she'd come back to life, but still. Attitude-wise, we'd taken a hit. Nancy had a can-do sensibility, while the rest of us were hesitant—with the exception of Thompson. He was still waiting impatiently for a chance to lob his grenade.

Anyway, Nancy got Miyoko on board—this scene too, she said, we needed to broadcast live; could Miyoko arrange for it?—and then she asked Raleigh for the loan of his beret-clad troops.

At first he hemmed and hawed, mulling it over since it wasn't exactly low-profile, but eventually, once he had enough mojitos/beers in him, he seemed to give his consent. You got the feeling the soldiers hadn't seen too much action, there in the British Virgin Islands. You got the feeling what they really wanted was just for something to happen.

Plus Miyoko had just agreed to go out to dinner with Sam, once the mermaid emergency was past. I think Raleigh wanted to show his solidarity.

IT WASN'T EVEN light out when Ellis came barging into our room. He and Gina'd been sleeping in the adjacent one, through the unlocked door, and now he stumbled across the threshold in a torn, oversize Sex Pistols T-shirt and Monty Python boxers, mumbling and pushing his bangs out of his eyes. He typically sports a tousled, Hugh-Granty look. "The deputy governor's here," he said, having reverted to his approximately Oxbridge accent and away from the fake cockney of indignation. "Also a minister. I rang them yesterday."

I was groggy, but awake enough to register shock: apparently Ellis had accomplished something. In general he carries off the dentistry, the accent, and the women; there the triple whammy ends. Things Ellis doesn't do and rarely remembers to delegate: Stock his refrigerator. Clean his condo. Pay bills. Fix what's broken.

Chip and I pulled on some clothes and joined Gina and Ellis in their room, where they stood at the door talking.

"Let them in!" said Chip. "Please. We're decent."

So two people entered, dressed business casual, both dark-skinned like most islanders, slight of build and faultlessly polite, a woman and a man. Their accents were a kind of soft quasi–Brit Creole; they had a genteel quality. (Ellis told me later they weren't elected officials but appointed by the Queen.) Gina tried to offer them coffee but gave up when she couldn't find any. They were very concerned, they said, that required commercial-fishing permits had not been even *applied for* by the parent company. There'd also been a number of related "irregularities," they realized, concerning the actions of the "constabulary." They'd be going out to investigate shortly, heading out to meet the armada in an unannounced visit aboard the U.S. Coast Guard's cutter.

The woman, who turned out to be the deputy governor, said we could hitch a ride, if we wished to. Could our party be ready by 6 a.m.?

It was then that Raleigh and Sam appeared at the open door; Raleigh winked at me. I grabbed Chip's arm and inclined my head in the soldiers' direction, impressing on him via sharp finger-squeeze that we probably shouldn't shout out a joyful greeting. These were the "higher-ups" Raleigh had been avoiding, I figured; orders had finally come down.

Luckily, the natives seemed friendly.

"Look here!" said Ellis to the bureaucrats. "I really am *dashed* grateful you took my phone call seriously. I'm chuffed to bits."

Usually when he went old-school Gina accused him of "getting lordy." But this time she let it sail right past.

Soon the others were up and bustling, Nancy "over the moon," as Ellis said, about the presence of the two civil servants (the man was the head of some government ministry). There was a shortage of vessels, she'd found out the night before, so if Ellis hadn't reached out to the colonial authorities a lot of us would probably have been stranded on land. Thompson's borrowed speedboat could have been called back into service, possibly, but its capacity was limited.

Before long we were driving straight to the main marina, no fear this time, no need to hide. We had the government with us; we had the troops. Steve and Janeane watched us motor away from the dock, as—Chip with one arm slung over my shoulders, the two of us floating in a crowd of soldiers—we stood at the bow in the leaping spume.

Janeane waved a yellow scarf in the air. It looked so old-fashioned, lifted by the breeze.

THE DEPUTY GOVERNOR invited us to call her by her first name, which was Lorna, but we both felt awkward so we avoided calling her anything. The minister guy didn't chat with us much, he mostly hunkered down talking to the Simonoffs, but the deputy governor talked to Ellis, and because we were near Ellis, she also talked to us.

This was on the deck of the Coast Guard cutter, you understand—there was a kind of excitement, a festive atmosphere, a bonded, band-of-brothers situation, though detail-wise, on a technical level, we weren't brothers or even all men and some of us didn't like each other.

But we dismissed the issue of not liking each other, then. Liking each other, not liking each other, who cared, was our thinking aboard that charging white vessel of law enforcement. It was beside the point. Gina's disgust with Thompson, Thompson's pathological fear/hatred of "the gays"—it was meaningless, on the deck of the Coast Guard cutter.

I thought of when I'd first met Janeane, harshly indicting her sandals, observing the plantlike tendrils as they wound up her fishbelly calves—my frustration as she talked to me during peeing. How small it seemed to me now. I felt a real pang of affection for her, the way I'd seen her just minutes before, standing on the shore and waving her yellow scarf. She'd looked nostalgic then, as though we'd boarded the *Titanic* and away we steamed.

I'd first deployed my devil/Gina half, judging Janeane, but then my angel/Chip half had taken over. Yet seeing Gina and Janeane together, I'd noticed there wasn't any conflict between them. Sure, they were opposites—Janeane deploring polymers while Gina ironically loved them, Janeane getting choked up over industrial meat production while Gina ironically ordered full plates of bacon at the all-American diners she frequented.

But still there was a kind of understanding between them, right? I thought of Gina raising a sly eyebrow at what Janeane was saying; of Janeane, sometimes, gazing at Gina in startled confusion.

We didn't know what was going to happen, but at last something would—we had a trajectory. We had new strength with the government on our side: from what Nancy said to me, passing us on the deck, it seemed the civil servants might be interested in her idea for a mermaid sanctuary. They already had some plan in mind, she said, for "marine protected areas."

We were aloft, moving forward at last, and not a single one of us was currently dead.

As we neared the armada, though—the first time I'd approached it in daylight—my mood changed rapidly. Damn! It was a floating citadel. It was a whole city on the ocean, with nets and crane-like structures, complicated metal architectures of utility. Small boats were moving among the larger ships, serving them, ferrying. My stomach flipped when I saw the armada/citadel. Who were we, really? And what was the law, even? We were a handful of men wearing berets, we were two very polite civil servants, one of whom was named Lorna; we were a small group of tourists, vacationing from our lives.

As the yachts and the trawlers towered over us, some soaring up gracefully in their white fiberglass slickness, some stolid as factories in their black rust and barnacles, what I saw was mass—I saw solidity. The law was ancient runes on a parchment, a parchment you might see in one of Chip's gameworlds. Law was a tale and government was more a wish than a reality. A smart dresser, maybe, but simply not effective. For the first time I understood its quaintness.

Government! Once we'd believed in it.

Those ships were really big.

We did have guns, at least (I reassured myself, looking sidelong at Raleigh's face). He stood straight-backed at the prow, hands clasped behind him, jawline firm. The guns were a factor in our favor, I could see the logic there, but where there are guns there are always more guns. Seemed like another can of worms. The guns didn't comfort me, for that reason.

There'd been some radio communiqués back and forth, I guessed, because we had a destination in the vast armada: the flagship yacht, where management resided. Now we circled the periphery, engine rumbling and wake churning as we cut a swath. I looked down at the white curls, at my flip-flop-clad feet on the deck, damp from the spray. I thought of the defectors, those former dive companions and partygoers. Where were they now, the blond-headed profiteer Riley, the toe fetishist from the Heartland, the substitute teacher? Where was the Fox News spearfisherman who'd rummaged around in my tampons?

I looked up at the rails, the gunwales, idly hoping to catch a glimpse of a familiar face. But if there were any people there, they were hidden from my sight.

Then the bureaucrats were climbing into an orange rubber motorboat—a Zodiac, Raleigh called it. Then he was boarding, then Nancy, then a couple more soldiers. I thought we'd all be left behind, till Nancy waved impatiently at Chip and he gave me a quick kiss and hurried to board too.

My husband was among the chosen people, but I wasn't, apparently.

I raised an eyebrow at Gina and tried not to resent it, the fact that I hadn't made the cut. I did resent it, though. I wondered whether I had offended Nancy somehow (bad breath? Or had she read my mind about her caterpillar eyebrows?). I felt only a bit better when, as the boat sputtered away toward the flagship yacht, Raleigh turned, smiled, and saluted me mockingly/flirtingly.

"Man. You could totally date him," said Gina.

SO THERE I was, cooling my heels with the rest of the rabble. It was me, Gina, Ellis, Sam, Thompson, Simonoff, the good doctor, and some leftover soldiers, still standing at strict attention on the deck, waiting on Sam's orders. Thompson was talking to a crewman and Rick, with Ronnie's help, was busy filming Miyoko. That Japanese VJ never stopped working; right then she was broadcasting an update from the stern of the cutter, where the mics wouldn't pick up the interference of our background noise.

We watched quietly as the orange boat ferried

our diplomatic dinghy over to the yacht with soaring lines, a pearly white vessel whose name, emblazoned in ornate gold curlicues, seemed to be *Narcissus*. I wasn't sure why you'd name your luxury yacht that. Was it self-aware/ironic, or more straight-up toolishness?

I opened my mouth to ask Gina, but she was already talking.

"What are they going for, an injunction?" asked Gina.

"They're going to ask them to simply pull up the nets," said Ellis. "The minister says they don't have the legally required permits."

"And they think the parent company will just say, Oh, OK?" said Gina. "And, like, go gently into that good night?"

"Not really, no," said Ellis. "They're also filing for a PI. Not sure where that's at, though, judicially."

The arc of my confidence fell. Gone was the rush I'd felt as the Coast Guard cutter crested the waves, when speed was ours and we'd seemed to be duty-bound.

We'd had a higher calling, then.

"Hey," said Sam, squinting into his binoculars, "I can see them talking, there on the upper deck. I can make out Nancy . . . that'd be the deputy governor, yeah. There's the GM."

"GM?" asked Gina.

"The resort's general manager," I said.

"Sam!" called one of the cutter's crewmen, sticking his head out the door of the wheelhouse. "Get in here!"

Gina and I followed Sam over, looking side-long at each other—we were hoping to get in on the action, whatever that might be. No one stopped us.

Inside, near the control panel with the steering wheel, a TV jutting out from the wall was playing CNN. We hung behind Sam and the crewmen and craned our necks.

It was live footage of the airport in Tortola, according to the news ticker. Very crowded: people hurried along pulling their roller bags, hefting their suitcases, pink-faced from the strain of hefting their duffel bags. Disorder seemed to reign, and the reporter's voice was barely audible. Then the scene changed: the ferry dock, also Tortola. I recognized it, since I'd been there less than a week before. Two ferries were docked at once, full of people; crowds were still pressing to get on them, crew pushing them away.

Then there was a reporter talking, a woman who stood on the quay with strands from her mound of polished yellow hair blowing across her face. She had a British accent, not unlike Ellis's —and for all I knew, equally fake.

". . . tourists descending on the island in numbers that have simply never been seen before," I caught. "Every single hotel room on Virgin Gorda is full to capacity, according to the reports we're getting, and frankly no one knows where the rest of the arriving crowds will be accommodated. Some are based here on Tortola, of course, where hotel rooms are also over-booked. . . ."

"Feculent shite," said Ellis.

"It's happening," I said, and my throat closed gaggingly.

"*Shhh,*" Gina hissed.

". . . these are not all your friendly neighborhood scuba enthusiasts and beachgoers, which these tiny islands in the British Caribbean have depended on for decades," said the reporter. "No, many of them apparently have a very *different* reason for visiting this tropical getaway."

A man was talking, a microphone held up in front of his angry, slightly sweaty face; his backpack bobbed behind his head.

". . . gotta get in there and take care of these things. Get rid of them. Our mission is *annihilation*. What if they interbreed with humans? What then?"

The camera panned to the woman beside him, who smiled and nodded.

"What our *pastor* is saying," she offered eagerly, "is this could be the Fifth Trumpet. Like it says in Revelation 9, you know, a man's face with lion's teeth, the wings of locusts and the tail of a scorpion—"

"Point being *is,*" interrupted the man, "these

things are not the work of the Lord. These things are filth and abomination."

I felt cold, and my scalp tingled. I backed out of the wheelhouse, hitting the deck rail with the small of my back. There was dizziness: the sky was too white. The sky attacked my eyeballs. Light was everywhere, when all I wanted was shade. I thought I might faint, although I've never fainted my whole life. I'm not sure why it hit me so hard, but basically, when I heard the man say that, my personality collapsed.

"Hey, hey," said Gina, her hands firm on my shoulders. "Honey. You need to get a *grip*."

"They're coming," I said.

"Well, that's right," said Gina. "What of it?"

She put her face close to mine and gazed into my eyes in what was, for Gina, a pretty strong bid for sincerity. I looked into her brown irises, her warm, almond-shaped eyes, so familiar and comforting, with their impossibly thick eyelashes courtesy of Latisse.

"Listen. *Deb*. It's not your fault, sweetie. This was always going to happen. The mermaids were living on borrowed time. You see that, right? It's amazing they weren't gone centuries ago. Like the giant sloths. The mammoths. The saber-tooth cats."

It didn't comfort me.

It's only been days, I thought, a handful of *days* after probably tens of thousands of years we must have lived in parallel—we stumbled across them, we filmed them, and now their enemies are legion.

Here come my people, those teeming hordes, here come my people, brandishing their stupidity. Above their heads they raise stupidity like a flaming sword.

I couldn't help imagining myself below us, the vault of water above me, the dark weight of the armada bearing down, oppressive, the nets sinking, the nets surrounding us.

I really couldn't breathe.

"You're white as a sheet! Head between your knees," said Gina, and she shoved the top of my head and made me sit down right there on the gritty surface of the deck, where instantly my ass got wet and cold. I didn't care, I just kept trying to draw breath, maybe it wasn't a panic attack, maybe it was my heart! (So I thought, and then felt sheepish—I was playing Janeane's role, with my hypochondria/panic attack; I recognized for a second that I'd feared being Janeane as soon as I met her. Janeane embarrassed me like a bad play, a close relation trailing dirty underwear out the bottom of a pant leg: somehow I over-identified. That's why I brought my Gina side to bear. Then, wearing the muumuu for all the world to see, I'd fully realized my fears.) Still all I could feel was the nets closing above my head, as I swam with the mermaids in their blue fathoms.

I sensed the massive hulls of those greedy ships

above us, their shadows blackening the water and closing off the sky.

I'm not sure how long I sat there, enclosed in my private grief/panic cavern—at a certain point it turned out that I was crying and too ashamed to show my tear-streaked, contorted face. I felt like a child again, because I hadn't cried in front of a group of people, I figured, since then—at least, not so that anyone would notice. Now I'd made a fool of myself, as sadness overtook me; I'd let down the façade of cohesion.

And I was angry at Gina, even, Gina with her irony, even though she meant well, even though her gentle hand sat on my shoulder, lightly patting, while Chip was off with other people, pursuing more important aims. She raised the shield of irony to deflect her opponents. She and her other friends *all* raised their ironic shields, I thought—her fellow academics, for instance—instead of being willing to fight. Just lifted the shields and held them there.

On the one hand you had the religious hysterics, obesely advancing with their ignorance. On the other hand, to oppose them, all you had was some thin effetes from the city, hiding behind a flimsy row of high-irony deflecting shields.

It wouldn't save us, I thought. It wouldn't save anything.

I hit Gina's hand away, at one point, shaking my head, refusing to raise my face. But then I felt painful remorse, as I always do if I lash out at Gina D., remembering the onset of her irony. It was when her mother died. How Gina had adored her mother, a mother who *lived* for her and her two brothers, who laughed a lot and was good-natured, actually almost a saint, to be honest. How often her mother hugged them, always looking for opportunities. The love shone out of that woman.

Then withering, pain, a skeletal appearance. No more smiling. And gone.

From that time on Gina painstakingly built the shield, piece by piece. I couldn't stay angry at Gina D. Never. Beneath her irony, to me, she'd always be that desolate kid.

And anyway who was I to judge?

I was a tourist, I thought. Even at home. I'd always had that aspect, the aspect of a tourist.

"DEBORAH!" I HEARD eventually, once I was ready to absorb current events.

Gina had gone off somewhere, murmuring something about getting me a blanket. I'd been shivering for a good while on my piece of grainy dirty-white deck, my modest, wet square of misery.

The voice filtered down from above; it was Sam. He looked preoccupied. Of course: he was a soldier, not a nursemaid.

I raised my head, wiped my eyes and nose and stood up shakily, one hand braced heavy on the rail.

"Take a look," he said, and handed me his binoculars. "They're just standing there. I figure you can read your husband's expressions better than I can, right? He's nearest us, there's a pretty good view of him from the front. So take a look. You think those talks are going well?"

He wanted to draw me out of my personality breakdown by distracting me. I saw that, and I appreciated it. I decided to play along. I took the binoculars from him.

I can never quite get the hang of binoculars, don't like them, basically, and as I was futzing around trying to normalize my face and emotions and at the same time master the focus ring, I must have turned my body. Because as I fiddled I noticed the specs were pointed in the wrong direction now, the wrong direction completely. And when my view sharpened I was looking out over a network of nets across the open ocean. I swiveled, trying to find the *Narcissus* again, but then I swiveled back, hesitating. There was a large, flattish gray bump out there in the water. Actually a couple of them.

"I didn't know there were atolls out here," I said.

"There aren't," said Sam.

I blinked; my eyes were watering, but this time from wind or staring, not emotion. The flat gray things were moving; now they were curved, not flat, I saw.

I took the binoculars off my eyes and handed them back to him. The gray bumps, in fact, were visible with the naked eye.

"Then what *are* those?" I asked.

"Shit," said Sam, raising the binoculars.

"What?"

"No, that can't be," he said. "Wait. Wait a second." He was playing with the focus ring, or maybe zooming.

"Look!" said Gina. "What's going on? Water came out of it!"

"Whales."

"*Huge* whales," I said.

"We *never* see whales this big," said Sam, but he still sounded distracted, as though it was hard to muster the time/energy to talk to us. Then, under his breath: "What the *hell?*"

"What species?" burst out Ronnie, running up from the stern. "Rick's filming them. What are they?"

"It can't be," said Sam, shaking his head. He was still staring through the field glasses, all tense and pressed against the rails. "They're not—no way, not this far south this time of year, I never heard of that. It's not a finback, see, it's even bigger—that baby's ninety feet long at least. Maybe a hundred. Blues!"

"*Blue* whales?" asked Ellis, dubious. He shook his head. "In the Caribbean in summertime? Go on, mate. Pull the other one."

"I worked one summer on a whalewatch boat," said Sam. "I know my cetaceans. But you're right. I've never seen this before. They usually travel in pairs or by themselves—not pods like that. Not blues. And they don't stay up for so long, they're not typically so *visible*. What the *hell*."

"Five," said Ronnie. "Six. Seven . . ."

I couldn't get a sense of their size, personally. Out there on the waves they were a fleet of dark bumps—that was all.

"They're goddamn blues, all right," said Thompson, appearing out of the wheelhouse. He was holding a can of beer. (When it came to beer being handed out, why *him?* Where was the beer for me?)

"Oh shit, are they going to get caught? Caught in the fishing nets?" asked Gina. "Jesus. Really? *Enough* already."

"I never saw so many in one place," said Thompson. He had a brief coughing fit, then stuck his beer in one of his large cargo pockets and fished in his tobacco pouch. "And we're talking, I've seen 'em in the Antarctic. They make 'em even bigger down there. Course, we don't know much about blue whales. Goddamn mystery. Used to think they migrated, turns out not all of them do. Bunch off the coast of Sri Lanka never leave home at all. Pygmy blues, just sixty feet long. Regular ones have hearts the size of cars. Baby could crawl through one of their arteries. No sweat."

"Doesn't make *sense,*" said Sam. "A large pod of blues? I've never seen that. They're coming toward us, too, toward the nets—they're headed straight for the nets across the open water. See? Is your man Rick still filming?"

"He's getting it," nodded Ronnie.

"Blue whale calls are louder than jet planes, you know that?" said Thompson to me. I briefly eyed his beer. If I moved suddenly, I could grab it. "Songs carry thousands of miles. Freakish. Slow swimmers. Still, used to be faster than we were, before the steam engine. Before the explosive harpoons."

I glanced up at the yacht, where I could make out Chip—suddenly I was sure it was him—leaning over the side and gazing toward the whales, just as we were. There was Nancy, too. Behind them, other heads and shoulders.

"Can't we get closer?" I asked Sam. "Out by the nets? To see them better?"

"We could take the inflatable, maybe," he said.

He sounded dubious at first; then (seeing Miyoko's hopeful face as she came toward us) he seemed to get a rush of energy, sounding more enthused. "You know what? Let's do it. This is a once-in-a-lifetime sighting. Let's take the Zodiac."

He stepped away and talked into his radio; in no time the orange inflatable that had been bobbing alongside the *Narcissus,* nobody in it but one

306

sailor at the helm, was jumping over the waves back to us.

Miyoko wanted to come, of course, and Ronnie, and Rick lugged the video camera along—in no time we were all scrambling down the ramp into the smaller boat. As we poured in Sam tossed us lifejackets from a bin under a bench, and we sat down and clicked their plastic buckles. Then there was engine noise and bouncing and a wall of spray that drenched me—it'd been bone dry on the high-up deck of the cutter, by comparison, despite my ass that was now soaked and freezing.

We sped off along the edge of the nearest net.

I wished Chip was with us—I wished our phones worked out here on the waves, at least I'd have been able to *text* him then—but failing that I turned and waved at the crowd on the *Narcissus'* deck, as we left the yacht behind. I couldn't be completely sure—the heads and shoulders up there were blurry and interchangeable to me once again—but I thought he raised a hand and held it up to me.

We drew closer to those gray masses, and they, I guess, were moving closer to the nets and to us as we approached *them,* and I couldn't see much because Sam and Thompson were the only ones looking through binoculars as we motored. Just as we were getting in close enough for me to begin to study the weird curves of the tops of their bodies—because frankly I had no idea what I was looking at—one by one they dove, the edges of their massive tails leaving a waterfall of white as they sank beneath the waves. They were great smooth-moving crescents of gray-blue, and just like that those crescents slid under and disappeared from view, leaving only a faint, lacy wash of intercrossing waters on the surface. In fact there was hardly any turbulence at all. Those giants' movements were seamless.

The guy at the steering wheel slowed us down; now we were chugging along a line of green oval buoys that marked the edge of a net. Beyond them was nothing but water.

"*Damn* it," said Gina.

"Patience. We're not done yet," said Sam.

The sailor cut the engine and we sat there in the boat, the boat that was suspended on the water, dancing a bit, up and down, side to side in the lazy rhythm.

For a short time it seemed to me—and I remember this moment better than anything else from my honeymoon trip—as though the light over the ocean was a different light from any I'd seen before. It was morning, I know that rationally, but I have a strong recollection of a golden light, a gilded, amber light you might associate with retirement, peace and tranquillity. The light that seems to tremble in the air before the dusk descends, before a darkness falls upon the earth.

I've always liked to talk, as long as they're someone worth talking to. I've always been bored by silent people. But right then I was *so* glad that no one was talking, that no one in that lifeboat was saying anything at all . . . I wondered: What if we'd never spoken in the first place? Where would we be, our race? Would we have machines, even?

Or on the other hand, maybe we'd already be long gone. Fallen to stronger animals, the ones with smaller brains and bigger muscles, longer claws and teeth.

Still: right then I wanted nothing more than for the wordless quiet to persist. I wished we'd never speak again, at that particular second—that the pure silence of waiting for the appearance of the blue whales, that wide-open, neutrally buoyant hope, that expectation would stretch on forever and a day.

No. Breaking the peace was the loud, abrasive noise of a ratcheting, a winching, scraping cacophony—mechanical, groaning. I understood after a second that a thick cable was creaking, the net slung beside us in the water was being moved. I wondered why; had the parent company found something? Or was this just part of the process of reduction, the process by which it was shrinking its search area and supposedly also forcing the mermaids nearer the shore, bringing them closer in?

With the hawser, or whatever it was, grinding away I had the urge to cover my ears with my hands, and at the same time I was struck with the conviction that either the whales or the mermaids were getting caught down there, convinced that the hauling of the nets was intended for them, that we were about to witness their willful death, what you might call their murder.

I was terrified, and for a while—I can't say how long—that feeling of dread, plus the whine of the moving cable, was all I was really aware of.

Rick was filming, though there was little to see, he had the camera pointed at the patch of ocean where the whales had been. The rest of us did nothing, just watched and waited and endured the groan of steel.

With no warning except a single, slight back-and-forth rock, the Zodiac was pushed up onto one side, and we spilled out of it before we could register what was happening. It flipped on top of us, as we splashed, gurgled, and squawked. Blinded, choking on salt water and flailing around, I panicked—maybe I wouldn't be able to get out from under the boat again, the surprisingly bulky inflatable boat that hung above me, upside-down, as I struggled to find its edge, get up around it and into the air to breathe. I felt my flip-flops slipping off my feet, and saw belongings floating near me, debris I bumped into, someone's foot landed a heavy kick on my thigh, and then a hard, smooth surface scraped along me—not quite smooth, no, actually very rough at times, later I'd find I was bleeding all down the outside of one leg where barnacles had scraped the skin open.

There would be scars, I'd understand later. Gone, in a single instant and for the rest of my life, were the days of perfect legs. Those barnacles are sharp as hell. They're vicious, truthfully. But at the time I wasn't conscious of pain, only desperation as I tried to scrabble my way to the surface to breathe.

And when I got there—because I made it, obviously, since here I am, not dead, not telling my story as a sad ghost full of wisdom and longing from the grave—the water was still turbulent around me, and I was hearing shouts, faintly, and I was deeply relieved I'd put on the bulky, foolish-seeming lifejacket (Thompson, by contrast, had refused to wear one) because I couldn't grab onto the side of the boat at first, it was too far up there and too slick/slippery and I was weak and out of breath, though I must have had some adrenaline on my side. There seemed to be chaos, and I couldn't see right away, it took me a minute to blink the salt water out of my eyes and clarify the bobbing boat alongside and the floating objects that, I guess, had been dumped out when we were overturned (my eyes fixed, while I was getting my breath back, on a two-liter soda bottle, its brown syrupy liquid sloshing inside; a white first-aid kit with the telltale red cross on it; and a large running shoe). There was still the over-whelming racket of the cable grinding, too.

Was Gina OK? Miyoko? The others? I looked around, called out, sputtering. But I was too low in the water, all I could see was the churning froth itself, right around me—I had to have a better vantage point. With more scraping of elbows and knees I hoisted myself up onto the upside-down boat, I found a rope to hold on to and hauled myself onto its bottom, which had ridges, almost shelves along it that made it easy to get a grip on, once I was up there. For whatever reason I was the first of all of us to clamber back on.

The whales were surfacing again. It was a blue whale, of course, that had come up right beneath us—I realized it only when I saw them, it took me that long to get a clue why we'd capsized. The whales were rising from the depths, and there were a fair number of them—too many for me to count, given their size. The only thing that made them seem less than frighteningly huge was the fact that you didn't see their whole bodies at once, only sections as they arched out of the water and then under it again, sliding along like sea serpents in movies. They had risen. They rose still.

And the mermaids were with them.

They'd dived down by themselves and come up with mermaids.

The first two I saw were clinging to a dorsal fin,

really far back on the whale—those dorsal fins were pretty small, considering how massive the whales' bodies were. That whale dove briefly and the mermaids went under; then he/she rose and they were visible again. And so it went. Whales surfaced, then dipped under, with a few mermaids holding fast to those lone fins but most of them grabbing onto the great white armatures of barnacles across the whales' massive backs. For a mermaid, I guess, those crusted, razor-sharp crustaceans weren't too lethal to grab onto. There werc whole rows of mermaids arrayed along the whales' backs and sides, like so many kids in a full school bus.

I'd left my cell phone in my bag, on the Coast Guard ship, but Rick had brought his, and bizarrely enough it hadn't gotten completely waterlogged/ruined.

Later, turning the sight over in my mind, I'd figure the mermaids had to hold on somewhere;

they weren't big on sitting, being half-fish and all. You don't see a fish in a chair often. Maybe they could sometimes manage on a stable base, say a pile of rocks or a coral outcropping, to brush their hair and sing seductive ditties to sailors, but not on a moving whale. They didn't have asses. It was that simple.

I barely noticed as the others joined me on the capsized boat, scrambling atop it one by one— there was Gina, there was Miyoko, then Ellis, with one limp arm that seemed to be bothering him— and we stared as the whales came up, one after another. After a bit we understood that they were heading out into the open ocean. The whales were moving away from the armada and the nets, and with them went the mermaids.

I watched a pair near me, one particular whale and one mermaid—*my* whale and *my* mermaid, as I thought of them afterward, though the mermaid wasn't the same one I'd seen before. She was a different mermaid, younger and prettier. I saw her shining tail hanging along the side of the whale's great, flattened head, the whale curves I didn't understand anatomically (nostrils? ears? blow-holes?). Sun glanced off the scales on her tail and the mermaid's long, light hair was plastered down her back and sides. There were others like her on that whale, but she was the one near me.

There were far more mermaids than we'd seen before and far more whales than we'd seen before, too. I couldn't count them, it was too fast and too multiple for that—it was like a storm or a battle, a frenzy of movement, a confusion of images and sliding, foaming water. Struggling to stay on the overturned boat as the last stragglers climbed on, rocking it as they clambered, and at the same time watching the whales in a daze, I had no time to draw conclusions, right then. I vaguely registered some discord about organizing—whether we should jump off the boat again and work together to turn it right side up—but I ignored the shouts, tuned out the argument, I wanted it to stop. I was laser-focused.

In the sound and the noise, grasping at the hard plastic ridges as I slipped back and forth on the bottom of the Zodiac, I watched the whales recede, watched them dip and surface, dip and surface again in a graceful motion (Sam said later it wasn't the usual way whales swam but more the way dolphins did—possibly for the benefit of the mermaids). They quickly put a good distance between us, eventually a great distance, and I was just beginning to shiver and feel the sting of the cuts and scrapes on my leg and elbows when they grew indistinct. Soon they were nothing but ripples in the plain of ocean beneath the horizon line.

And finally they disappeared from my field of view and I knew I'd never see those whales or mermaids again. I'd never see another blue whale, the vastest creature ever to live on earth, and I'd never see a mermaid again, either.

They'd taken our mythological creatures, the blue whales had. They'd come to the rescue as the nets were closing in and the hordes were descending with their burning swords. They'd come to claim their own and taken the mermaids far from the armada—far from the Venture of Marvels. They saw what we were, those whales, and wanted nothing to do with it. They simply swam away, those ancient goliaths of the sea.

They took the marvels with them.

I'M A PERSON who doesn't like aftermaths, as I may have mentioned earlier—in general they're depressing. But this one wasn't like that, at least not for me. I could tell some of us were let down, some people felt kind of robbed—Ellis, for instance, who'd been nursing a possibly broken arm and hadn't seen much of anything—but I didn't feel that way at all. From the time we headed back to the cutter (we'd finally righted the rubber boat, but its motor wouldn't start so Sam, Thompson, Miyoko, and Gina paddled us in) I felt euphoric.

I was shivering in my wet clothes, even under the tropical sun, but a curious sense of peace kept me sitting quietly, contented. Blood ran down my leg from the barnacle scrapes: it welled up in thousands of microscopic pinpoints from one place where the outer layers of skin had been sheered off, plus there were thin, deep lines scored into my thigh and calf that drooled blood all the way down to my ankle and heel.

I barely noticed it. I mean, I *did* notice—sitting on the wet bench-seat of the Zodiac I stretched out the leg and peered down at the red lines and ribbons of blood—but it was less out of urgent concern than with a sense of friendly interest.

I knew I *shouldn't* feel peaceful, necessarily, because those mermaids wouldn't be safe now anyway, no matter where they went. Still, for today they were safe, and somehow the knowledge that the blue whales had taken them far away comforted me.

What if the whales, I thought dreamily (happily resting my dripping leg on the side of the boat and letting the others handle the paddling), what if the whales were in charge of the whole she-bang? Those behemoths had obscure ways of knowledge, obviously. Somehow they'd heard a mermaid distress call: that alone was astonishing.

I let myself daydream that the whales had great, all-encompassing wisdom, far greater than any commanded by the race of men. The whales weren't going to fall prey to our mischief this time (although they often had, in centuries past and even more recently). Their songs carried hundreds of miles; we hadn't even known about those songs until the 1960s. Sam and Thompson had both trotted that out.

So we knew little of them, and for eons they'd wandered the quiet deep, masters of that dark and liquid kingdom.

They might be anyone. They might know anything.

WE MADE IT back to the cutter just as Gina was becoming annoyed by having to paddle; we toweled off and sat in the sunlight with towels wrapped around us, tamping the moisture from our soaking clothes.

In due time the rest of our party returned from the *Narcissus*. Though our Zodiac was out of service now, the yacht had her own inflatables; so over they chugged, finally, aboard one of those (larger, newer, and cleaner than the one we'd capsized in). When Chip came back aboard the Coast Guard boat again I saw he was elated too, just like me. Behind him was Nancy, satisfaction shining from her like a beacon. She went up to her father right away, for he and the doctor had stayed on the cutter this whole time, and they shared a heartfelt, emotional greeting: each grasped the upper arms of the other, briefly yet firmly.

Gone were her hopes of a sanctuary, I assumed, and yet—and yet I could tell she was pleased.

We'd been far closer to the spectacle than they had, but aboard that yacht, with its lofty decks, the diplomatic party had had the boon of height, a panoramic view. Chip had made a phone video; on the small screen the whales weren't anything, you couldn't see the mermaids at all, but it was HD, he said, it would look better on his laptop screen.

As the cutter headed back to shore, he knelt down beside me and tended my hurt leg, smearing on some antibiotic ointment and then wrapping my calf lightly in bandages from the cutter's well-stocked first-aid cabinet. The thigh would be harder to bandage, he thought; we'd get the doctor to handle that.

Chip took a lot of care over the cleaning and bandaging, talking to keep my attention off the pain; he said he'd practically had a heart attack when he saw the rubber boat flip. He'd watched the whale's head rise beside it, the great whale-chin ridged with curving lines, and he'd been thunderstruck. He realized I could swim perfectly well, but who knew, he said—I might have been knocked unconscious by a hard blow to the head, I could have sunk beneath the waves, drowning.

It was the worst minute of his life, he said, waiting for me to come up again, waiting to make sure it was me heaving myself onto that bobbing orange oval.

Negotiations hadn't been going that well anyway, he added, when the whales came. He looked around then, not wanting to hurt anybody's feelings. The civil servants had been very polite, said Chip—well, too polite, honestly. They'd been so polite it was hard to tell what they wanted, if anything. Their words, as they spoke to the representatives of the parent company, were so matter-of-fact, so bureaucratic (Chip said these words included *stakeholders,* as well as *win-win* and *orientated toward the long term*), that even to Chip it wasn't clear they had a compelling interest in progress. So yes, they'd *spoken* to the GM, Chip said, the guy from the beach who really *was* a ten-gallon ass hat.

But on the other hand it was as though they hadn't spoken, pretty much.

There'd been no forward motion at all until Nancy, out of sheer frustration, had broken in, and just as she was taking the conversational reins away from the civil servants, just at that very moment the blue whales had arrived.

They'd all stopped talking and stood at the rails and watched, and the GM went from disbelief to astonishment to rampaging anger, so that by the time the mermaids were riding into the distant horizon he was in the grips of a temper tantrum, Chip said, you really could call it that—he raced around yelling at underlings, expressing his outrage. He tried to rally crewmembers and volunteers alike, tried to rally them to the cause of chasing down the whales, somehow trapping the whales or possibly attacking them, making them yield up those mermaids; but heads were shaken, for once no one cooperated with him, Chip told me.

It seemed more like a strike than like a mutiny, but either way it was calm and reasonable, and in the face of his crew's indifference the GM blustered uselessly.

Gina hovered over me, along with Chip and Raleigh; Raleigh had a glass of water, some painkillers he wanted me to take, where Gina mostly wanted to gape.

"That's gory," she said, admiringly, and raised her phone. "I'm going to post it to Facebook, when I have bars again. Do they have toxins in them, barnacles? Like sea urchins?"

As we sped shoreward, I turned back and gazed at the armada. On our approach it had soared above us like a citadel. There'd been no doubt in my mind that it was a seat of power, that armada, a bastion of mindless force. It was impervious to our opinions, cold to the good of others. Yet with the mermaids gone—for all of us knew there were none left behind—it struck me as a ghost fleet. Even a ghost city.

Thompson had talked about diving in the sunken warships of Truk Lagoon, full of the skulls of Japanese fighters . . . Thompson had told the tale, that night after first contact at our drunk party, of how he had swum through those mossy, rusted hulks, seeing small fish dart through the eye sockets of sailors. Those sailors killed a lifetime ago in a distant war, long forgotten by all who knew them, the forgetters even forgotten.

And here I was looking at a new fleet of ghosts, the remnants of a rapacious army of commerce. Already it was floating around uselessly on top of waves that had been stripped of assets. The whales were gone, and so were the mermaids; the coral reefs were on their way out. I felt like I saw the future of these ships, from the private yachts to the workhorses of the fishing industry, and it seemed to me that future was a sad one, in some respects—a future of decay and dereliction, a future where the ships floated on the vast waters with nowhere to sail to anymore.

For the yachts, no pleasure stops along the sumptuous coasts. For the fishing ships, no schools to catch in their high-tech nets, those endless skeins of white monofilament that would drift for millennia in the oceans, immortal.

I was waxing pretty eloquent, in my mind, about all this, when we got back to the marina. We stepped onto the jetty and said our goodbyes to the civil servants. With Chip's arm around me I hobbled into the Hummer.

Ellis and I got the places of honor, being the injured ones: he perched in the front passenger seat, gritting his teeth and trying to hold his arm immobilized, while I stretched out in the very back, my scraped-up leg propped up on a pile of dusty blankets. The good doctor said he'd tend to our wounds back at the motel, that he thought Ellis's wrist was fractured; he'd borrowed some supplies from the ship's first-aid station.

I lay on my side looking out the rear windows—there were a pair of them, the Hummer had two doors at the back—and seeing the sky, with occasional pieces of tree looming. The rear of the Hummer was sandy, full of diving gear, wetsuits, knives, guns, and ammunition, and the fine white sand got all over me. At first I brushed at it irritably, but then I let it stick. I should appreciate the sand, I thought. The parrotfish expert had said it before she died: the white sands would be leaving us soon.

Maybe they would appear in another time and place, I comforted myself. There were so many stars. These days the scientists said a zillion planets might support carbon-based life, out there. Maybe a planet in a triple-star system would grow these fish with pouty lips, these hills of white sand beneath clear saltwater.

Over the history of the earth, I learned in high school biology, the eyeball has evolved, died out, and then evolved again. The eye can't be kept down.

Maybe the fish couldn't be kept down either, the fish and their beautiful reefs.

One time, not long before our wedding, Chip had come home from work with a factoid he'd learned, a piece of new research uncovered in the course of doing business (insurance adjustment). Ashes had been discovered in some cave in South

Africa, ashes from cookfires a million years ago, he'd read it in a magazine. Or he had found it on Wikipedia. Something. Anyway, that was us, Chip said—our grandparents, practically.

We'd had short foreheads then, eyebrows that were even bushier than Nancy's. A million years ago.

"Did we talk?" I asked Chip, propping myself up on an elbow.

I may have sounded fuzzy. My leg was stinging a lot by that time. It really hurt quite a bit.

Chip was chatting with Raleigh in the backseat, and at first they didn't hear me, so I repeated my question.

"Chip. When we were *Homo erectus*. Did we know how to talk back then?"

"Relax, honey. Lie back. She may be delirious. Just rest, OK honey?"

"I mean it, Chip, did *Homo erectus* talk?"

"Uh, hmm. Let me think. I mean no one knows for sure about this stuff. And *Homo sapiens* were the first real talkers, right? Like maybe fifty thousand years ago. But some people think maybe the later specimens of *erectus* spoke some kind of pre-language. Like *maybe* they didn't just grunt like apes. Still, even if that's true, it wouldn't have been anything fancy. They didn't *write* or anything. It took us, like, five million years to learn how to do *that*. Evolution-wise. If you count australopithecines."

Five million years, I thought, lying back again.

It was warm in the back there, stuffy and warm, and as the sting sharpened and then abated, sharpened and abated, I wondered if I was falling asleep. The Hummer bounced over potholes, leaving behind an invisible stream of global warming . . . it had taken our ancestors four million years to figure out fire. It took them five million to develop writing. And then, in a great acceleration—just a brief, screaming handful of seasons—we got electricity, nukes, commercial air travel, trips to the moon. Overnight the white sands of the parrotfish were running out. Here went the poles, melting, and here, at last, went paradise.

The writing gave us everything all of a sudden, then nothing forever.

I WOKE UP to a mild wind sweeping in from the open doors of the motel bedroom. I lay alone on our bed, my leg wrapped in gauze. It was dusk, I saw from the pink sky. No one was in the room with me, but I could hear their voices outside, where they were milling around the pool.

I must have needed the rest, I thought; maybe it was the shock of the injury. I didn't have much experience with pain, accident, or trauma—I've had an easy life, let's face it. I'd thought the leg was no big deal. But still I'd slept through the afternoon.

I didn't want to move yet; I saw my cell phone lay on the bedside table, and I reached out for it. There was a text waiting: *Call me when you wake up. <3 C.*

So I did, I lay there on my back on the cool linens and I called Chip, and he came in. He sat on the side of the bed, then lay down beside me, careful not to nudge the hurt leg; he asked if I wanted more painkillers.

It wasn't so bad, I said.

He said that was because they'd given me codeine.

I wanted to know what I'd missed.

"The crowds—the haters?—they're not accepting that the mermaids are really gone," he said. "They're everywhere, looking for them. Trying to hire out boats, dive equipment. It's a madhouse at the marina. A lot like it was before. The armada's come back in, mostly to service them. So even without the mermaids, the Venture of Marvels is making a tidy profit. Right now, at least. It's going to be all the local authorities can do to keep the crowds from destroying the reefs here."

"Oh," I said weakly. I closed my eyes again.

The sense of peace I'd had after the whales took the mermaids was dispersing like smoke.

"The good news is, the Coast Guard's going to be pitching in and Thompson's reinforcements came through. Wild, right? Can you believe the old guy actually has pull? So there's a Navy boat on its way. That's the good news, honey. There's pretty solid help coming."

I was tired. It wasn't just the codeine, the leg ache—I was more tired than that.

"But there's not so much you and *I* can do," he added. "I mean, Nancy's staying. She's on sabbatical anyway, so she doesn't have to go back and teach. And she feels like she has to go to bat for her parrotfish. Plus the locals can use her biology expertise. But I was thinking—since obviously we don't want to go back to the resort, and this motel's booked up now, even *this* crappy place is full, so we're going to be kicked out in the morning—well, I was thinking we'd get on the ferry and go to the U.S. Virgins, just the two of us plus maybe Ellis and Gina. We can spend the rest of our vacation there. I'm thinking the best would be St. John. I was going to book us there in the first place, you know, before I saw how Gorda had that floating restaurant."

"Aren't there crowds on St. John too?" I asked.

I still wasn't opening my eyes; I lay tucked into Chip like a small child. I've always liked that about Chip, his height and broad shoulders, the fact that he can enclose me.

"No, the haters are only in the British Virgins. None of them really went farther west than Tortola, apparently. It's too far away from where we saw the mermaids, you know, in the U.S.

Virgins—people wouldn't have the access they're looking for. But listen. On St. John there's a two-bedroom bungalow on the top of a small mountain that had a last-minute cancellation—we can rent it for a whole week. I checked. It has a private yard, these flowering bougainvillea vines all over the place, even a rose trellis. It has one of those infinity pools, Deb. You always wanted to swim in a pool like that, didn't you?"

"I've always wanted to swim in an infinity," I murmured.

"And it has a great view of the ocean."

"Chip? Sweetheart? I wonder if we should just go home," I suggested. "*Home* home. Back to the Golden State."

I thought of those angry crowds teeming onto the coral heads out there, slashing the corals with those long rubber fins, of Nancy's silly-looking parrotfish with their bulging lips, those innocent fools of fish. Poor things. Just swimming around with no idea what was coming.

I felt like crying again.

"Deb, no, hey—this was a victory. Maybe not ours, exactly, but still, it was a victory for the mermaids. The Venture didn't get to them, and maybe some small part of that timing was us. Maybe, partly, with our distractions and our interference, we held them off until the whales came. Think of it that way, babe."

"I've always loved your optimism," I said.

"Deb, look. The reefs are going to weather this invasion. All right? So don't be discouraged."

"But if we hadn't gone public with the mermaids, there wouldn't *be* these crowds," I said listlessly.

"But if we hadn't gone public with the mermaids, who knows? Maybe the GM wouldn't have had to take time out to intimidate us on the beach, with his posse. Maybe they would have found the mermaids themselves. Before the blue whales ever got there. And the mermaids would be in a cage right now. And a lot of them might be dead."

I shook my head. It sounded paper-thin, to me, Chip's logic. The truth was, I thought, we'd tried our best, we really had. But we'd been bulls in a china shop, and now the reefs were being invaded by hordes of our very own barbarians.

For the first time I had a glimpse of something: I got an inkling of why Chip was obsessed with the Heartland. He knew it was our fault, the ape denial, the fear of science, the epidemic of obesity. He knew we'd done it to ourselves, made our own village into idiots. We'd put our best-looking idiots on thrones, those empty pawns and shiny dolls. And then we had the balls to act surprised— even superior!—when people began to worship them.

Some people worshiped the false idols and in the face of that some other people turned away.

We weren't this sordid mass, they wanted to think, we were children of God, special and better than the rest. Once you weren't beautiful, you needed God to love you.

Between the two groups a fault line rumbled, ominous.

". . . I know your leg hurts," Chip was saying. "But the doctor says it's going to be fine, maybe some light scarring. As early as tomorrow, he said—as long as you keep a waterproof bandage over the part without the skin—you can maybe go swimming. I'll take care of you, honey. Let's relax, OK? We'll have that lazy honeymoon you wanted, I promise. We really will. St. John's is like, rainforest green, one big national park with mountains, and around the edges is a ring road that stops at tons of white-sand beaches. You can snorkel on every one of them, if you want. We won't do any diving. We'll take it easy."

We lay there for a while, with the babble of conversation from the pool, a splashing, every now and then, and the whir of the ceiling fan.

Chip kissed me, and so forth.

"OK," I said finally.

FOR OUR LAST night with everyone he carried me out to the pool—just for the hell of it, since of course I could have walked, albeit painfully. The leg looked savaged, but it was just lacerations. He laid me down on a chaise and people took turns coming over to see me. I felt like a gimpy queen.

Someone had picked up takeout food, on the pretext of taking the burden of cooking off Janeane, and everyone (except Janeane) was chowing down on pulled pork and fish tacos. A few of the soldiers had come, dressed in their civvies, cargo pants, swim trunks, et cetera, which made them look much younger—like college kids with neat haircuts, I thought, or maybe high school jocks.

Guns age a person, I decided. If you want to look young, you probably shouldn't carry one.

Miyoko was talking to Sam, who looked enthusiastic about the conversation; Thompson and Gina seemed to be playing darts, with a board stuck up on the trunk of a palm tree. Rick and Ronnie were talking to Janeane, who lay in a hammock knitting, as Ellis (one arm in a sling), Simonoff and Nancy pored over some maps spread out on a table and the doctor floated in the pool ensconced in a pink lifesaving ring. Raleigh leaned over the food table, putting together a plate for me.

Of all of them, I thought, watching people stand around in their drinking-and-talking gaggles, I'd miss Steve and Janeane the most. Their niceness was warming. Even their boring-ness grew on you after a while, because they meant so well. They really did.

And Raleigh: I liked him too. I liked so many

people, when I got to know them, and when I was drinking.

When I was drinking I could almost be Chip, I thought, almost that nice.

But not quite.

I wouldn't think of the crowds, I told myself, I wouldn't think of them, the crowds with their swords burning.

That's right. I would refuse to think of them.

I watched as one of Gina's darts struck Thompson on the hand. He shrieked. I nursed my smooth bourbon on the rocks, looked up at the darkening sky. There was the planet Venus, and a few stars were out; purple was turning black. The end of our day was ending.

"You should come down and see us, man," said Chip to Steve.

They were sitting beside me in yellow-and-white deck chairs; Steve was squeezing some kind of resistance ball that's supposed to make your hands stronger.

"You live in the Bay Area, right?" persisted Chip. "Five-hour shot straight down the 1. We're *literally* just a couple minutes off the PCH. Brentwood. Stay overnight! Plenty of space. We'll move Deb's Pilates machine out of the guestroom. That thing's gathering dust anyway, isn't it, honey?"

"Kind of it is," I admitted.

"Hey, I really wish we could," said Steve. "Just not sure there'll be time."

He looked up then, tipping his head back pensively, and Chip and I did the same.

In the sky the asteroid was blazing. That earth-crosser was so near, these days. I'd almost forgotten.

"True dat," said Chip, nodding.

"You read the GAO report?" asked Steve.

"Of course," said Chip.

We'd all read the report, something from Congress that the papers and blogs picked up. It'd been translated into more than a thousand languages; when Chip saw that figure he said he didn't even know there *were* that many. (Gina ridiculed him.) Anyway the study said the asteroid could probably have been stopped, the impact prevented if we'd prepared in time. Well, technically it could have been redirected, not stopped per se, deflected just microscopically along its path so that it wouldn't hit and wouldn't bring on the extinction event. Like in a high-concept blockbuster movie, we could have knocked it off its course with a missile, or maybe a few. Apparently, some of that Hollywood shit was true.

But the time for whining had passed.

So in the end we'd failed the whales, much as we'd failed the mermaids. I wondered if they already knew. Did they see to the end, the way we did?

I wished there were some perfect retreat for

those whales and those mermaids—the beauty we knew, the beauty we thought we'd made up or maybe only dreamed, we'd never been quite sure. I wished there was a safe haven for them, locked deep in the endless blue.

We smiled at each other, Chip and Steve and I, sadly. I flattered myself that the men were thinking fondly of each other and of me, as I was thinking so fondly of them—of all the milling friends and partygoers—longing for what couldn't be.

When it came to the future, we all acted *as if*. Only way to proceed, said Gina firmly, and Chip and I agreed.

So we did the wedding, we did the honeymoon. There'd never be a better time for it.

Still there are instants when it pierces me, it pierces all of us—we all have those instants of remembering—a terrible love that passes in a flash, our terrible love of everything.

It brings us closer than we've ever been.

But the closeness is fleeting.

Tears stood on my bottom eyelids again, twice in a single day now, but I wouldn't let them spill over—not this time. This time I restrained myself, determined to keep my personality intact. From now on, that's what I'd do. No more slipups. It wasn't the best personality, I'd been reminded of that recently, but it was mine. You work with what you've got.

I'd keep my personality intact, I decided. Give it the old college try.

I raised my cup and toasted; the others raised theirs too. We went on smiling, smiling, and smiling, until the very moment when the whiskey touched our lips.

Center Point Large Print
600 Brooks Road / PO Box 1
Thorndike, ME 04986-0001 USA

(207) 568-3717

US & Canada:
1 800 929-9108
www.centerpointlargeprint.com